SEA OF LIES

AN ALLISON HART NOVEL
BOOK 4

ROBIN MAHLE

HARP HOUSE PUBLISHING, LLC.

Published by HARP House Publishing
February 2021 (1st edition)

1

The music exploded with relentless bass while people on the floor basked in the sound. Hands raised high as lights flashed and bodies pressed against one another. Acrid air that fused booze, sweat, and coconut sunscreen fazed no one. The dance floor pulsated beneath Jessica's feet inside the boardwalk bar. Her long red hair, shiny and straight, clung to her face as she drank from her Solo cup. The young man who danced next to her devoured her with his eyes. This was Daytona Beach, and it was Spring Break.

He moved closer and leaned toward her ear. "I like your necklace."

Jessica looked down to see the pendant bounce from her chest as she danced. "Thanks."

"You with anyone?" His tone raised so she could hear him over the crowd and the beat.

"Came here with my friends. They're over there." Jessica pointed to them near the bar. "You?"

He shook his head and his eyes diverted when he caught sight of someone approaching.

"Jess! We're leaving. Come on." Nia snatched Jessica's hand and yanked her away.

She peered at the handsome blonde-haired man and shrugged. "Sorry. Gotta go." Jessica turned back to her friend. "Where are we going?"

Nia pulled her through the crowd toward the exit. "To the next bar. Everyone's outside waiting for us."

They spilled out onto the boardwalk, laughing and stumbling over each other. The five young women attended the University of South Florida in Tampa. A Spring Break destination in itself, Daytona was hours away from family and school and offered a sense of freedom. And in the few hours since their arrival, all five were already having the time of their lives.

"Who was that guy?" Nia Brown, the popular senior who was recently accepted into law school, considered herself the glue that held this wild bunch together. The first in her family to attend college, she bore the weight of her family's future, though she was not the only strong black woman in her family. That honor also belonged to her mother who raised Nia and instilled in her the importance of education. The weight of that aside, for now, Nia had only just begun to let down her hair.

"I don't know. He was hot, though, right?" Jessica Healey, the 20-year-old junior had grown up in the Sunshine State. On scholarship, the Computer Science major rarely put down a book. She needed this more than she knew. "Sophie? Where are you going?" Jessica laughed and started trailing after her roommate. The two shared a dorm room and were as close as sisters.

Sophie Matthews even looked a little bit like Jessica, though her hair was deep brunette. They dressed in similar styles and right now, Sophie was on a mission.

"Guess she's ready for the next bar." Madison Graves was Nia's roommate. Both were seniors and 21. The only two of the bunch who were of drinking age, though all had been served without a second glance of any bartender. She was athletic, strong, and didn't take guff from anyone. Madison never backed down and would defend her friends until the end. She hurried to catch up, pushing away her ash-blonde curls that had frizzed out in the humid air. "Hang on, my flip-flop came off. Wait up, guys." She looked back to the last one of the group. "Harriet, let's move!"

Then there was Harriet Torres. Sensible Harriet. A curvaceous beauty with thick black hair that hung in tight ringlets past her shoulders. Hard worker, on scholarship like Jessica. Avid bookworm. "I'm coming, I'm coming."

———

STEINBRENNER FIELD WAS PACKED for the minor league baseball game pitting the Tampa Tarpons against the Clearwater Threshers. And Allison Hart, 48, former fraud investigator turned P.I., was there to see the debut of her son, Nolan. The sunny day gave her a reason to wear the baseball hat he'd given her, and she wore it proudly. Her long brassy blonde hair was pulled into a ponytail and pushed through the back of the cap.

"Can you believe it?" Allison gazed out onto the field. "He's wanted this for so long and it's finally here." With her ex-husband sitting next to her, she patted his thigh with enthusiasm.

Leo Hart hadn't quite taken the same care in his appearance as Allison had. She was trim and fit. Not so for Leo, the newly betrothed high school P.E. teacher looked every bit his 49 years. Slightly plump and with thinning hair, he wore the same ballcap.

"You've always been a huge advocate for him, Leo," Allison added.

"As long as he keeps his head on straight, he'll do just fine. And avoids injury." He tapped on his knee, a painful reminder of how he ended his own minor league baseball career.

"He'll be great." Allison spotted Leo's fiancé approach with a beer in her hand. "How were the lines?"

"Busy. Took almost 10 minutes." Jenny sat down. "Here you go, Leo."

Jenny was a younger, firmer version of Allison. Although Charlie, Allison's best friend and partner, insisted Alli was much more attractive. She was biased. Allison had wished Charlie was here now. But she had two teenage boys who were always busy with their sports, leaving Charlie little time to squeeze in Nolan's big debut.

Allison could take solace in Lucy Boyce, though, who sat next to her. The "L" in ACL Investigative Services, Allison's P.I. firm, Lucy and Nolan had been dating for the past few months. She was the same age as Micah, Allison, and Leo's daughter, who was currently attending Florida State. Allison reached for her purse. "Lucy, do you want anything? Maybe I'll go up now before he gets up to bat."

"No thanks. Don't think I could eat or drink right now anyway. I'm so nervous for Nolan." The daughter of Tommy Boyce, a hard-boiled P.I. and mentor to Allison who had recently passed, Lucy had been instrumental in helping Allison's private investigating firm get off the ground using her dad's old contacts for a leg up.

"How did he seem earlier?" Allison asked. "You talked to him outside the locker room, right?"

"He's better than I thought he'd be. Relaxed. Calm. Not at all like me." Lucy tucked her long dark hair behind one ear and tugged down on her snug blue tank top. Her brown eyes and smooth face lit up with a wide smile.

Allison recognized that smile. She'd held that very same look for Leo for many years. But their 20-year marriage fell apart almost six years ago now. The notion that Lucy and Nolan would stay together was sweet, but the reality was that they were still young, and each was on a very different path.

"He's up!" Leo nudged Allison. "Are you recording this?"

She fumbled for her phone. "I got it. I got it." Allison aimed the camera at the batter's box. Her heart pounded and she could hardly hold the phone still. The grin on her face was bigger and brighter than it had ever been. She was proud of both her children, but right now, Nolan's accomplishments tugged at her heart. It didn't even matter if he struck out. The point was, he'd made it.

———

UNDER THE BRIGHT light of the noonday sun, Jessica Healey shielded her eyes with her hand as she lay on a towel atop the soft white sands of Daytona Beach. "I forgot my sunglasses." Her pale skin was scantily covered by the two-piece her mother would not have approved of, and her red hair pulled back into a low bun.

Music played from radios and echoed from the restaurants on the boardwalk. Girls in tiny bikinis walked by. Admiring young men took notice.

"You want mine?" Nia asked.

"No, thanks. I could use some headache tablets if you have any." She peered at Nia who lay next to her on the towel. "I drank way too much last night."

"Didn't we all?" Nia reached into her beach bag and pulled out a bottle. "Here, take these." She smiled. "Last night was lit, though, right?"

Jessica raised her lips into a crooked smile. "Hell yeah, it was."

She popped the tablets into her mouth and took a swig of her bottled water. "Maybe I'll see that hot guy again tonight."

"Which one?" Nia laughed. "Besides, aren't you into someone else right now?"

Jessica cocked her head. "Huh? No. Who told you that?"

"No one. I just thought...It doesn't matter. There's plenty of guys here." Nia peered out over the shoreline. "Those guys are crazy."

Jessica turned to see the other girls tossing around a Frisbee. "Neither of them can catch for shit."

"Hey, Jess, your phone's ringing." Nia raised her sunglasses to see. "You want me to get it?"

"Could you? I just put on sunscreen and my hands are still sticky," Jessica replied.

"Well, if you had my beautiful caramel skin, you wouldn't need so much of it." Nia smiled and answered the call. "Jessica's phone. Yeah, she's right here. Hang on." She turned to her with a serious mien. "It's your mom."

Jessica wiped her hands on her beach towel and took the phone but before letting her mom speak, she preempted her. "I'm fine, Mom. I already told you, you don't need to worry about me. I got my girls here." She listened while her mother spoke, and the color drained from her face. "Oh my God. Is he okay?"

Nia whipped around and peered at her.

Jessica quickly nodded. "Okay. Okay. Yeah, I can come home. I've gotta pack... Okay. I'll be home as soon as I can." She stared out over the water with her mouth open, pulling in deep breaths on the verge of hyperventilating.

Nia grabbed her arm. "Jess, what's wrong?"

Ghostly white and wide-eyed, she turned to her. "My dad had a heart attack. He's in the hospital."

"Oh no. Jess, I'm so sorry. Is he going to be okay?"

"They don't know yet. I have to go home."

Sophie walked toward them, still wet from the blue ocean waters. Harriet and Madison trailed, and all wore smiles until Sophie saw the look on Jessica's face.

"Jess? Are you okay?"

"She has to go home," Nia said.

"What?" Madison squeezed the water from her hair.

Jessica waited for them to move in. "My mom just called. Dad had a heart attack and he's in the hospital." She couldn't blink. Even in the bright sun, her eyes remained fixed on the waves as they crashed against the sands. "I have to go home."

Sophie dropped to her knees on the beach blanket. "Jess, oh my God. Is he...?"

Nia reached out to her. "They don't know if he'll be okay."

Jessica seemed to regain her senses and flinched. "I have to go to the room and pack."

Sophie and Nia helped her to her feet while Madison and Harriet packed up their things. Sophie turned to them. "If you guys want to stay here, I can help her pack."

"No way," Madison said. "We're coming with you."

"Yeah. We're all here to help, Jess," Harriet added.

Sophie wrapped her arms around Jessica. "Your dad will be okay, Jess. I know he will."

———

WIRES POKED and prodded Jim Healey as he lay in the hospital bed. The machines that monitored his vital signs beeped like a metronome. His wife, Mary Ann, sat beside him and clutched his hand. Peering through the hospital window, she noticed the sun setting and dusky light drove scattered rays inside the room. Her brow knitted as she checked the time.

In all the chaos of Jim Healey's admittance to the hospital, Mary Ann had only just realized that Jess should have been back from Daytona by now. It was only an hour and a half drive, two hours tops. Maybe there had been an accident and she was delayed in traffic. Leave it to a mother to assume the worst.

Mary Ann released her husband's hand and stood from the chair. Her back popped as she pushed up. The 56-year-old had felt her age at the moment, though she kept herself moderately fit. Stress, worry, fear—they took their toll on her, but what weighed on her mind now was that Jess hadn't yet arrived.

Her purse lay on a shelf along the windowsill and she retrieved her phone. No missed calls. Mary Ann now regretted deleting the tracking app she'd had on Jess's phone. But Jess insisted she was grown up now and in college and deemed it a violation of her personal rights. Perhaps it had been, but at least Mary Ann was able to sleep at night knowing she could easily find Jess. Now, the girl was almost two hours late. She made the call and pressed the phone against her ear. "Come on, sweetheart, answer." Mary Ann smoothed down her short auburn hair as she waited for Jess to pick up. Instead, the call went to voicemail. "Jess, honey, it's Mom. Where are you? It's almost 6 o'clock. Please call me as soon as you get this message. Dad's doing okay at the moment. Please, honey, get here soon." She ended the call and held onto her phone as she returned to the chair.

Jim's eyes fluttered open for a moment and in a gravelly tone, he began, "Where is she?" His gaunt features and dark circles under his eyes aged him beyond his 58 years.

Mary Ann took his hand again. "She'll be here soon. You just rest now." With her hand on her phone, she waited for the returned call.

"Hello?" A nurse pushed through the door and walked inside. "Sorry for the interruption, but I need to check his vitals."

"Of course." Mary Ann stood again. "I think I'll grab a cup of coffee and let you do your thing." She turned to Jim. "I'll be right back, sweetheart. I know the nurse will take good care of you." He muttered an inaudible response as she walked out of the room. What she needed wasn't coffee, but some fresh air.

Mary Ann made it to the lobby and walked through the glass doors out into the cool evening air. She peered up at the sky, unable to see the stars yet as the sun continued its descent. "Please make sure she arrives safely. I can't handle any more stress." She wasn't a regular attendant of church, but Mary Ann believed in God and she looked to him now in one of her darkest moments. Jim had been in her life for 30 years and while it appeared that he was doing well, the doctors still insisted he wasn't out of the woods. Now to worry about Jess. Mary Ann didn't need coffee. What she needed was a good stiff drink to settle her nerves. She wouldn't have either, but it was a nice thought.

———

SOPHIE PICKED up a French fry from her plate as the friends sat inside the cantina. "What are we going to do? I mean, we've only been here for 2 days. Do we just leave?"

The bar and grill had a beachy vibe and grew busier as the day neared its end and Spring Breakers flocked in from the water.

"Has anyone heard from her yet?" Madison wore the kind of concern unfamiliar to most college kids.

"No. I was kind of afraid to text her thinking she probably went straight to the hospital." Nia sipped on her Diet Coke. "Do you guys want to go back home?"

They glanced at each other with uncertainty before Sophie

answered. "I think we should stay. I mean, there's nothing we can do for Jess. She's got her mom. I don't think she'd want us to leave."

"Maybe you're right." Harriet inhaled a deep breath. She felt a kinship with Jess because of their similar backgrounds. Neither came from money and both had worked hard to stay in school. "We planned this for, like, months. And Sophie's right, we can't do anything more for her. I just feel guilty, is all."

"Look, Jess will be fine," Nia began. "I agree that we should stay. I know it won't be the same, but Jess would only feel bad if we all went back and just hung around, you know?"

Madison nodded. "Okay. So we stay. But let's call her in the morning after things have settled down. Make sure she's okay."

"Yep. Good idea." Nia raised her glass of iced tea. "To Jess."

———

A GLIMMER of light sparked in Officer Stewart's eye as he drove along the highway. The Florida Highway Patrol officer turned to his partner. "Hey, did you see that?"

"See what?" Officer Tillman pulled his gaze from his phone.

"There's something up there. Off the side of the road up there. I think we should check it out."

"Sure. Why not?" Tillman asked. "It's been a quiet day. Let's take a look."

About 200 yards ahead, Stewart pulled onto the side of the road. "I think it came off the embankment." He stepped outside and waited for Tillman to join him. "Dangerous stretch right here. Could be an overturned car."

"If the roads were wet, that's possible." Tillman walked alongside him as they approached the embankment drop-off. He peered down over the rocks. "I don't see anything."

Stewart cast his gaze around the area. "Well, hell. I guess my eyes were playing tricks on me. I don't see Jack squat." He turned and started back toward the cruiser but stopped cold. "Oh boy."

"What is it?" Tillman caught up to him.

"What's that?" Stewart pointed to the other side of the highway. "Looks like we got ourselves an abandoned car."

"We'll have to turn around and check it out." Tillman returned to the vehicle and waited for his partner. "At least we didn't stop for nothing."

Stewart turned the engine and pulled back out onto the highway. "I guess so." He continued about one-quarter of a mile until he reached the turnaround. "Time to check it out."

The stretch of highway between Daytona and Tampa off the I-4 saw heavy traffic most days and especially during Spring Break. Stewart drove toward the off-ramp and near the entrance to a construction site. "Looks like it broke down."

"I'll bet the owner hoofed it from there." Tillman watched as his partner pulled up behind the vehicle. He stepped out and joined him at the front of their patrol car. "Should we run the plates?"

Without a response, Stewart placed his hand on the butt of his gun and started toward the car. Each step was cautious and calculated. He'd known too many of his colleagues who got mowed down or shot during routine traffic stops. While this was different, he was cautious, nonetheless.

His brow furrowed, he approached the passenger side from the rear. Tillman stood ready to make his way to the driver's side when he got the go-ahead.

Stewart flipped the strap of his holster and wrapped his fingers around the handle of his gun as he reached the passenger door and peered inside. His shoulders dropped and he released his gun. "Son of a bitch." He turned back to his partner. "Looks like we got a suicide. Gun's still in her hand.

Tillman shook his head. "I'll run the plates and see what turns up." He returned to the vehicle and keyed in the plate number into the laptop. "Shit." He stepped out of the car again and walked to Stewart. "If that's Jessica Healey inside that car, then we're the lucky ones to find her. She was reported missing more than 24 hours ago."

"Call the ambo. We'll need to get her out of here."

Tillman started away with Stewart at his side. "A clean shot to the head. Frickin tragic."

"If it were anything but suicide, color me dumbfounded. I don't see any signs of another vehicle. An accident. Nothing." Steward peered over his shoulder at the red Mini Cooper. "How old you think that girl is?"

"Records say 20," Tillman replied.

Stewart sighed. "I'll call it into the station and talk to the detective in charge. He'll want to inform the family."

———

DETECTIVE BRENNER ARRIVED on scene and stepped out of his car while the Coroner's office prepared to load the body of 20-year-old, Jessica Healey. The stout veteran homicide detective, early 50s and strikingly rugged features, wore aviator sunglasses and a rolled-up blue Oxford shirt. "Officer Stewart?"

"I'm Tillman, he's Stewart."

Brenner nodded and walked ahead toward the trooper. "Officer Stewart?"

"That's me." Stewart, a solid 6 feet, loomed over the detective who was 5 feet 9 inches on a good day. "You must be Detective Brenner. I was the one who made the call."

"Good to meet you." Brenner removed his sunglasses and looked at the car ahead. "You're calling this one a suicide, huh?"

"That's right. Single shot right to the head. The victim still has the gun in her hand." Stewart started toward the vehicle. "Come see for yourself. Coroner is ready to load her up, but we've been waiting for you to take a look."

The driver's side door was open, and Jessica Healey was slumped low into her seat. Her head drooped and red hair covered her face. Her hand lay palm up with the gun resting on it in her lap. Blood soaked the girl's yellow t-shirt and trickled down onto her denim shorts, her pale thighs dotted in red. Spray broadcast on the windshield, dash, and the driver's window.

Brenner squatted low and looked inside. From this angle, the girl could have been simply asleep. The hole in her head was on the right side and were it not for the blood spatters, it would have been an easy assumption. He noticed the chocolate bar wrappers, the Diet Coke can in the cup holder, the miniature Beanie Boo unicorn hanging from the rearview mirror. He closed his eyes and stood again. "Note?"

Stewart took a couple of steps forward. "What's that now?"

"A note. Did anyone find a note? If it's a suicide, typically, there would be a note somewhere."

"No one's found one yet," Stewart replied. "Forensics already swept the scene. Took a few samples. That was it."

Brenner grunted his acknowledgment and walked around the car to the other side. The passenger door was open, and he again peered in. "Parents say she was on her way back from Daytona. Was there with some girlfriends for Spring Break. The only reason she was coming back was that her dad suffered a heart attack." He continued to examine the car's small interior. "Kind of unlikely she'd decided to up and kill herself while hurrying back to see her ailing father." Brenner stood again.

Stewart and Tillman stood next to each other and traded glances before Stewart spoke. "I'd tend to agree with you, Detective, but frankly, the evidence is fairly clear on the matter. You got the point-blank star of the entrance wound. You got the fact that there are no signs of an accident of any kind. No signs of any other vehicle."

"Meaning it wasn't road rage or we'd likely have some tire marks on the asphalt," Brenner said.

"Exactly. Then you got the one thing I think stands out the most."

"Which is?" Brenner continued.

Stewart turned to his partner. "Show him the phone."

Tillman walked to his cruiser and retrieved a plastic bag. Inside the bag was Jessica Healey's cell phone. When he returned, he began. "We figured you'd want to see this before we handed it over to Forensics."

Brenner took the phone. "I hope you didn't jeopardize the prints on this, if any."

"No, sir. Forensics used gloves and put it straight into the evidence bag. But when I initially picked it up, wearing gloves, the phone displayed an incoming message. "Course, it's password protected, but the notification appeared, along with the first few words of the message. Take a look for yourself. Just press..."

"I know how phones work." The detective took the bag and pressed the button on the side to illuminate the phone. A partial message appeared that read, "Don't do it, Jess..." Brenner peered at the officer. "Anyone look into whoever this Sophie person is on the caller ID?"

"Figured that was up to you. Just thought it was interesting and that you'd definitely want to see it," Stewart added. "See, the way I read that is this Sophie was telling this young girl not to do something. Until you get a look at what's on that phone, it's just a guess, but it looks like she was asking the girl not to kill herself."

Brenner examined the phone again. "That's possible." He

turned to the red Mini. "Along with the rest of the evidence, your theory could be on the nose. I'll hand this over to Forensics and see what they can find. In the meantime, if we can rush the autopsy, all the better." Brenner started back to his car. "I'll find out what happened to this girl."

2

Cause of death was suicide. A bitter pill that Mary Ann Healey was forced to swallow down. The idea that Jessica shot herself on the drive home to see her father was inexplicable. The police shut down the investigation. Now, Mary Ann was forced to come to terms with caring for her recovering husband and the suicide of her only child.

In the two weeks since this unimaginable nightmare began, sleep had become a luxury. When it did come, it brought terrifying images of Jessica pleading for help while the hole in her temple seeped with blood. It was all Mary Ann could do to keep from collapsing in a huddled mass. Jim still recovered from what had been called the "widow maker" heart attack. He was lucky to have survived it and she knew that right now, he wished he hadn't. She had to be strong for him. If he was gone too...

"I'll be back soon. Do you need anything?" Mary Ann stood over Jim as he lay propped up on their bed, watching the news.

"No, I'll be fine." He picked up his phone. "I'll call Mike next door if I have to." He eyed her. "Where are you going?"

"The funeral home. They're letting us bury her now and I need to pick out..." she couldn't finish the sentence.

"You shouldn't go alone." Jim heaved up, ready to swing his legs over the bed.

"No. No, you have to rest. You know what the doctor said. Stay here. I'll take care of things."

He held her gaze, his own eyes welling with tears. "I want to be with you."

"I know you do, but I'll be all right. I promise." She bared a faint smile and walked away. Her heart broke even more with the lie. The arrangements were already made and all they waited on was for the coroner to release Jessica's body, which was scheduled for tomorrow. But today, Mary Ann had made a decision. She wasn't one of those mothers who *thought* she knew her daughter well. She *did* know her daughter well, damn it. And there wasn't a chance on God's green earth that Jessica killed herself, and with a gun, no less. No one in her house possessed a gun. It made no sense. A bright, loving girl who did well in college and loved her friends. No. Mary Ann couldn't bring herself to believe that something dark lay in Jessica's thoughts and she decided to end her life as a result. The time had come to do something about it even if the police said there was nothing more to do.

Mary Ann arrived at the door of the ACL Investigative Services office. Her chest was heavy with emotion, she took in a deep breath and reached for the handle.

"Good morning." Lucy Boyce peered up from her desk. Her youthful smile was warm and welcoming. "How can I help you?"

"This is a private investigating firm, right?"

"Yes, ma'am. I'm Lucy Boyce. Allison Hart and Charlie Wells are the other two partners but I'm afraid they're out on a call. They should be back soon." Lucy pushed back her long black hair and offered her hand.

"My name is Mary Ann Healey. May I wait? If it isn't inconvenient." She clutched her handbag as though frightened.

"Absolutely. Not inconvenient at all. Would you like a cup of coffee? Water?" Lucy started toward the credenza behind her desk.

"Coffee, please. Black is fine."

"You got it." Lucy prepared the cup. "Please feel free to take a seat over there."

Mary Ann noticed three chairs lining the wall. "Thank you."

"Here you go." Lucy handed her the steaming mug. "I'll give the ladies a call and find out when they might..."

The door opened and Allison and Charlie walked inside.

"Perfect timing." Lucy peered at them. "This is Ms. Healey. She just arrived."

"Ms. Healey, I'm Allison Hart." She offered her hand. As was Allison's style, her blonde hair was piled on top of her head and she dressed in light spring clothing. A grey slip dress with a denim jacket over top.

"Please, call me Mary Ann."

Allison nodded. "Mary Ann. This is Charlie Wells."

Charlie Wells, the middle-aged divorced mother of two boys, continued inside. Her black hair was cut short and spiky, which complimented her round face and thickset figure. She preferred comfort to high style, though her look was always well put together. "Good morning, Mary Ann."

"Hello. I hope I haven't come at a bad time."

"It's never a bad time. Please, come over here and take a seat." Allison started toward the new conference table they'd recently purchased. "What can we do for you, Mary Ann?"

As the partners gathered at the table, Mary Ann began. "Well, my daughter, Jessica..." She placed her hands on the mug as if the warmth soothed them. "About two weeks ago, she was found dead."

"I'm so sorry," Allison said.

"Thank you. But you see, Ms. Hart, the police say it was suicide. I know my Jessica. I can assure you, it wasn't suicide."

Allison rendered minor apprehension. "You believe your daughter was murdered?"

Mary Ann, the petite mother who wore her auburn hair full and short, turned resolute in an instant. "Yes, I do. With my whole heart. She was murdered."

Allison glanced at her partners. "Had she mentioned having a problem with anyone? Did she fear anyone? A stalker. Someone she had a fight with. A boyfriend."

"No, she never mentioned anything like that, but I'm telling you..." Mary Ann's eyes pleaded with Allison. "Jess had everything in this world going for her. She was coming home from a shortened Spring Break trip with her college friends due to my husband having suffered a heart attack." She held up her palms. "He's okay now. He's recovering. But Jess was coming home because I called and told her what happened. She left immediately, but never showed up."

Lucy swallowed down the lump in her throat, seeming to harken back to the death of her father. "I can't imagine what you must be going through. I recently lost my father to a heart attack. But for this to happen too, well, I couldn't imagine."

A gentle smile appeared on Mary Ann's lips. "I can't believe it myself, to be honest." She turned back to Allison. "The police talked to her friends. They checked her phone."

"And there was no suggestion of foul play?" Charlie asked.

"No, ma'am." Mary Ann shook her head in certitude. "Not a single thing turned up that suggested suicide either, except the obvious. She had even been texting her friend on the way back. Something I'd told her not to do while driving countless times..."

"Then why did they rule it that way?" Charlie pressed on.

"The coroner said that was how she died. There was gunpowder residue on her hands. The way the bullet..." She cleared her throat. "I'm sorry. It's still very difficult to talk about."

"Of course it is." Allison reached across the table for her hand. "You want us to look into this. Is that what I'm hearing?"

"Yes." She tugged at her blouse as if confirming her assertion. "I need to know why my daughter was murdered and who the murderer is. He or she is out there. I promise you."

"Who's the detective in charge of your daughter's investigation?" Charlie asked.

"Brenner. Detective Howard Brenner, Tampa PD."

Allison peered at her colleagues and it looked as though everyone agreed. "Well, Mary Ann, I'd like to get some more details from the police, and then discuss it with my team."

"You'll get back with me soon?" she asked. "I am supposed to bury Jessica next week."

"We'll have an answer for you by end of day tomorrow. If what you think happened to your daughter was murder, then there's no time to waste."

———

IN THE FEW months that had passed since Allison attained her P.I. license, she grew confident in her relationships with the guys at the station. She'd already worked with a few of them and word got around that she wasn't the dumb blonde they thought she was going to be. Maybe Detective Shane "Sully" Sullivan had a small part in that. Nevertheless, Allison was sure it was her professionalism and respect for what the detectives did that showed them she was a force with which to be reckoned.

Now, as she walked inside the Downtown Tampa police station once again, it was to meet Detective Howard Brenner. He worked in Major Crimes, which also happened to be where Shane now worked, thanks to his recent promotion. It had been a shaky move and more than once, Shane had felt that his new boss had it in for him since he took part with another detective in taking down a bad federal agent. That was all in the past now and Allison was glad he'd found his footing. However, she wouldn't get away with going upstairs to see Brenner without stopping to talk to Shane first.

His desk was in the bullpen where the newbies were relegated, and not one of the offices where Brenner could be found. Allison reached the top of the stairs and caught sight of him. Shane could make any woman catch her breath, including Allison. And the two had shared moments when their spark was evident. But it had been her decision to keep as they were, friends. No matter that the 40-year-old detective with big brown eyes, a jaw that could cut glass, and a body—well—she started to blush.

"Allison. Hey. What's going on?" Shane stood from his desk and greeted her with a friendly hug.

"Looks like I have a new case. Detective Howard Brenner. You know him?" she replied.

"Sure. Haven't worked with him yet, but the best homicide detective the department has."

"Wow. That's good to know," Allison began. "I'm going to ask him about a case he ruled a suicide."

"A suicide?" Shane asked.

"Yep. Mother doesn't think so and hired us to look into it." Allison noticed his expression shift. "What?"

"Nothing. Hey, it's your business. Not mine."

She wanted him to elaborate but didn't have the time. "I don't want to be late. I'll catch up with you later?"

"Sure. See ya." He returned to his desk.

Allison felt Shane's eyes on her as she turned into the hall and reached the detective's office. She knocked on the door that was already open. "Detective Brenner?"

He peered up at her from his desk. "Ms. Hart, come in."

"Thank you."

Brenner stood and offered his hand. He was older than she expected, though his veteran status should have given away his age. And while he was stout, he was an attractive man with dark hazel, almost brown eyes, that captured her attention.

"I've heard a thing or two about you, Ms. Hart. Have a seat and let me know what I can do for you."

"Well, Detective, a woman by the name of Mary Ann Healey came into my office today. Her daughter..."

"Jessica Healey. I'm familiar." He sat back down at his desk. "Suicide. Very tragic."

"Yes, well, that's what I'm here to discuss with you."

———

Charlie peered through the restaurant window that offered a stunning view of the bay. The lunchtime break was to form a consensus as to whether the partners would accept the Healey case. She sipped on her iced tea and gauged Allison and Lucy. "So, what do we think, ladies? Is there a case here?"

"Not according to Detective Brenner." Allison tossed a fry into her mouth. "He said he initially considered the possibility of a homicide, but the more he looked into it, the forensics, the less convinced of it he became."

Charlie peered at her. "You don't agree?"

"Well, it's just." Allison shook her head. "What still gets me is why she would choose that very moment to take her own life. A moment when her mother needed her most. When her father needed her. By all accounts, this girl loved her parents. She was close to them. Never had a problem with suicidal thoughts in the past."

"According to her mother," Charlie added.

"I have considered the mother's bias," Allison continued. "We have no hint of foul play either."

"I don't know about you, but I'd like to see the files before we come to a decision. What have Jessica's friends said about all this?" Charlie asked.

"Brenner only gave me a brief rundown, but he said the friends suggested it was possible Jessica had the mindset to take her own life. Well, let's just say that they couldn't rule it out."

Lucy grunted. "Just playing Devil's Advocate here, but she was about my age. In college. It's stressful, I know."

"What are you saying?" Allison regarded her. "That there might be more explanations as to the fact that she could have done this, despite what Mary Ann believes?"

"I'm just saying, this isn't easy any way you look at it. And because of that, maybe it isn't at all cut and dry." Lucy set down her glass of water. "Maybe there is something there. Something worth looking into deeper. I'm just not sure the detective had a desire to dig into this based on the coroner's report."

"The kid could be right," Charlie said. "Maybe we won't turn up anything more than what the detective has, but..."

"And Mary Ann would've paid us a lot of money for nothing," Allison replied.

Charlie raised her index finger. "Not for nothing. For either confirming her suspicions or for confirming the police's investigation. Maybe she's just looking for a second opinion. The cops don't always get it right. And when it's a suicide, sometimes they don't see anything but that. But if we also come to that conclusion, it might help Mary Ann rest easier." Charlie peered at her partners. "I say it's worth looking into. Hell, we spend two days on it, don't charge her anything, and if something points us to a different conclusion, then we turn up the heat. Take it seriously. That's my two cents. And you know me, that's about all I got."

Allison nodded. "Okay. I can live with that. Lucy?"

"I think that's fair."

Allison picked up her cheeseburger. "Then let's talk to Mary Ann and get the ball rolling."

———

ALLISON PEERED through her office window down at the parking lot. "Mary Ann's here. She's coming up now."

Allison and Charlie took a seat at the conference table while Lucy stood ready to greet their client. The door opened and Mary Ann walked inside.

"Ms. Healey, it's nice to see you again. Please, come in." Lucy ushered her inside. "Can I get you a bottle of water?"

"Thank you, Lucy. Yes, that would be nice." Mary Ann approached the table and glanced at the files. "Hello. It looks like you have a lot there."

"Mary Ann, please sit down." Allison gestured to the chair. "We'd like to talk to you about how we want to approach this."

"Okay." She took her seat and Lucy placed the water in front of her. "Thank you, Lucy."

Allison cleared her throat. "I know you're anxious to learn our decision and as we know, time is never on our side in these situations. So, we'll get right down to it." She eyed her colleagues. "After we spoke yesterday morning, my partners and I did some digging. I spoke to the detective who had been in charge of Jessica's investigation. We were given access to the statements of her friends and reviewed them just before you arrived."

"And?" Mary Ann peered at her with anticipation.

"While we didn't find any evidence of foul play, in our opinion, there was also not enough evidence to rule it out," Allison replied.

Mary Ann's heavily lined face assumed relief. "So you'll take the case? You'll find out who murdered my daughter?"

"We'll do our best to get to the bottom of what happened to Jessica," Charlie interjected. "The answers we get may not be what you want to hear, but it'll be the truth."

"Fine. Fine. When will you get started? I can't live like this anymore. I have to know the truth." She glanced at each of them. "And if it happens that you find true evidence that suggests Jess did take her own life, then I will accept that. I will learn to live with that."

Allison nodded. "Then we will take the case and we can get started as soon as today."

———

THE ON-CAMPUS COFFEE shop was where Lucy was set to meet Sophie Matthews, roommate and best friend of Jessica Healey. With her long black hair, stick-straight, and trendy clothes, Lucy blended well with the rest of the college crowd. Her eyes drifted around the café until landing on a dark-haired girl who appeared downhearted. She made her approach. "Sophie? I'm Lucy Boyce. We spoke on the phone."

There was no life behind the young woman's brown eyes. No glow on her otherwise youthful skin. Only melancholy remained. "Hi. You can sit down."

"Thank you." Lucy joined her. "I'm very sorry for your loss."

Sophie nodded. "I've been hearing that a lot lately. They always seemed like empty words until now. I never lost anyone before." She let her eyes rake over Lucy. "Jess's mom hired you guys?"

"She did."

"And you're, what, like a private detective or something?" Sophie pressed on.

"I work for a private investigating firm. My dad was a P.I., but he passed away a little while ago."

"I'm sorry for *your* loss," Sophie replied.

Lucy revealed a delicate smile. "Thanks. I'm here because..."

"Because you want to know why she did it. Why Jess killed herself, right?" Sophie absentmindedly stirred her iced coffee.

"Something like that, yeah," Lucy added.

"No offense, but I already told the cops everything I know. Jess got a call from her mom and drove home an hour later. That was the last I heard from her."

Lucy retrieved a small notebook from her purse. "But you did text her after she left, right? You didn't want her to do something? I don't have the records yet."

"Yeah. Look, I know you're not supposed to read texts while you're driving, okay? But I had to just tell her that I didn't want her to go see him. I told her not to do it. Not to see him."

"Who? A boyfriend?" Lucy pressed on.

"Ex-boyfriend." Sophie pushed back her hair and wiped a finger under her nose as though her emotions were about to become overwhelming. "They broke up over Christmas break. He goes to a different college. Things got too hard and so she broke it off with him."

"Then why would she want to see him and especially at a time when you'd think she'd only be concerned for her dad," Lucy said.

"She was upset. It all just sort of came crashing down on her, you know?" Sophie replied. "I didn't hear from her after that. She didn't reply."

"Had she met anyone in Daytona?" Lucy pressed on.

"No, not that I'm aware of. We were there all of two days when this went down. We were just there to party. Nothing serious. I mean, you get it, right? You look like you're about my age. We just needed to blow off steam." Sophie stared at her drink. "That's all it was supposed to be."

Lucy studied her a moment. She looked like an average college girl. No underlying agenda, tone, or mannerisms. Her dad had taught her how to pick up cues like that. "If Jessica hadn't driven her own car on this trip, would you have offered to take her back home? You drove, too, right?"

"Yeah, I drove. And hell, yes, I would've driven her back home. It just so happened that there were five of us going and our cars only fit four. So we both drove."

"Who else knew you were going to Daytona Beach?" Lucy asked.

"I don't know." Sophie peered around. "Like, everyone. Everyone was going somewhere. Either home or to a beach someplace. No one stays on campus during Spring Break."

Lucy nodded. "You told the police you didn't think Jessica had enemies, so to speak. No one she was beefing with, right?"

"Yeah, I mean, everyone loved Jess. She was the kindest person..." Sophie wiped her eyes as she trailed off.

"You also don't think she had contemplated suicide."

"Never," Sophie began. "We talked about everything. Boys, school, family. Even if one of our friends was being bitchy or something, we'd vent about it. She had no reason. None that I could see or that I knew about to kill herself. It still doesn't make sense to me."

"Thank you, Sophie, for talking with me. I know it's not easy. By the way, what's the name of the ex-boyfriend?"

"Huh?" She looked up again, appearing to have momentarily drifted away.

"Jessica's ex. The one you told her not to see in a text that day."

"Oh, right. Tony. His name is Tony Cruz."

Lucy stood from the chair. "Thank you again, Sophie." She started away.

"Hey, Lucy?"

She stopped in her tracks and turned around. "Yeah?"

"Not that I think this is really anything, but you should probably talk to Nia. She drove to Daytona with Jess and, I don't know, they might've talked or something."

"I will. We plan on talking to all of you who went on the trip," Lucy replied.

"Oh, okay. Cool."

Lucy nodded and walked outside, returning to her car. She stepped inside her dad's old black Monte Carlo SS. Not exactly what a young woman would choose to drive, but he left it to her, and driving it was how she chose to honor him. Inside, she waited and watched Sophie Matthews. After another minute or two, Sophie did nothing but stare at her drink. Didn't even look at her phone. Lucy's brow knitted and she finally turned the engine.

A quick call to the office before she pulled away. "Hey, it's me."

"What'd you find out?" Allison asked.

"Nothing we didn't expect. Except for maybe one thing. You remember that she had sent a text to Jessica?"

"Sure. What did she have to say about that?"

"She told Jessica not to meet up with her ex-boyfriend. I guess they split up over Christmas break. So, I was thinking..."

"Go. Find out where he is and meet with him. Charlie and I are headed back to the office. We have more details that we need to sort through. We'll see you back there soon. Good work, Lucy."

3

The phone records arrived in an email from Tampa PD homicide detective, Howard Brenner. Since the case had been ruled a suicide and closed, all he needed to release the files was a signed affidavit from Jessica's parents, which Mary Ann willingly provided.

"I got them. I'll forward it to you to take a look." Allison sent the email to Charlie who was at her desk. "I'd like to see just how often Jessica had been communicating with her ex-boyfriend. Could be worth knowing especially after Lucy gets in touch with him."

"Assuming he'll talk to her," Charlie replied. "No reason to believe he won't, but there's no active official investigation here. Just us chickens."

"Right now, Charlie, everything is on the table."

"What has Sully said about all this?" Charlie asked. "He works with Brenner, doesn't he?"

"They're in the same department, but I haven't told him we're officially on the case yet."

"What? Why? He's going to find out," Charlie replied.

"I know, but I just wanted us to start this off on our own. We've asked Shane for a lot these past several months. It's time we stand on our own two feet."

"Hey, there's nothing wrong with getting an inside track." Charlie eyed her over her dark-rimmed reading glasses. "What's going on with you?"

"Nothing." Allison shrugged and looked away.

"Don't tell me 'nothing.' I'm your best friend. I'm your partner. You two get in a lover's spat or something?"

Allison pursed her lips and cast a scornful gaze on Charlie. "We aren't lovers, and you know that. I just think we can do this on our own. Brenner's been helpful, cooperative. Not like some of those guys we worked with in the past. Brenner doesn't seem to feel threatened by us."

Charlie pushed off her chair and walked to Allison's desk with her arms folded across her stout midsection. "Wait a minute. You like this Brenner, don't you? That's why you haven't told Shane." A wide smile lit up her face. "You think he's cute."

Allison rolled her eyes. "I don't think he's cute, and last I checked, we weren't in high school. Look, I'll grant you, he's attractive, but that's beside the point. You know how much I care for Shane. We've been friends for a long time. Long before we started ACL."

"And he's been after you pretty much since the day you two met," Charlie added.

"Exactly. With Leo getting married..." She inhaled a breath. "I don't know. I just don't think I want another man in my life. Not right now. And Shane, he's great, but he's younger than me."

Charlie shrugged. "I don't see that as a problem at all."

"Well, it is for me. All I need is to get involved with a man 8 years my junior who will eventually tire of looking at my worsening wrinkles before deciding to dump me for a younger woman."

"Like Leo did?" Charlie perched on the edge of Allison's desk. "Leo cheated on you. He begged for your forgiveness. You made the decision to end your marriage because of it." She held up her hands. "I'm not saying that was the wrong decision. Obviously, it wasn't. But what I am saying is that just because Leo is getting married to a younger woman doesn't mean all men are like him. I don't see Shane like that at all."

Allison lowered her gaze. "Despite the fact we know he's a player."

"Yeah, um, you can't really pull off that phrase, Alli."

Allison laughed. "Maybe you're right. But it still doesn't mean I'm ready to start a romantic relationship with him. And from a professional standpoint, we need to do this on our own."

"Fair enough." Charlie stood again and with a short burst of strides, walked back to her desk. "You should still tell him about the case. If he hears about it from one of his colleagues, or from Brenner himself, he'll be hurt, Alli."

"Okay. I'll tell him we're on it."

"Good." Charlie grunted as she sat back down. "Now that that's settled, we have a job to do."

———

Harriet Torres stood behind the counter wearing a green apron and holding a plastic cup with a pen. Her curly hair was pulled back into a low bun with fringes of curls resting against her full cheeks. "What can I get for you, ma'am?"

Allison squinted to see the menu above. "I'll take a Grande iced mocha half-caff latte, please."

"And your name?"

"Allison."

"That'll be right up." She spun on her heel and started away.

"You're Harriet, right?" Allison asked.

The young Latina turned back. "That's what the name tag says."

Allison raised a corner of her mouth into a smile. "I don't suppose you can take a quick break. I wanted to talk to you about Jessica Healey."

Harriet froze in place and lost all expression. "Are you a cop?"

"No. I'm here as a favor to Jessica's mother, Mary Ann."

She eyed a co-worker who appeared to offer a nod in return. "Yeah, okay." Harriet stepped out from behind the counter and removed her apron. "We can sit over here."

"Thanks." Allison sat down. "I'm sorry to drop in unexpectedly. I see how busy you are."

"What do you want to know? I already told the detective everything I knew, which wasn't much."

Allison regarded her a moment. Her olive skin and shiny dark hair. She seemed older than her years and it was her eyes that were the most telling. They were a deep brown that appeared to hold too many secrets. "First of all, I'm sorry about what happened to your friend. I didn't know her, of course, but she seemed to have been her mother's whole life. I can understand that. I have two grown children."

"I miss her." Harriet nodded slowly and pressed her lips together. "It's just all so weird, you know?"

"I'm sure it must be," Allison replied. "Did you talk to Jessica a lot? I know she was close with your other friend, Sophie."

"They shared a dorm room," Harriet replied.

Allison nodded. "Right. But did you two have a close relationship?"

"I think so. There's a group of us. We're all pretty tight,"

Harriet added. "I mean, we all hung out a lot. We always went to parties together. And we were, like, fierce in the way we protected each other. College campuses can be, well..."

"Yeah. I have a daughter at FSU. I know what you mean," Allison said. "Sounds like you guys looked out for each other."

Harriet's lips quivered. "We did. Totally."

"It must have come as a shock then to learn what happened. What Jessica did."

Harriet looked away. "It didn't make sense. I mean, I get she was upset about her dad and all, but why? Why then? She wanted to see him, to make sure he was okay. Not to..." She inhaled a deep breath. "I'm sorry."

"No need to be." Allison placed her hands on the table and laced together her fingers. "Look, I don't want to get you in any trouble with your boss, so I'll just ask you this." She paused a moment. "Was Jessica doing well in school? Getting good grades and getting along with her professors, things like that."

Harriet appeared to ponder the question. "Um, actually, I don't know. We all sort of bitched about our classes and stuff. That's just what you do."

"But nothing that stood out to you?" Allison pressed on.

"Not really. No. Jess was smart. Smarter than the rest of us, that's for sure. I don't think she had any trouble with, you know, like adjusting to college life."

Allison nodded and retrieved her business card. "Okay. I'll let you get back to work. Do me a favor, though. Call me if you think of anything else?"

Harriet took the card and examined it. "Do you think Jess was, like, murdered or something?"

"I don't know." Allison peered at her. "Do you?"

The young woman shrugged. "It would make more sense than her killing herself." She stood from the table. "I gotta go now."

"Thank you, Harriet. It was nice talking to you."

"You too, Allison."

————

CHARLIE MEANDERED in the lobby of the dormitory. She peered at a wall where a large, framed photograph of Tampa Bay hung.

"Ms. Wells?"

Charlie turned. "Guilty as charged." She smiled and extended her hand. "You must be Nia?"

"I am. Madison's upstairs. Come on. We can talk in our room." Nia started back toward the elevators. The short shorts and tank top showed off her youthful caramel skin. Her naturally curly hair was full and hit her jawline. "I can't believe Mrs. Healey hired a private detective."

"Why?" Charlie asked, trying to keep up with the young woman's long strides.

"I don't know. It's just kind of crazy. This has all been really stupid crazy." She stepped onto the elevator. "We didn't know any of this had happened. We all thought she got back home and helped her mom, you know?"

"When did you find out?" Charlie followed her into the elevator.

"Jess's mom called Sophie, of course, the day after when she didn't turn up."

Charlie raised a brow, picking up on a hint of resentment. "What do you mean, 'of course'?"

"Nothing. They were best friends, shared a dorm room. It made sense. But we were due to come back the next day anyway. And none of us wanted to admit it, but it wasn't the same without Jess there. We were all bummed out."

The elevator door opened, and they stepped out into the corridor. The halls were painted a sunflower yellow and the floors were like concrete. Drum lights hung from the ceiling as they passed beneath them. The modern and bright dormitory was refreshing. "Our room is just down here."

"So you and Madison share a room, too, huh?" Charlie asked.

"Yep. We're all here in the same hall, just different floors," Nia continued on.

"That must be pretty cool. All you hanging out together."

"It is—was, until this happened." Nia opened her door. "Hey, Maddie, the Private Detective is here to talk to us."

Charlie looked at Madison. "Hi. I'm Charlie Wells. Nice to meet you."

They traded a handshake, but Madison didn't reply and only nodded.

The room was cramped. Twin beds placed on opposite walls. A set of desks with chairs. It wasn't much bigger than a prison cell but was decorated nicely with hues of grey and pink.

"Okay, well..." Charlie began. "I know you both have already spoken to the police and I'm sure this feels a little unnecessary."

"No, it's not," Madison interjected. "No way Jess killed herself. No frickin way."

Nia shot her a glance. "Maddie..."

"No, Nia. We all know it. Sophie knows it. Harriet knows it." Madison stood about 5 feet 8 inches, a little thicker around the waist with more of an athletic build. Her ash blonde hair was pulled up into a haphazard bun with wisps dangling against her cheeks.

Charlie pulled out a desk chair to sit on while the girls sat on their beds. "Are you saying that you believe someone killed Jessica?"

"I do." Madison thumbed to Nia. "They don't."

"And is that what you told the police?" Charlie asked.

"Well, no. My mom said my opinion didn't matter and that I should just tell them what I knew, and I did."

"I see." Charlie looked through the window for a moment and watched the tall palms in the distance sway in the breeze. "You didn't believe Jessica could ever do such a thing. I can understand that. That's the main reason why I'm here. Why Mrs. Healey hired our firm. She didn't believe it either, but what we want to believe and what is the truth sometimes aren't the same thing."

"You didn't know Jess. And to be honest, her mom didn't know her either," Madison continued.

Nia reached out for her friend's hand. "She's just upset. We all are. None of us want to believe that we missed the signs. We were around Jess all the time. And none of us thought we were that self-absorbed."

Charlie nodded. "Well, I'll tell you one thing, the last thing any of you girls should be doing is blaming yourselves. I came here to ask you a few questions. So, Madison, I'll start with you."

"Okay."

"The way we currently understand it, is that Jessica had no enemies that any of you knew of, is that right?"

"Yeah. Jess didn't have a mean bone in her body. No one disliked her. No one could."

"Of course. And I think Sophie, who one of my partners already spoke with, mentioned an ex-boyfriend. That maybe Jessica wanted to see him when she returned home. Do you know anything about this ex?"

Madison glanced at Nia. "I knew they broke up a few months ago. But I don't know if Jess was still talking to him or whatever."

Charlie turned her attention to Nia. "Sophie also mentioned that you might know something about Jessica's state of mind since you two drove to Daytona together."

"Sophie said that?" Nia asked.

"Yes. You two did drive together, right?" Charlie added.

"Yeah, that's right. And I didn't notice anything different. She was just like always. We had fun. It was a great road trip." Nia wiped away a tear.

"I don't mean to upset you," Charlie said. "Is there anything else you can tell me? Do you know if she met anyone there, in Daytona?"

Madison jumped in. "No. I mean, like, we always flirt and stuff, but nothing serious. Not that I knew of, anyway."

"Yeah, me neither," Nia added. "Jess wasn't the type to hook up. That wasn't who she was. I mean, no judgment, but most girls here are."

"Hey." Madison shot her a look.

"I didn't say you. Geez. Sensitive much?" Nia rolled her eyes.

"Okay. I think I understand," Charlie said. "No enemies. No hookups with strangers in Daytona. Just an ex-boyfriend who she was thinking about visiting."

Madison peered at Nia again. "What about Professor Lyman?"

"What about him?" Nia replied.

"Jess said something about him. I don't remember exactly when, but something like she thought he was hot or whatever."

"We all have hot professors. What's your point?" Nia pressed on.

Charlie's interest was piqued. "Had she seen him outside of class?"

"I have no idea," Madison continued. "I just remember her saying something. I think it was maybe a month or so ago. I can't remember. It wasn't like she said his name all the time or anything. But I don't know if that helps."

"Right now, everything helps." Charlie stood. "Thank you both. I know how hard this must be for you. I appreciate you talking to me. Here's my card. Call me if you remember anything else."

————

THE LATE AFTERNOON sun cast bright warm rays through the window of ACL's office. The partners had returned and now sat at the conference table. Charlie pulled off her reading glasses and rubbed the bridge of her nose. "It's easy to understand why Detective Brenner didn't pursue the case as a possible murder."

"I didn't hear anything that tripped my senses," Allison replied. "With one exception. Harriet Torres didn't believe Jessica could have killed herself."

"None of them did, by the sounds of it," Lucy added.

"The girl—Madison—was adamant Jessica couldn't possibly have done that to herself. She was angry about it," Charlie continued.

"That could be the grief talking. I think they're all still in a state of shock over it," Allison said. "No surprise there."

"Well, my nose is good for more than just holding up my glasses. I got a little whiff of something interesting," Charlie began. "I don't know if it meant anything or not, but when we started talking about this ex-boyfriend Jessica had broken up with months ago, Madison looked at Nia. I don't want to say it was a suspicious look, but more like an unspoken knowledge they had about this ex. It was a fleeting expression, but it was there. It reminded me of my two boys when one of them was covering for the other."

"Lucy, have you tracked down the ex yet?" Allison asked.

"I called and left a message on his cell phone, but I haven't received a call back. That was just a few hours ago, so I'm trying not to read anything into it yet."

Charlie held out her fingers to count off. "So we have the ex-boyfriend. We have statements from Jessica's closest friends that they didn't think she could take her own life. Oh, and then we have a professor."

Allison narrowed her eyes. "A professor?"

"Yeah, it's probably nothing, but again, Madison brought up one of Jessica's professors. Apparently, Jessica thought he was hot. Madison's word, not mine."

"Harriet didn't mention a professor." Allison turned to Lucy. "You? Did Sophie mention one?"

"Nope. This is the first I'm hearing of it," Lucy replied.

"Interesting." Allison cast her gaze to the ceiling while an idea took shape. "Madison seems to be the only one casting serious doubt as to suicide. The others didn't think it was possible, but based on your impression, Charlie, she seemed to be adamant about it. You say she pointed to the ex and now a professor. I'm starting to wonder if we should speak to her alone. I'm wondering if she might open up if her friends aren't around."

Charlie nodded. "Good idea. I can probably arrange that."

———

THE DINING HALL was serving dinner and in the dorm room, Madison slipped on her flip-flops and checked her reflection in the mirror. "Hey, we gotta go down now or the line will be a nightmare." She turned around. "Nia? We need to go."

Nia sat cross-legged on her twin bed with her laptop open. "I'll catch up with you. I have to turn in this assignment before 6. Kleinman's an asshole about turning in things late. Go. I'll be down soon."

Madison tucked her thick hair behind her ears and tugged on her bra straps. "Fine. I'll try to save us a table." She walked out of the room.

Nia reached for her phone and typed a text message. Waiting for a reply, she chewed on her nails. The nasty habit worsened when she was under stress.

When the bing sounded, she peered at the screen to view the incoming message. *"I already got a message from them. I haven't called back yet."*

With speedy thumbs, Nia typed her reply. *"Are you going to tell them we've been hanging out?"*

A swift reply was returned. *"Why should I? They aren't cops. Don't worry so much. We didn't do anything wrong."*

Nia closed her eyes for a moment and whispered to herself. "We didn't tell Jess."

4

Her cheeks flushed a light pink when she set down Shane's beer on the table. The 20-something dark-blonde waitress, sporting a black polo and khakis, smiled at him.

Shane had seen the look in women's eyes before. A desire bubbling just beneath the surface. Nevertheless, it was always flattering, and he was of the age knowing those looks probably wouldn't last too much longer. He would relish in them until the very last one.

"Is there anything else I can get you?" she asked.

"Not just yet. I'll wait until my friend arrives. Thank you, though." When she started away, he added. "You know what? How about a glass of chardonnay? For my friend."

"You got it. I'll be right back with that." Her eyes lingered for a moment longer than they should have until she turned away.

Shane "Sully" Sullivan was used to drawing the attention of women. Except for the one woman he wanted, Allison Hart. She'd rebuffed his advances on more than one occasion. Each time stung a little more than the last. And just when he thought he might have gotten under her skin, she pulled away again. Now, he'd discovered that she was keeping from him a new case her team had been working. A case that derived from his own department.

"I'm sorry I'm late." Allison slipped into the booth "I hope you haven't been waiting long."

"Not long. It's nice to see you." He took in the beauty of her face, her wonderfully messy blonde hair, and her figure that was incredible for a woman of any age, let alone one who was close enough to smell 50.

A crooked smile appeared on her light rose-colored lips. "You know, don't you?" She tugged at her white sleeveless top and pushed away the wisps of hair on her face.

He shrugged, not wanting to take his eyes off her. "Word gets around. I'm just surprised I didn't hear it from you first."

"Shane, I'm..."

"Here you go." The waitress set down the glass of wine for Allison. "Are you two ready to order?"

Shane looked up at her and noticed the earlier craving in her eyes had been replaced with a friendlier one, as though she thought he might have been taken. "Just the drinks, for now, thank you." As she stepped away, he turned back to Allison. "I took the liberty of ordering you a glass of wine. I hope that's okay."

"It's great. Thank you." Allison sipped on the drink, appearing to bide her time, but Shane wasn't having it.

"You were saying about this new case?"

"Right. I was about to apologize for not telling you about it first." Allison batted her eyes in a hollow attempt at gaining his forgiveness. "I'm sorry, Shane. I really am. This is going to sound like an excuse, but we've been running full steam ahead with it and this is the first opportunity I've had to let you know we took it on."

"You're right, that does sound like an excuse." He tossed back a swig of his beer, appearing ready to let her off the hook, but not just yet. "Look, Allison, you don't have to come running to me every time you start working a case. I get that. But when you mentioned you were meeting with Brenner, I guess I thought you'd fill me in on what happened. But I didn't hear a word from you."

"Considering all that you've done for me and ACL, putting yourself in danger, risking your own job, you're absolutely right. That's the least I could've done." Allison reached for his hand. "You're my friend. My intent wasn't to slight you. It was to prove to myself and maybe to the guys at the station that I didn't need to consult with Detective Sully, that ACL could stand on its own two feet."

"I get it." He eyed her hand on his and when she pulled it away, he felt the pang of regret for being upset with her. "Well, Allison Hart, here's your chance to make amends. So, tell me all about it."

————

Dr. Jacob Lyman was the university's Data Analytics professor. The 30-year-old former CEO of a software upstart sold his company to Microsoft and made a fortune from it. He chose to bring his skills to the classroom and was hired by the school as an adjunct professor. His relative youth, wit, and good looks made him popular with the students. And it seemed a lot of young women took his class regardless of whether it was a graduation requirement. One of those women was the now-deceased Jessica Healey. It wasn't until last week that he received the news of her death.

Lyman inserted his key into the front door of his home near

campus and walked inside to the delightful aroma of sauteed onions and garlic. He set down his carrier bag at the entry and continued inside the two-story townhome. "Something smells great in here." He flashed a white smile through perfect teeth and his blue eyes gleamed as he peered at his wife.

Brianne Lyman turned from the stove. Equally attractive, put their images into a 3D printer and Ken and Barbie would pop out. "I thought I'd try my hand at a new recipe I found online."

He approached his wife of three years and kissed her tanned cheek. "I can't wait to try it. I need to get changed first and I'll be right out. Maybe I'll open a bottle of wine."

"Sounds great."

Lyman walked upstairs and loosened his tie, pulling it over his head before unbuttoning his dress shirt. A quick swipe of his phone and he noticed a missed call and voicemail message. As he continued to undress, he placed the phone on speaker to listen to the message.

"Hello, my name is Lucy Boyce. I work for ACL Investigative Services. I'm calling to see if you could set aside a little bit of time to meet with me and/or my partners in the next day or so. I apologize for the short notice, but we were hired by Mary Ann Healey, the mother of one of your students, Jessica Healey."

The name quickly drew his attention as he reached for his phone to take it off speaker and place it against his ear.

"We're looking into Jessica's unfortunate suicide and talking to some of her friends as well as her instructors. We'd be grateful for a call back just as soon as you can."

Lyman finished listening to the message that relayed Lucy's call back details and returned the phone to his bed. He sat down on its edge and stared through his bedroom window. Clouds rolled in with the tide and he quickly regretted having just washed his Range Rover.

He pushed back his dark, wavy hair that brushed atop his shoulders and remained motionless. It took a moment for him to realize Brianne had called his name as her voice traveled upstairs. Dinner was ready.

The t-shirt and board shorts he always wore lay across a side chair in his bedroom. He slipped on his clothes and started back down the stairs until arriving in the kitchen.

"There you are. What took you so long?" She set down the plates at the table. "You were supposed to open a bottle of wine for dinner." When he didn't respond, she peered at him with a creased brow. Her bleached-blonde hair was pushed to one side over her shoulder. She cocked her head. "Are you feeling okay?"

"Huh?" Yeah. I guess." He grabbed a bottle of wine from the fridge. "I just got a weird call."

"Oh?"

"A student of mine killed herself over Spring Break."

"Oh my God." She shot him a glance. "And you're just now finding this out?"

"Well, no. I got word of it last week when the students returned, but then I just got this call."

"Who was it from?" Brianne asked.

"A private investigating firm. They're looking into the student's suicide and want to talk to me." He set down the bottle on the kitchen island and searched for the opener.

"Why on earth would they want to talk to you?" she pressed on.

"They said they're talking to people she knew. Friends, instructors, too, I guess. I don't know what they hope to find."

"I'm sure it's nothing. You look really upset about this. Do you want to sit down a moment?"

"No." Lyman placed his hand on her shoulder. "I'm fine. I

think it just sort of hit me. Just now. The reality of it all. Such a shame."

"Did you know her well?"

"Not particularly. She was one of my students. A good student, at that. On scholarship too. But we were never chatty with each other."

"Then I guess that's what you'll have to tell this private investigator." She peered at him with pursed lips and growing concern. "Come on. Let's sit down and eat before dinner gets cold."

———

SHANE FINISHED off his second beer and set down the glass. "You're in a tough spot."

"Tell me about it," Allison replied. "I don't know how this is going to play out, but we have to follow the crumbs."

"What crumbs? You don't have any crumbs to follow. Allison, all you're doing is confirming what Brenner already knows."

"Maybe." She sipped on the few drops of wine left in her glass. "We have to finish the process and try to make a determination. I'm almost thinking the girls and I should make a trip to Daytona too. Take a look at the hotel surveillance footage. See if we pick up Jessica anywhere and find anything unusual."

"That's actually a good idea," Shane replied.

Allison chuckled. "Why, thank you. I'm smarter than I look."

He raised his hand to garner the waitress's attention. "Two more over here, please." Shane turned back to Allison. "Sorry. Do you want another? Do you have time?"

She offered a half-smile. "I have time."

"Great." Shane wrapped the paper from a straw around his finger, fidgeting as if ready to speak, but unable to find words that didn't make him sound like an idiot. He'd never had trouble talking to women, but it was different with Allison. A hard-core bachelor, Shane was in real trouble with her, and the worst part about it was, she didn't feel the same. "How are the kids? Nolan doing well with the team?"

Her eyes lit up. "He's doing great. He made his big debut a couple of weeks ago and absolutely killed it. I'm so proud of him."

"And Micah?" Shane asked.

"She didn't come home for Spring Break. Had a big thing going on with her friends. I tried not to be offended, but..."

"But you were anyway."

"A little. She's an adult now. And while our relationship is better than it was, I think she's still trying to pull away from me. But I understand that's a natural thing for her to do. She only has one year left at FSU and that's it."

"How is everyone adjusting to the engagement?" he asked.

"Everyone, or me?" She laughed. "No, it's fine. It's Leo's life now, and it has nothing to do with me anymore. He can marry whoever he wants." Allison waited while the waitress returned with their drinks. "Thank you." A long sip and she closed her eyes for a moment. "Besides, I can get a man if I want. I think I still got it...somewhere," she laughed.

A sly grin formed on Shane's lips. "Are you kidding? They're all lining up for you, Allison. Trust me on that."

———

BRIANNE LYMAN WALKED outside her front door and squinted from the rays of a setting sun. Jacob was due home in an hour, and she had already called in for delivery. Indian food tonight. It was Jacob's favorite. She didn't mind it so long as it wasn't too spicy.

She continued down her driveway to the gates at the end. Slipping outside of them, Brianne opened the mailbox and retrieved the day's mail. Inside the gates again, she shuffled through the various bills, flyers, and occasional credit card offers.

Brianne didn't work a regular job anymore, not since Jacob sold the business. She used to be the vice president of marketing, which suited her well considering her master's in marketing from Berkley. That was where she'd met Jacob. He was 2 years older and was already a senior at the university when they met. The business he'd started was still in his parent's garage at the time. Soon after, he graduated and focused on it full-time. Brianne soon went to work for Jacob. By then, they'd gotten pretty serious, but she wanted to get her master's before anything else.

That seemed like a lifetime ago. Now they were wealthy, and she could buy anything she wanted. And usually did.

On returning inside, Brianne walked to the kitchen and grabbed the letter opener from a drawer. She sliced open the credit card statement and dropped onto the kitchen chair to open it. "Looks good. Looks good. Oh, crap, I forgot about that." She peered up for a moment. "I need to send back that dress, come to think of it."

This was her life now. Buying nice clothes, brunches with her friends, sometimes yoga. Jacob wasn't thrilled when she suggested getting another job. He'd insisted they hadn't needed the money, so why bother? He didn't understand that if she didn't go back to work, who was she? She wasn't a mother—yet. So who was she, really?

Brianne continued to peruse the statement until coming across a charge. She fixed her eyes on the line item. With her phone next to her, Brianne picked it up and dialed the 800 number for customer service.

"Yes, hello, I'm Brianne Lyman. I wanted to let you know that there's a charge on my statement that I don't recognize. I know I didn't make that purchase." She nodded and listened while the service representative spoke. "No, I didn't purchase that. It's a mobile phone store. No, I have a phone. I didn't buy another. Yes, please, I would like to file a dispute on this charge. Great, thank you so much." She ended the call, returned the statement to its envelope, and stood from the kitchen table. A glance at the street before she shoved the statement in the bottom drawer of the kitchen desk beneath several papers. "Takes care of that."

———

CHARLIE HONKED her horn in the driveway of Lucy's home. A gentle beep to remind her they were in a crunch for time. They needed to get to the professor before his first class this morning if they'd hoped to catch him at his office. After no returned call last night, they were about to take the matter into their own hands. She smiled at the sight of Lucy emerging from the home. It was a wonder how she handled all this. The loss of her father less than a year ago. Losing her mother to cancer several years before that. Lucy was alone in that house she once shared with the venerable Tommy Boyce and Charlie was amazed by her ability to cope.

Lucy's long black hair was pulled into a braid and she smiled apologetically when she opened the passenger door. "Sorry about that. Figured you might want some coffee." She held out a travel mug. "Brought one for myself too."

"A woman after my own heart. Thanks, kiddo." Charlie took the mug and sipped on the brew. "You ready to talk to this guy?"

"He left us no choice." Lucy closed the door and buckled her belt.

Charlie shifted into Reverse and backed out of the driveway. "'Leave no stone unturned', someone once said. I have no idea who."

"And where is Allison hoping to catch the ex-boyfriend? Did she mention it when you spoke to her last night?" Lucy asked.

"Apparently, he lives not far from the Healey's and stays with his folks while attending college. No call back from him either, so she's taking a shot that he'll be on his way to class this morning. Going to try to catch him at home."

"Interesting how neither of these men got back to us, don't you think?"

Charlie turned to her and grunted. "Typical, as far as I'm concerned."

Lucy eyed her for a moment. "You don't think much of men, do you? Not that I blame you."

"Me?" Charlie pressed her hand against her chest. "That's not the case at all. Despite the fact that I was recently kidnapped by a man who finally cracked, was married to a psycho, that says nothing of how I feel. I have two sons who I adore and can't wait to see the men they become. My ex is pretty much a dirtbag, but again, I don't paint all men with that brush." She grinned. "You'll find out for yourself soon enough. Although Nolan is a great kid and there's no doubt in my mind that he'll continue to treat you well."

"I know he will, too." Lucy returned her gaze to the road. "That's it, up ahead."

"Yes, ma'am. Professor Lyman should be in that building right there." She pulled into the parking lot and cut the engine. "Right now, all we know is that this Professor Jacob Lyman had Jessica in one of his classes. According to her friends, she was at least a little attracted to him. What I don't want to do is go in there with any sort of accusations. Remember what it is we're trying to do..."

"Confirm it was a suicide or find reasonable evidence to suggest it could have been murder," Lucy added.

"Bingo." Charlie opened her door. "Now, let's go have a chat with this man and since he's not expecting us, we'll be able to tell a lot by his reaction."

They started toward the administration building where several professors held their offices. Charlie double-checked her notes. "His office is in the C Hall, number 209." She slipped on her reading glasses and glanced at the directory next to the doors. "Second floor and to the right."

When they arrived at his office, the door was open, and the bright light of a clear day shone inside.

Charlie peeked in. "Excuse me? Professor Jacob Lyman?" The attraction of his female students became quite clear. He was hot. And by no small measure. In fact, she was sure her heart skipped a beat, but that could've been the caffeine.

"Yes?" He shook away the hair from his face and peered up with curiosity. "Can I help you?"

She started inside and Lucy trailed. "Pardon the interruption. My name is Charlie Wells, and this is my partner, Lucy Boyce. I believe you received a call from our office yesterday. ACL Investigative Services."

Lyman cleared his throat and thrust back his shoulders. He wore a light beard, just slightly thicker than a 5 o'clock shadow, as though he hadn't had time to shave today. "Yes. I'm sorry for not getting back to you. As you can probably imagine, the loss of one of my students has been difficult to come to terms with."

They both moved inside and stood just feet from the professor's desk. Charlie continued. "I'm sure it has been. But we'd just like to ask you a few questions and then we'll be out of your way."

He appeared to study them with some thought as to the consequences of a refusal. "Of course. Please, take a seat. Can I get you anything to drink?"

"No, thank you." Charlie sat down and motioned for Lucy to do the same. "This won't take long."

"Then what can I answer for you?" He pulled his chair closer to his desk and rested his elbows on top of it. "Ms. Healey was in one of my classes, but I didn't know her that well."

"I suppose you just answered my first question," Charlie began. "You didn't know her well. Have you ever spoken to her outside of class?"

"Yeah, sure. Students always come to me with questions. That's not unusual."

"I didn't say it was," Charlie added. "From what I hear, your female students are a little enamored with you. Do you think Jessica Healey was also?"

He smiled and a hint of pink rose in his cheeks. "I have no idea. I can be oblivious to that sometimes. I'm happily married." Lyman raised his left hand to show off the ring on his finger.

"That's nice to hear," she continued. "I think what I'm getting at is do you believe Jessica Healey paid you any special attention? And if she had, were you quick to shut it down to avoid any misunderstandings?"

"I'm always quick to shut that down. Like I said, I'm a happily married man and I suppose I do see what you're talking about. Although, I really can't say if Jessica held feelings like that for me." He glanced at the time. "I do have a class I need to get to."

"Sure, I understand. There's one last thing I'd like to ask." Charlie eyed Lucy for just a moment. "The police believe Jessica Healey committed suicide. In your opinion, in however brief your encounters with her were, did she strike you as mentally unstable to that degree?"

His eyes flickered with emotion. "No. Not at all, actually. Jess was bright smart, and incredibly talented. To hear she could have done that to herself just seems impossible."

Charlie nodded. "That appears to be the general consensus. Thank you so much for your time, Professor Lyman. I'm sorry we barged in, but this is for the Healey family. They're looking for closure." She stood. "We'll let you get to your class. Lucy?"

Lucy joined her and peered at the professor. "Thank you, sir."

"Anytime."

The partners returned to Charlie's car and stepped inside. Both turned to each other, wearing the same look.

"You picked up on it too, huh?" Lucy asked.

"Jess. He called her Jess." Charlie started her car. "That seems very familiar for a man who hardly spoke to her and couldn't recollect any real conversations."

Lucy buckled her belt. "I have a feeling Professor Lyman knew Jessica Healey better than he let on."

5

In her old blue Honda Accord, Allison parked on the opposite side of the street from the home of Antonio Cruz, the former boyfriend of Jessica Healey. The high-school sweethearts broke up only a few months ago, making his insight into Jessica incredibly valuable for the ACL partners.

At 7:30 on a Wednesday morning, Allison hoped the catch the young man on his way out the door to head to the local community college. And as she spotted someone emerge, Allison realized her intuition was right. While she hadn't seen a picture of the ex-boyfriend, this one looked to be the right age.

She stepped out of her car and walked across the street. "Antonio?" Allison spoke up as she made her way toward him. "Antonio Cruz?"

"Yeah?" He peered at her with concern.

"My name is Allison Hart and I'm a private detective. I wanted to ask you a couple of questions about Jessica Healey."

With a backpack slung over his shoulder, the olive-skinned,

dark-eyed young man stopped at the end of the driveway. "You're the one who called. Why? Who sent you here?"

"Antonio..."

"It's Tony," he added.

"Tony, Jessica's mother hired my firm to look into other possible reasons as to how Jessica died."

"What do you mean, how? She killed herself." He pushed on ahead. "I'm sorry, but I have a class I have to get to."

"Tony, please. I'll only take up a moment of your time." She reached out for him as he brushed past her. "Please. It's for her mother. As you can imagine, she's very upset by all of this."

"We're all upset, Ms. Hart. I went out with Jess all through high school and up until a few months ago. I loved her."

"Then you must have been surprised to learn that she had taken her own life."

He stopped again and lowered his head before turning back to Allison. "I'm not all that surprised, to be honest."

This was a first. So far, everyone they'd spoken to was completely caught off guard as to the matter of Jessica's suicide. Allison stepped closer. "Why were you not surprised? Had she said something to you?"

"No." He looked away as if suddenly recalling an unpleasant memory. "She was just under a lot of pressure, you know? School, grades. She was on scholarship too. That put a lot of pressure on her. And her parents, well, they expected a lot from her. Always had."

"You knew her well, didn't you?" Allison asked.

"Of course, I did. I thought I was going to marry her someday," he replied.

"I know you have to get going, but can I ask, and you'll forgive me for the personal nature of the question, but why did you two break up?"

Tony shoved a hand into the pocket of his shorts and pressed his lips together. "She said she outgrew me. That she'd changed since being at the university. But I don't think that was why she broke up with me."

"What do you think her reason was, then?" Allison pressed on.

"I think she liked someone else."

"Do you know who?"

Tony shook his head. "She never said, but you just feel that sort of thing, you know?"

Allison knew all too well. "On her drive back home, she and her friend, Sophie, were texting each other. Apparently, it was about you."

He rolled his eyes. "I'm pretty sure Sophie was part of the reason Jess wanted to break up, so I'm not surprised."

"It turned out that Jessica contemplated coming to see you after she visited her dad in the hospital."

"She did?" He shrugged. "She never texted me. Is her dad doing okay? I really liked him."

"Yes. He's recovering."

"That's good." Tony's eyes reddened. "I always thought of him like a dad. My dad took off when I was five."

Allison felt his heartbreak. "I'm sure he'd appreciate it if you stopped by."

"Maybe." He started away again. "I'm sorry, but I really have to go. I'm going to be late for class."

"Tony?" Allison stepped quickly to catch up to him. "You mentioned Jessica was under a lot of stress. Do you think her mom put a lot of that on her shoulders?"

"Some, yeah. But Jess was always hard on herself. Never thought she was good enough, smart enough." He shook his head. "I always believed in her, though. I guess it wasn't enough."

———

ONE OF THE skills that had made Allison ideally suited for P.I. work was her ability to read people. She'd employed her talent while working as a fraud investigator for the state and now used it as a means to determine the intent of those she interviewed. Not infallible, her accuracy rated around 90 percent or so. An informal spreadsheet she kept track of in the back of her mind. And on her return to the office, she felt 100 percent confident that Tony Cruz had no part in whatever had happened to Jessica Healey, except for perhaps contributing to her emotional state.

As the team reconvened at the office, it was Allison who began. "Aside from the fact that you guys think the good-looking professor might have known Jessica better than he admitted to, none of us, at this moment, believe this was anything more than a suicide."

Charlie appeared to accept the premise. "Everyone liked her. I realize that's hardly definitive, but it's all we know right now. I don't know, Alli, if it looks like a duck..."

"I do think it's worth checking to see if Professor Lyman had an alibi," Lucy added.

"You're right," Allison began. "And we already know Jessica's closest friends were with her on the trip and stayed behind when she left. Pretty solid alibis there, too."

"And the ex-boyfriend?" Charlie asked. "I mean, if we're checking things out, we should check him out too. Especially in light of the fact Jessica and Sophie texted each other about him."

"Yep." Allison checked the time. "It's almost noon. We've talked to everyone in Jessica's circle. Time to move onto motive, if any. Lucy, would you mind digging into the background of Tony Cruz? Let's find out where he was when Jessica left that afternoon. Charlie, I think you should take the lead on looking into Professor McHotty."

Charlie laughed. "You're starting to sound like me. I'm on it."

"Good. I'm going to drive to Daytona and check out the hotel where they stayed. Talk to anyone who met the girls, the staff, whoever. I realize it's been more than 2 weeks, but I'm hoping someone will remember them."

———

WITH 23 MILES of white sandy beaches, it was no wonder Daytona Beach was called the "Spring Break Capital of the World." When Allison passed under the expansive welcome sign, she was transported to another realm. One where life wasn't bogged down with worrisome notions of suicide, death, and pain. If only life was as carefree as the local tourism board advertised.

While the students had returned to school, the beaches still teemed with visitors. Daytona also catered to other walks of life such as biker's clubs and NASCAR enthusiasts. The Ocean Walk Shoppes still bustled. But where Allison headed was just outside this upscale location. Farther down the stretch of beach lay smaller hotels. A comparison could be made to youth hostels in some cases. These were the hotels that catered to the college crowds. The less-affluent ones, anyway.

Allison arrived at the hotel as it reached about 2:30 in the afternoon. She had to confirm the name of the place with Mary Ann Healey as well as the exact dates the girls had been booked for. One room, five girls. Fun. But now she was armed with all the details necessary to piece together the two days they had stayed here with Jessica. There were no guarantees, but if she could scratch this off the list, it would bring them that much closer to confirming the truth.

"Excuse me." Allison pulled off her sunglasses and retrieved her credentials. "Allison Hart. I'm a private investigator. I'd like to speak with the manager about a young woman, women, actually, who stayed here for Spring Break a couple of weeks ago."

"Do you happen to have the name of the registrant?" the man asked. "Sorry, but we were at 100 percent capacity over Spring Break. It'd be nice to narrow it down."

"Of course. I don't know who booked the room, but I do have the names of the girls staying in it." Allison slid a piece of notebook paper across the counter.

"Great. Let me take a look." He keyed in the names listed. "And you say it was two weeks ago?"

"Just about," Allison replied.

"All right." While his fingers typed quickly, he nodded. "I see it here. The name on the room was Sophie Matthews. Guests were listed as Jessica Healey and Nia Brown. I don't see the other two girls on there." He peered at her. "Although, that's not too unusual. The more people, the more we have to charge. We see it all the time."

"Then it sounds like they're the ones I'm looking for," she added.

"So how can I help you, then?" he pressed on.

Allison gauged the immediate area. "Again, this is probably something that I should discuss with your manager if it's okay with you."

He peered at her with some irritation. "Of course. I'll go and get her. Just a moment."

Allison waited while the 30-something man in a short-sleeved dress shirt and black trousers headed back. The good news was that he found the record of Jessica's stay. Now, to convince the manager to let her view security footage. Allison could be persuasive when the need arose. She spotted the return of the front desk staffer and his boss. A woman. Even better. Older too, perhaps a mother herself.

"Good afternoon, I'm Linda, the day manager. You're Ms. Hart?" She offered her hand.

"I am. Thank you for agreeing to see me." Allison returned the handshake.

"Of course. What can I do for you, Ms. Hart? Austin tells me you're a private detective."

"That's right. I don't suppose we could talk someplace a bit more private?"

"Certainly. Follow me. We can talk in my office." Linda started ahead wearing beige stiletto heels and a snug-fitting blue dress. Her figure filled out the dress, and she was a well-put-together, attractive woman in her forties. "Right through here. Please, have a seat." She walked inside and closed the door, returning to her desk. "So, this is about a guest we had a few weeks ago, I understand?"

Allison sat down. "Yes. Five girls from the University of South Florida. Unfortunately, one of them never made it home."

"Oh my goodness." Linda pressed her hand against her bosom. "Forgive my crassness, but I assume it didn't involve this hotel. I'm sure I would've heard otherwise."

"I suppose that's why I'm here. I'd like to be certain that the young woman, who was found dead on a roadside on her way back to Tampa, hadn't been followed, or stalked. And if that did happen, I would hope your company would want to assist in finding out if that was the case."

Linda averted her eyes for a moment. "I think I understand. And yes, of course, I can help, but I do have some limitations."

"All I ask is to see the surveillance footage from the two days this young girl was here," Allison replied.

"I can help you with that."

———

CHARLIE ENTERED the restaurant and spotted Shane at the booth. "Hey. Thanks for meeting me. What did you find?" She sat down.

"Nice to see you too, Charlie. Right down to business, I see."

"No time for our usual witty banter, Sully. What did you find out about Professor McHotty, I mean, Lyman?"

Shane cast her a sideways glance before swiping open his phone. "Dr. Jacob Lyman, USF professor, adjunct. Founder of SpearLink Data Systems. Sold his company to Microsoft two years ago for a cool $20 million."

"Cheese and rice." Charlie's eyes widened. "He's rich?"

"Rich? No. He's incredibly wealthy," Shane added. "He took the professor job to keep himself busy enough until he comes up with his next multi-million-dollar idea, I'm guessing."

A waiter approached with a broad smile. "You two ready to order?"

"You know what? I could eat. I haven't eaten all day," Charlie began. "I'll take a cheeseburger and an order of fries. Oh, and a Diet Coke."

"And for you, sir?"

Shane glanced at the menu briefly. "The hoagie with a side of fries. Iced tea for me, thanks. Unsweetened."

"Got it. Be right back."

After he stepped out of earshot, Charlie continued. "Super-rich guy. Super good-looking. Part-time professor. Wife. He made that point abundantly clear when Lucy and I met with him this morning."

"Interesting. He's really good-looking, huh?" Shane asked.

"Oh yeah. You should see this guy. We were drooling."

"Allison too?" He turned sheepish.

"Don't worry, Sully. Alli still thinks you're attractive too." Charlie rolled her eyes. "Sheesh. Didn't think you were so insecure. What else did you find out?"

Shane cleared his throat, attempting to regain his composure. "No kids. And he's only been married for three years."

"So she married him before he made all that money?" Charlie asked.

"Looks like it. It's one way to be sure someone's not after your money. Don't have any."

"Any tickets, speeding, parking? Anything at all remotely shady that popped up for you?" Charlie asked.

"Sorry, but no. Guy's clean as a whistle," Shane replied. "What makes you think he had anything to do with Jessica's death, assuming it wasn't suicide?"

"We don't know he did, but he seemed to be more familiar with her than at first glance."

"How so?" Shane asked.

"He referenced her by her nickname. A name we've only heard her friends and family call her. Not something an instructor would say, at least, we didn't think so. And it was just odd how he made sure to let us know he was happily married more than once."

"He didn't just say he was married, he said he was 'happily' married?"

"That's right. Like he was putting a fine point on the subject." Charlie considered an idea. "I wonder if we can find out whether he's had any complaints from students. If he'd been investigated or suspended. Anything like that."

"That wouldn't be in the public domain, not the details anyway." Shane sipped on his iced tea that had just arrived. "Luckily, I know a guy who could find that out for us."

"You know a guy? Who's this guy?" Charlie asked.

"He works for the Athletic Department at the university.

We're old friends from school. I'll bet he could look into it for me." Shane glanced away for a moment. "Unless you don't want my help. Allison made it clear she wanted ACL to stand on its own two feet."

"She said that?" Charlie asked.

"In no uncertain terms."

Charlie eyed him. "You know, Alli doesn't want to be seen as needing anyone. You get that, right? That includes me and you."

"I guess I thought, after all this time, and us all working together on stuff. I guess I thought she'd welcome my help."

"She does, Shane. She does. But it's hard for her to admit it. This whole thing. The agency, us, it took her last dime to make this happen. She's put everything at stake, including her home. It was a hard decision for her because if it failed, Leo would blame her for losing the house. The kids would blame her."

"No, I don't think that's true at all. Nolan and Micah wouldn't do that," Shane added.

"I don't think so either, but that's what Alli believes. Listen, just cut her a little slack. She does need you. We all need you. There are things you can do that we simply don't have access to. The partnership is real and it's important."

"Thanks, Charlie. I needed to hear that. Even if it didn't come from Allison." He stirred his iced tea with his straw. "You know, I really thought I got through to her after the last case."

"What do you mean?" Charlie asked.

He shook his head. "Nothing. Yeah, let me get in touch with my buddy. See if he can root around into Lyman's history at the school. It might take a day, maybe two, but I'll get back to you."

The waiter returned with their plates.

Charlie peered up at him. "Perfect timing. I was about to start eating the table."

———

LUCY HAD DONE as much leg work as possible on Tony Cruz, Jessica's ex-boyfriend. She'd spent the better part of two hours researching his social media to find out who his friends were and whether he was anywhere near Daytona when Jessica and her friends were there. Sophie Matthews had already admitted to texting Jessica and advising her not to see Tony when she returned home. But what Lucy didn't know was Jessica's response. Sure they had phone records, but all they indicated were that texts were exchanged. And Jessica had sent the final one, they now knew. This was something Sophie insisted hadn't happened. Now, Sophie would have to offer up her phone to see the message and right now, Lucy had no cause to ask for that, or warrant, or any of the other things usually required by law.

So the question remained, did Tony Cruz receive a text from Jessica before her final moments on this earth? And would he admit it?

According to Tony's Instagram account, he played baseball for his community college team. He would be at practice this afternoon. That was where Lucy was headed now. However, she had no intention of speaking to him. Allison had already done that, and he would get suspicious if Lucy made another go of it.

She reached the field and walked to the bleachers. The team was already on the field and running drills. Several observers were on the bleachers. Mostly girls. Probably girlfriends of the players.

According to Allison, Tony seemed genuinely upset by Jessica's death. By all accounts, he loved her and her family.

The coach called for a break and Tony and several players walked to the dugout and grabbed sports drinks. Tony shook the sweat from his hair, the black strands clinging to his neck. Lucy immediately thought of Nolan. They were about the same age, similar build even. But Nolan quit school when he made the Triple-A team. She'd never watched so many baseball games in her entire life as she had since she and Nolan started dating. Now, this.

It wasn't until the practice ended, after much too long, that Lucy spotted a young woman step off the bleachers and walk toward Tony. She reached for her phone and snapped a few pictures. Tony kissed her lightly on the lips and put his arm around her. "They're dating," Lucy said.

As she waited for the team to disburse and Tony to head to the locker room, she followed the pretty girl while she waited nearby. Lucy peered down at her phone intentionally, attempting to accidentally bump into this girl. She hadn't seen her on Tony's Instagram page, so this could be a new relationship.

"Oh, my gosh. I'm so sorry." Lucy pulled back. "I wasn't paying attention and I ran right into you."

"That's okay. Hey, I do it all the time, right?" The young woman with light brown hair pulled in a long ponytail smiled.

"Dangers of phones, I guess," Lucy quipped. "I write for the school paper and I was watching the practice."

"Oh really? That's cool. Did you see Tony Cruz?" she asked.

"He was number 12, I think," Lucy said.

"That's right. Wears number 12. You should pay attention to him. He's going to the Major Leagues someday."

Lucy smiled because that was exactly what she thought about Nolan. "I don't mean to pry, but are you his girlfriend?"

She smiled and turned a little flush. "Yes. We just started dating about a month ago, actually. I'm Hailey. Hailey Buford. I'm on Insta. You should find me."

"Nice to meet you, Hailey. I'm Lucy. I will. I'll look you up." Out of the corner of her eye, she spotted someone approaching and from here, it looked like it could be Tony. "Listen, I need to get going, but it was really nice meeting you, Hailey."

"Wait, Tony's coming right now. You two should talk."

"I actually have an appointment to get to. How about I go through you and arrange an interview soon?" Lucy started walking away. "Take care, Hailey."

As she hurried ahead, Hailey was greeted by Tony. "Hey babe. Who was that?"

"She writes for the school paper. She wants to interview you soon and said she'd contact me."

Tony nodded. "Cool. Come on. Let's go."

6

I nside a small room with no windows, Allison sat beside Linda, the hotel manager. Their security room wasn't much more than a closet. Several monitors lined the wall, each showing different angles and views of the hotel grounds. They'd been reviewing the footage for hours. Scouring every frame in search of Jessica Healey and anyone who might have been seen with her.

"I wish we had more to show you, Ms. Hart."

Allison took in a deep breath. "Me too. To be honest, I'm not sure what I was hoping to find. A clue, anything I suppose, that might lead to a different conclusion."

"Do you happen to know where the girls went at night? There are a lot of bars and clubs here and they're especially packed during Spring Break," Linda said.

"Jessica wasn't 21 yet, but some of her friends are," Allison began. "I'd be naïve to think she wasn't drinking while she was here."

"Yes, I'd just assume she was," Linda replied. "You could hit some of the hot spots. I know a few if that helps."

"I can make a call to her friends and find out where they were but thank you. I'm so sorry to have wasted your time." Allison pushed back in her chair and glanced again at the monitors. "Hang on." She lowered back down and pointed to one of the screens. "When was this?"

Linda paused the video and checked the timestamp. "Saturday. So, I guess that would've been their first night here." She peered at the screen. "What am I looking for, exactly?"

"I'm sure it's nothing, but that girl there. That's Nia Brown, one of the group of friends. She's got her back turned but is looking over her shoulder at Jessica and the others." Allison eyed the screen and cocked her head. "She looks upset. Angry, even."

"You know what girls that age can be like. They're still so insecure and vulnerable to peer pressure," Linda replied. "It was probably a minor argument that, after a couple drinks, was all but forgotten."

Allison nodded. "You're probably right. I have a daughter that age and I remember what I was like, too." She stood again. "I appreciate your time, Linda. Do you mind if I contact you again should I need anything else?"

"Not at all." Linda joined her. "I'll show you out."

Allison returned to her car and started back toward Tampa. The footage didn't offer anything more than what she already knew. Maybe she was looking in the wrong place. The only people who knew Jessica was returning home, from what she had been told, were her group of friends who'd traveled to Daytona. Was it possible a random attack might have occurred on the side of the road? A road rage incident? It was possible, but according to Detective Brenner, no evidence suggested that. No skid marks on the road near Jessica's

Mini Cooper. No damage to her vehicle. The grassy shoulder revealed flat patches indicating a car may have been there at one point in time, but with the rains, there was nothing definitive. And the car hadn't broken down, wasn't out of gas, so the idea Jessica tried to flag anyone down for help didn't jibe either. What was worse was that particular stretch of highway was absent any cameras. It was just outside the city and only a few speed cameras were dotted around. None, of course, anywhere near Jessica's car. If Allison was a betting woman, she would wonder what the odds of that were.

Brenner's initial determination seemed all the more likely with Allison having come up empty-handed as to another theory. Jessica Healey pulled off the side of the road and aimed a gun at her head. As unlikely as that was. What was she missing? Was there anything missing? Allison pressed together her lips until they turned white. "Damn it."

As Allison drove on, she couldn't help but think back to the surveillance footage of Nia Brown and her reaction to what appeared to have been a disagreement between her and Jessica, specifically. While it was impossible to know what was said or the pretext behind it, the issue concerned her. Had whatever was said or done contributed to Jessica's state of mind? There was no mention of any arguments among the girls and Nia was the first one, by all accounts, to help Jessica pack and get ready to go home. Allison knew she'd begun to overthink it, looking for any reason that Brenner might have been wrong. She hadn't yet found one.

———

IN THE LATE AFTERNOON, Allison returned to the office. "You two haven't been waiting long, have you?" She hurried to her desk and set down her bag. "I started to hit rush hour traffic and it took me longer than I thought."

"I got back about an hour ago, but have kept busy," Charlie began. "Lucy's been back, what two hours?"

She nodded. "Yeah, but I've had plenty to do." Lucy turned to Allison. "I hope it wasn't a wasted trip."

Allison walked to the conference table with her files in hand. "We should lay out everything and see where we're at. We're going to need to update Mary Ann soon and I'd like to have something tangible for her."

Charlie stood and straightened her lightweight tan blouse that rested nicely over her full figure. "Then we should get down to brass tacks."

Lucy grabbed her folders and started toward the table and took a seat. "I did find out some interesting details."

"Then you should start," Allison replied. "Tell us what you found."

"Before I did anything, I checked out Tony Cruz's social media." Lucy eyed them. "If he's mourning Jessica, he's not showing it. In fact, I couldn't find a single reference to her death."

"They had been broken up for a few months. Maybe it was all too personal for him?" Charlie asked.

"I thought about that, but I know my generation pretty well. It's all about online attention, as much as I hate to say it. Likes, comments. They post things that should be kept offline, in my opinion. Dad hammered that into me pretty hard. So, I guess my point is, there's no mention of Jessica anywhere. And what's even more strange, he said he'd been dating her since high school. Well then, he must've scrubbed everything they did together off his pages. I didn't find any photos showing the two of them together at all."

"That is interesting," Allison replied. "I talked to him directly. He seemed genuinely distressed by Jessica's death. Maybe Charlie's right. Maybe it is too painful for him to talk about or remember. He just wanted to erase her from his life."

"Okay, say I agree with that," Lucy began. "If he was so distressed, his girlfriend didn't see it."

"Girlfriend?" Allison lifted a brow.

"That's right. Her name is Hailey Buford. She seemed happy and made zero mention of anything that Tony was going through at that moment. Almost as if she hadn't known."

"Did you tell her who you were?" Charlie asked.

Lucy turned sheepish. "Yes and no. I told her I wrote for the school paper and was interested in Tony's position on the school baseball team."

"He plays baseball?" Allison asked. "You did learn a lot. I'm impressed."

"She is Tommy Boyce's daughter." Charlie rewarded her with a crooked smile and a nod. "Good work, kiddo."

"Thanks, but I didn't get enough information to mean anything."

"Sure you did. Tony's got a girlfriend now and he's all but erased everything about Jessica Healey." Charlie eyed them both. "That's something."

"But does it amount to murder?" Allison asked.

"We'd have to know where he was when she died. And we don't know that right now," Charlie replied. "What about you, Alli? What did you come up with?"

"Not a lot. Spent a couple hours reviewing surveillance footage and the best I could do was pick up on an apparent disagreement, argument, or something of that nature between Nia Brown and Jessica."

"How do you mean?" Charlie asked.

"There was no audio and they got out of the frame quickly, but I picked up on a disgruntled look from Nia directed at Jessica."

"A look?" Charlie asked. "There could be something to that. Like I mentioned earlier, I could've sworn I picked up on a look between Madison and Nia. Like these girls are all in on something."

"If they are, they did a good job of hiding it. Nothing else caught my eye. Absolutely nothing. The hotel manager suggested I visit some of the popular nightspots and ask to take a look at their footage, but I didn't see that it was worth it." Allison took a deep breath. "I had initially thought that maybe someone had spotted her. Picked her out and followed her unnoticed. But the more I think about it, the more it looks like what it is..."

"A suicide," Lucy said.

Charlie's phone buzzed on the table. "It's Sully. I'll put him on speaker."

Allison peered at her with concern and Charlie seemed to pick up on it. "I asked him to look into Lyman for us. What? We needed the help, Alli." She swiped to answer the call. "Sully, hey, I've got you on speaker, so no badmouthing Alli, okay?"

He chuckled. "Hey, Allison."

"Hi, Shane. Lucy's here too. Charlie said she asked you to check out something for us?"

"She did. I know a guy at the Athletics department at USF and asked him to see what he could find out about Dr. Jacob Lyman."

"And?" Allison asked.

"Interestingly enough, my contact had attended a fundraising event for the school shortly before Christmas break. He recalled seeing the professor there along with his wife."

"Sounds legitimate enough," Charlie said.

"It does, with the exception that there was a somewhat public display of discourse between Lyman and his wife," Shane replied.

"What happened?" Allison asked.

"He grabbed her arm and she pulled it away before leaving in a huff. He didn't see the wife after that, but it was clear a lot of people noticed what happened. Even the professor looked a little red-faced about it. Like he was embarrassed to have caused a scene."

"So much for his insistence that he's happily married," Lucy said. "He was quick to point that out to Charlie and me."

"Every marriage has its troubles," Allison added.

"There's something else too," Charlie began. "I forgot to mention it, but this guy is stinking rich."

"Lyman?" Allison asked.

"Yep. Right, Sully?"

"That's right," he replied through the phone. "I can check out a few more things about him if you want."

Allison leaned over the table just enough for her voice to better carry through the speaker. "The most helpful thing for us to know would be if he had an alibi for the day of Jessica's death. I think it's time we start looking at alibis because we aren't getting very far with assumptions about these people. Peeling back these layers is only revealing more layers."

"Well, we know where her friends were," Lucy said. "They were still in Daytona."

"I know Brenner didn't look for alibis because he was convinced it was suicide based on the evidence," Shane added.

"We still need to be convinced of that," Allison replied. "I think we'll need your help with that, Shane, if you wouldn't mind."

"I don't mind at all. I'm always here to help."

"Thank you, Shane. Hey, we'll catch up with you later." Allison ended the call and glanced at her partners. "Okay. We still have our work cut out for us. Let's do what we can on our end to gather alibis and then we make the call to Mary Ann."

———

Tony Cruz sat at the dinner table with his parents and younger brother. The chicken on his plate had already turned cold and his appetite was non-existent in any case.

His mother, Estelle Cruz, furrowed her brow. "Tony, did you eat after practice again?"

"I had a snack, is all," he replied.

"A snack huh?" She eyed him. "I know what your snacks look like. I wish you wouldn't do that after I spent an hour making you a nice homecooked meal."

His father cast him a disappointed gaze. "You see what you've done to your mother?"

"Sorry, Dad." Tony stabbed a piece of chicken and shoved it into his mouth. "There? Happy?"

"I'll be happy when your plate is clean," Estelle replied.

Tony's phone buzzed in his pocket and when he retrieved it, another disapproving glance came at him by way of his mother. He noticed the caller ID. "I have to take this. It's Coach."

"Fine," she replied before turning to her younger son. "Don't you start picking up on your brother's bad habits."

Tony pushed away from the table, walked to his bedroom, and closed his door. "Hey. I'm eating dinner right now."

"It's important," Nia replied.

"What is it?" Tony sat on the edge of his bed with his phone to his ear.

"Did they talk to you yet?" she asked.

"Who? The cops?"

"No, the private detective. You said they called and wanted to talk to you."

"I didn't call them back, but the lady just showed up at my

house this morning. I talked to her for, like, a couple minutes then I told her I had to go to school."

"What did you say to her?"

"Just that me and Jess dated for a long time and I was sad. I asked how Mr. Healey was. I don't know. I didn't say much."

"Did you tell her about us?" Nia asked.

"It didn't come up, so I didn't say anything."

"Good. Let's just keep it that way, you know? I don't want anyone to think we had some sort of reason to do anything to Jess."

"Who says we did? Jesus, Nia. We didn't do anything wrong. I wasn't even going out with her anymore when we started up. Why are you so freaked out by this?"

"I'm not. It's just...it just freaks me out that they think Jess might've been murdered," Nia replied with fright in her tone.

Another call beeped in on his phone and he glanced at the screen that read, "Hailey." He returned the phone to his ear. "Nia, I gotta go. Just calm down, okay? This is all going to be over soon. I promise. I gotta go. Bye." He clicked over to the other call and his tone was immediately changed. "Yo, Hailey, what's up?"

———

WITH A DISHTOWEL IN HER HAND, Mary Ann Healey wiped down the kitchen counter. It was after 7pm and her husband had been fed. For now, he needed help eating, bathing, and going to the bathroom, which Mary Ann willingly did for him. She'd only eaten a couple of bites and had hardly eaten anything over the past two weeks. How could she? Her daughter was dead. Her life was unrecognizable.

She walked into the living room to see her husband laying on the sofa. "Do you need anything else, sweetheart?"

He managed a faint smile. "No, I'm okay. You should go rest for a bit. I'll be fine watching the news."

Mary Ann nodded and started up the stairs. Her husband slept in the guest bedroom downstairs because it was easier for him to move around on his own. At least he was no longer a prisoner on the second floor. Now, she was relegated to the entire second floor all alone. Jessica's room was still exactly as she had left it.

At the top of the steps, Mary Ann turned left instead of right. It was a daily ritual, standing in Jess's bedroom. Sitting on her bed. Peering into her closet. Anything to remind her of Jess. She pushed inside the room and the fresh floral scent tickled her nose. Jess loved scented everything and had candles, potpourri, anything that smelled nice. The fragrances lingered even though she hadn't been home in several weeks. Jess would come home on some weekends, mostly to do the laundry. She didn't like the dorm facilities. But Mary Ann was pretty sure she just didn't like to do laundry herself. Mary Ann didn't mind it, though. In fact, Jess came home less and less this school year. Mary Ann supposed she was getting used to college life and preferred to hang out with her friends instead of her parents.

She went about her usual ritual and started at the closet first. Not many clothes still hung there, except for a few winter pieces that Jess hadn't needed. Her shoes were lined along the floor. Mostly flip flops. Mary Ann smiled and noticed a pair that still had sand on them. Jess loved the beach and had grown up around it. She'd given her daughter a far better life than she had herself. That was how it was supposed to be, though. That was what all parents strived for. Only the child wasn't supposed to die before the parent.

Mary Ann's eyes welled as they had every time she walked into that bedroom. But she moved on to Jess's dresser. White with pretty trinkets on top. A few seashells. She opened one of the drawers for the first time. There was no telling how much stuff would need to be boxed up and donated. She hadn't even cleared out the dorm room yet, which must've been hard for Sophie. "I have to go and do that tomorrow. No point in putting it off any longer."

A few pairs of sweatpants, a couple of old t-shirts. A bathing suit she hardly ever wore. The remnants of a life only partly lived.

Mary Ann picked up one of the shirts and peered down at what else was inside. She spotted a small glass ornament. A mermaid, but it was inside a drawstring fabric bag, as though it had been gift wrapped. A present to her maybe. A tag hung from the strings. Mary Ann opened the small, folded tag. "To Jess, I hope this will be a reminder of our amazing weekend. Can't wait to do it again."

She flipped it around in search of a signature. A name of whoever gave Jess this gift, but there was nothing to be found. She had no idea who had given her this but suspected it must've been Tony, even though they'd broken up months ago. Mary Ann would return it to him. He would want it back; she was sure of it.

7

Getting comfortable with the idea of being an empty nester was a big adjustment for Allison. With Nolan traveling for baseball and Micah at school, she did her best to cope with the silence of an empty house. And she couldn't help but wonder how Mary Ann coped with the loss of her daughter, who was the same age as Micah. In fact, the parallels between them were striking, no matter how hard Allison tried to cordon off that idea in her mind.

She had begun to have doubts about the investigation and pondered whether to pull the plug, but she'd given her word to Mary Ann that she would exhaust all leads. None of the people in Jessica's circle had been absolved of anything. Not until all alibis had been established. Once that happened, Allison and her team could present the findings to Mary Ann with confidence that they'd done all they could do to help the grieving mother.

She walked to her kitchen and poured a glass of wine, knowing it was best to put something in her stomach first, but ignoring her pragmatic side. Allison pulled out her hair tie and let her long blonde locks cascade down her back. When the knock on the door came, she took in a breath and padded in bare feet to open it. "Hi. Come in."

Shane walked inside. "I was a little surprised by your invitation."

"I didn't like how our call earlier went down and I thought we should sit and talk about a few things." Allison returned to the kitchen. "Do you want a beer? I've opened a bottle of wine, too."

"Beer's good, thanks." He pulled out a stool at the island counter. "I'm not upset about earlier, if that's what you were thinking, Allison. Like I told you the other night, I understand where you're coming from with wanting to handle things on your own."

She handed him a bottle. "We're still finding our footing and have tackled some challenging and dangerous cases already. I feel like we're starting to earn the trust of the detectives and I don't want to do anything to damage that."

"I'm one of them too, remember?" Shane tipped back the bottle at his lips. "And I have you to thank for my promotion to Major Crimes. So, it's me who's indebted to you. Not the other way around."

"I don't see it that way." Allison rested her elbows on the island and leaned over. "I can't have any of those guys thinking you and I are—an item. My credibility would be..."

"I get it, Allison." A hint of regret surfaced in his eyes. "But if you need help, don't let your need for independence hinder getting answers for your clients."

She creased her brow for a moment. "I didn't think that was what I was doing."

"That's how it looks to me. Allison, if you don't want us to be anything more than friends, then fine. I'm a big boy and I can handle that. But you can be stubborn when it comes to certain things. Don't let it get in the way of your goal. That's all I'm saying."

Allison felt as though she'd just been admonished. "I think you've made your point. I'm doing what I think is best for my team and while I appreciate your input, I have my reasons. None of which will jeopardize my client's interest. So, how about we move on and talk about why you're here."

"Fair enough. I can see when I've pushed the wrong buttons. That wasn't my intent. I'm sorry," he replied.

She thought about responding but the horse was dead, no point in beating it. "Did your friend at USF offer any more details on Professor Lyman?"

"Not yet, but I spent a little more time looking into him. It was pretty easy. The guy's been in the public eye and with is business dealings, information was plentiful." He swirled around his empty bottle. "Hey, you got another one of these?"

"Yeah, sure." Allison grabbed another bottle from the fridge. "Here you go."

"Thanks. We know the guy's rich. Philanthropic. Goes to lots of benefits for non-profits."

"A real do-gooder," Allison added.

"Looks like it. Given his moderately high-profile, it's unlikely he'd be careless, if you know what I mean."

"Sure. But with money comes the ability to sweep things under the rug. And lots of people to do the sweeping for you. Shane, do you know where he was the day Jessica was found dead? That's what I really need to know."

"It just so happens that I have some idea." He reached for his phone and swiped it open. "I got access to the school's security footage."

"How did you do that?" She raised her palms. "Wait. Do I want to know?"

"Probably not, but suffice it to say, I owe someone. Nothing I can't manage, though."

She felt a twinge of guilt for chiding him, even if it had been a rebuttal of his own words. But once again, he'd risked something for her. No matter the size of the risk, the fact that he did so served as a reminder of how much he felt for her as a friend if not more. "What did you find on the video?"

"I saved it." He handed her the phone. "See for yourself."

Allison pressed the button and the video played. "It's a parking lot."

"Yep. It's the teacher's parking lot. Keep watching."

Allison continued to view the small screen. "Is that him? What day was this?"

"The day of," he replied. "About an hour before Jessica's stated time of death."

"So he was still in Tampa, at the school." She peered at him. "But it was Spring Break. Why was he there?"

"I couldn't tell you that. You'd have to ask him for yourself. Point is, he's present and accounted for."

Allison nodded and tossed back her hair. "But this was an hour before Jessica died. She was only about an hour away from home when it happened. It's possible..."

"It's possible, but you would have to find motive, Allison. He could've gone home, to a store, whatever. There's a thousand places Lyman could've driven to after he left the school."

"But this doesn't let him off the hook," she added.

"No. You have a shot, yeah. But still a longshot."

"What do I do with this?" Allison returned his phone. "I'll have to talk to him again. If he comes up with a legitimate alibi, then that's it. For him, anyway."

"Right now, he's under no obligation to even talk to you. The cops have closed this case. You need to be pretty damn certain about this, Allison."

She nodded. "You're right. I really had hoped to cross him off the list, but this only presents more questions."

"That's usually how it works." He smiled. "It's the best I could get for you now."

Allison reached for his hand, as she had done countless times before. "Thank you, Shane. I'm sorry for being so pigheaded."

He pulled his hand away. "I'm used to it."

———

Sophie Matthews should have been studying for her poly-sci test tomorrow, but after getting a call from Mrs. Healey, her plans changed. She rounded up a few boxes that the students on her floor had to spare and decided to pack Jessica's things. The idea of Mrs. Healey arriving tomorrow to do what should have been done a week ago was unacceptable. She couldn't sit back and watch the mother of her dead best friend pack up her things. So, she wanted to make it easier and carefully placed Jessica's belongings in the boxes, packed and ready to go when Mrs. Healey arrived. It would be too hard on the both of them otherwise.

A knock sounded on her door and Sophie opened it. "Hey, Maddie."

"Hey." Madison walked inside.

"Thanks for coming over. I didn't want to do this alone."

"I get it. It's no problem. I haven't heard from Nia tonight. I don't know where she is." Madison slipped off her shoes and pulled back her ash blonde hair with the scrunchie she wore on her wrist.

"That's okay. Harriet's working too, so it's just us." Sophie set down an empty box in front of her. "Let's just get through this."

"Yeah, sure." Madison pulled down the pictures from the wall. "Did Mrs. Healey say when the funeral was going to be?"

"No, but I'm sure she'll say something about it tomorrow. Since the police closed the case, she said they finally released Jess's body."

"I hate that." Madison's voice cracked. "Her body, as if she wasn't a human being. As if she wasn't our friend."

Sophie placed her hand on Madison's back. "If this is too much..."

"No. No, I'll be fine. I came here to help and that's what I'll do," she replied.

Sophie returned to her task and folded Jessica's bedding. "She loved this quilt. Said it reminded her of summers at a beach house. Anything to do with the beach." She turned to Madison. "What do you think about Mrs. Healey hiring that private detective?"

"I don't know. I guess if it was my kid, it'd be hard to accept the truth." Madison placed the throw pillows in a box. "Have you talked to them again since that lady, Charlie, was here?"

"No. I did get a text saying they might have a few more questions. That was earlier today, I think. I was in class and didn't respond. Did they text you too?"

"Not yet."

"Maybe because I was her roommate," Sophie added. "I don't know anything besides what I told them already."

"Yeah, I know. That's all you can do," Madison replied. "Where is Nia, anyway? Have you heard from her?"

"Not in the last couple days. It's weird, though, right? Like the way she's been not hanging out with us. I kind of feel like she's blowing us off."

"Maybe it's her way of dealing with this," Madison replied. "We're all messed up over it. The whole dorm is messed up."

"Still, it's not about her. She always thinks it's about her." Sophie shook out a towel with noticeable force.

"That's not true. Come on. Nia's been there for all of us. We all just need some time."

"Yeah, maybe. I'm just pissed that she's not here helping us."

"She didn't know we were doing this tonight," Madison pressed on. "Look, I know what happened in Daytona—the fight Nia had with Jess. She probably feels guilty as shit, you know? I mean, wouldn't you?"

"Yeah, but it was all over when we were at the beach that day. The day Jess got the call from her mom. No one was still mad. We were drunk. Shit got said. That's all it was. But I guess you could be right. She probably said things she regrets."

"Right?" Madison added.

Sophie turned to her and offered a tender smile. "I'm glad you're here, though. I'm not sure I could do this alone."

"I wouldn't want you to. We're in this together, okay?"

———

MARY ANN GRABBED her handbag and car keys from the side table. "I'm going to the school now, but I'll get back as soon as I can."

"I'll be fine for a few hours," Jim replied, still lying on the couch. "I think I might try to do some walking today. Just around the house, of course."

"Honey, please wait until I get back. If you fall..."

"Fine. I'll wait." He reached for her hand. "I hate that you've had to do all of this on your own, Mary Ann. You shouldn't have to."

"We don't get to choose when our strength will be put to the test. We just have to live up to the demand." She smiled at him.

"I'll be home soon, my love." Mary Ann walked to her car and stepped inside. She choked back the tears that threatened to overwhelm her and started the engine.

There was one stop she needed to make ahead of the trip to see Sophie at Jessica's dorm. Mary Ann eyed the glass mermaid trinket wrapped in tissue paper resting on top of her open purse. She knew Tony had a later class this morning. He'd called to check on her and her husband several times since all of this happened and Mary Ann knew his Thursday class schedule. He lived around the block with his parents and she pulled to a stop in front of the house.

She stepped out of the car and started toward the door, the wrapped trinket in her hand. Before she had the chance to knock, the door opened. "Estelle, good morning."

Tony's mother wore a kindhearted smile and pulled Mary Ann into an embrace. "Good morning. Oh, honey, how are you holding up?"

Mary Ann shrugged. "About as you'd expect. I'm sorry to drop by unannounced, but is Tony here?"

He appeared from beyond the hall and approached the front door. "I got it, Mom." He looked at Mary Ann and stepped outside wearing his backpack. "Hi. I was just leaving..."

"I know. Do you have just a moment to talk?"

"Sure." He looked back. "It's okay, Mom." Tony walked along the path. "Is everything okay? Is Mr. Healey all right?"

"Oh, yes. He's doing fine, thank you for asking." She reached into her handbag. "I actually wanted to return this to you."

Tony peered at the wrapped item. "What is it?"

"I found it in Jessica's dresser yesterday. I finally started packing up her things. In fact, I am heading to the university after this to see Sophie. Poor girl shouldn't be forced to look at Jessica's things every day like she was only out for lunch or something. So,

I'm going to clear out all of it. But I wanted to stop by first to give you this. I figured you might want it back."

Tony took it in his hands and unwrapped the trinket. He held it between his thumb and forefinger, examining it. "What is this?"

"You don't recognize it?" A hint of uncertainty laced her words.

"No. I've never seen it before. If this is Jess's, it didn't come from me." He handed it back to her.

"Oh. I see. Well, I'm so sorry. I just... Well, it came with a note about a lovely weekend and I just assumed..."

Tony pursed his lips and nodded. "Jess and I haven't had a weekend together. Not in a long time. Not since before Christmas. And I didn't give her this. She was probably seeing someone else, Mrs. Healey. I kind of figured that was why she broke up with me. She was with someone new already."

Mary Ann's eyes reddened as she took back the trinket and placed it in her purse. "I'm so sorry, Tony."

"Don't be. I've had time to get over the breakup. I mean, with all that's happened now, it's brought back a lot of feelings, but I get that Jess didn't love me anymore."

"Do you know who she might've been seeing? She didn't tell me about anyone new," Mary Ann asked.

"No. We hadn't talked in a long time, Mrs. Healey. I heard Sophie and Jess texted that day about her coming to see me, but she never asked to see me. So, I don't know what happened there." He checked the time. "Listen, I really have to go now. Are you going to be okay?"

"Yes. Yes, of course, sweetheart. You go on to school now. I'll figure this out. I am sorry to have bothered you, Tony."

He leaned in and kissed her cheek. "Don't apologize, Mrs. Healey. I'm here whenever you need me. My parents are too. We all love you and we loved Jess." He started away.

87

Mary Ann watched as he drove away and returned to her car. From behind the wheel, she peered at the trinket. "I thought I knew everything, Jess. Why would you keep anything from me? Who gave this to you?"

She started on toward the university and considered that Sophie might know if Jess was seeing someone new. Was it possible Jessica's best friend was hiding something, too? It didn't make sense, but then they were young women who were learning to live their own lives. Maybe Sophie didn't think it was important. Regardless, Mary Ann would pose the question because now the hairs on her neck tingled. The idea there was someone out there who was involved with her daughter that no one knew about frightened her. In her heart, Mary Ann believed Jessica had lost her life at the hands of someone else. Perhaps she was right.

The campus was just ahead, and Mary Ann parked in the visitor's section. She blotted her eyes and stepped out of the car. "You can do this. Go and get your daughter's things."

Mary Ann arrived at the dorm room and took in a calming breath. She knocked softly on the door and waited. Sophie appeared on the other side. Her beautiful face smiled warmly, her brunette hair was pulled back in a ponytail. "Mrs. Healey. Come in."

"Good morning, sweetheart. How are you?" Mary Ann walked inside. "Oh, I see you've done everything all ready."

Sophie closed the door. "I hope that's okay. I just thought it might be easier for you. Maddie came over last night and we put everything in boxes. It was actually kind of cathartic for the both of us."

"I'm sure it was." Mary Ann peered at the boxes in front of Jessica's bed, not quite sure how to feel about this. "It's perfectly fine you two did that. I'm glad it helped. I should've let you do it much sooner. I'm sorry for that." She turned to her and withdrew the trinket from her bag. "There is something I'd like to ask your help with."

Sophie peered at the glass mermaid. "What is that?"

"I was hoping you might know," Mary Ann said. "It came with a note from a boy, I assumed. Something to the effect that the two had shared a memorable weekend together recently."

"Recently?" Sophie asked.

"That's right. I thought it was from Tony, but he claimed it hadn't come from him." She reached for Sophie's arm. "Honey, if you know anything. If you know Jess was seeing someone else, please, please tell me."

"I—I didn't know she was. I promise you, Mrs. Healey. If she was seeing someone, it was completely on the down-low."

"I'm sorry?"

"I mean, she kept it quiet. I was her best friend and we told each other everything. I'm sure she would've said something to me."

"Then she might have been seeing someone who she didn't want anyone to know about. Why would that be?" Mary Ann asked.

Sophie appeared to think on it, shaking her head. "I just don't know."

———

ALLISON SET down her phone and peered at Charlie and Lucy. "That was Mary Ann." She stood from her desk. "Apparently, she discovered a gift left for Jessica that she had kept in a drawer."

"A gift." Charlie nodded. "And who was this gift from?"

"Well, that's the $64,000 question. A note came with the gift and suggested a romantic weekend was shared between Jessica and an unknown person."

"She was seeing someone," Lucy said as if confirming their suspicions.

"Mary Ann ruled out that it came from Jessica's ex-boyfriend. And she asked Sophie Matthews about it too. She had no idea who it could have been from."

"Okay. So it was someone Jessica didn't want anyone to know about," Charlie added. "Not even her best friend."

Lucy stepped toward Allison's desk. "Does Mrs. Healey still have the note?"

"As far as I know," Allison replied.

"We should get a copy of it ASAP." Charlie peered at Allison. "There's only one reason a young woman would keep a secret like that."

"A relationship that might have been considered taboo," Lucy said. "Like with a professor."

"You got it, kiddo." Charlie took in a deep breath. "We need to get a sample of ol' Lyman's handwriting."

"Yep." Allison picked up the phone. "I'm on it."

8

Allison stood before the desk of Detective Brenner. The trinket lay on his desk alongside the note attached to it. Her confidence was undeniable. "Look, I realize this doesn't definitively mean anything. But the idea that Jessica Healey was seeing one of her professors, a wealthy man who alleged he hardly knew her, that should raise a red flag."

Brenner sighed a little too loudly. "Even if she was seeing this guy, forensics show the girl pulled the trigger herself. I get that if she was dating him what that might have done to her mental state at the time, especially if they'd had a falling out, but..."

Allison sat down in the chair, never surrendering her gaze on him. "But doesn't that mean you should take a deeper look at her phone records? You had no reason to consider Dr. Lyman but now you do."

"Ms. Hart, I can't arrest a guy because he dated a student. Do you know how often that happens? Frankly, the worst that could happen to him is he might lose his job. It's not a crime to date a woman who was of age." He peered at the note. "And are you positive this is his handwriting?"

Allison opened her carrier bag and retrieved a folder. "I asked Mrs. Healey for Jessica's school papers. She collected her daughter's things earlier today. There was a stack of graded assignments that she kept. Mrs. Healey sent me copies of the papers from Dr. Lyman's class." She pulled them out. "See for yourself. The notes from him on her papers. The writing matches."

The detective eyed Allison before taking the folder and examining the contents. He nodded slowly as he flipped through the papers, reading the notes and comparing them to what was written to Jessica. "Okay. Maybe you're right about this. Again, it doesn't..."

"What do I have to do to get you to take this seriously, Detective Brenner?"

"Look, Ms. Hart, don't mistake my caution for complacency. I am doing my job, thank you very much."

"Of course. I'm sorry, Detective. I'm just—I want what's best for my client."

He pulled back in his chair and peered at her. "Here's what I can do, Ms. Hart. I'll review the phone records again. See if Lyman communicated with Jessica on a regular basis. Then, I'll talk to him, get a feel for his reaction."

"I learned that Dr. Lyman was at the university until about an hour prior to Jessica's time of death. He was getting into his car."

"How did you come by that information?" Brenner asked.

"I'm a private investigator. I investigate," she replied. "Point being, I couldn't account for his whereabouts after that time. Suggesting..."

"Suggesting you think the professor happened upon Jessica on the road back to Tampa and killed her."

"Well, I..."

"That's what you're implying." Brenner scratched his head while he kept his dark hazel eyes glued to Allison, his features suddenly appearing harsher. "That's a big leap, if you ask me. Again, you're going against the forensic evidence."

"I understand, but don't you think we should know where he was when she was killed? Like I said, I can get a lot of information on my own, but some things are out of my periphery. I'd like to ask you, on this point, will you help? At the very least, to consider ruling out the possibility."

He dipped his head while his lips drew up into a knowing smile. "No wonder Sully likes you."

She leaned in just a little. "What's that?"

"Detective Sullivan. He speaks very highly of you."

Her brief flash of concern passed. "Oh. Yes, we've been friends for a long time, and he's helped out with some of our earlier cases."

"And the mayor. That was a big feather in his cap," Brenner replied. "I'd say Sully has you to thank for a lot of things, including his move up to Major Crimes."

"He's done a lot for us, too. But I'm glad to know that he respects what I'm doing."

"We all respect what private investigators do, Ms. Hart. It's just sometimes, your colleagues have been known to be a tad overzealous. It'd be a shame for you to travel down that same path."

Allison stood. "I blaze my own trail, Detective. Thank you for your help. It won't be forgotten." It was a good thing Shane wasn't at the station as she turned to leave. She was grateful he'd spoken so kindly of her, but the immediate assumption was that the two were more than friends. Regardless, the answer she wanted to hear from Brenner came and it was time to head back to the office. She returned to her car and picked up her phone. "Hey, Charlie. I'm leaving the station now. Brenner says he'll talk to Lyman and find out where he was that day."

"Good. I thought you might get pushback," Charlie replied.

"Oh, I did. I just didn't accept it." Allison smiled and slipped into her car.

"Why does that not surprise me?" Charlie laughed. "That's one thing off our plates. We still have Jessica's friends. We know they were at the beach when she got the call. I think it's time we follow that up and find out what they did for the rest of the day."

"Agreed. I think Harriet is probably at work, so I'll head there now."

"Then Lucy and I will track down the other musketeers and see if they'll give us a minute of their time."

"That leaves the ex-boyfriend," Allison began. "But I think I'd like to find out where the girls were exactly, then follow up with Tony Cruz."

"Why wait?" Charlie asked.

"I don't know. I'm not feeling it from him. I don't want to rule him out because we can't, but let's put our focus on the rest of Jessica's circle and see what we can turn up."

"You got it, boss. Catch you on the other side." Charlie ended the call. "Okay, we're up, kiddo." She grabbed her things. "It's time we learn what exactly Jessica's girlfriends were up to when she was driving alone and somehow decided it was time for her to end things."

"That was Allison? What did she have to say?" Lucy closed the lid to her laptop.

"She got the detective to agree to follow up with the professor and she's going to meet Harriet at her work. So, it's up to us to find the other three and get them to tell us where they were. You ready?"

THE DOOR OPENED to Sophie's dorm room and Charlie noticed all the girls were together. "Hi. I didn't expect all of you to be here." She glanced back at Lucy. "Guess it'll make our jobs easier."

"Come in." Sophie stepped aside. "We thought it would be easier for you rather than having to track us down individually."

"Sure. No, that was very thoughtful, thank you." Charlie noticed the other half of the room, Jessica's half. "I heard Mrs. Healey came here this morning to collect Jessica's things. It looks pretty empty in here."

"Yeah, we thought it was best to help Mrs. Healey and so Maddie and I packed up her stuff last night. I don't know how else we can help her, so we did the best we could."

"I'm sure she appreciated that." Charlie turned to Lucy. "You all remember my partner, Lucy Boyce."

"Sure," Sophie replied. "Nice to see you again, Lucy."

"You, too. And the rest of you. Thank you. We just had a couple of follow-up questions."

Sophie sat down on Jessica's bed alongside Nia. Madison sat at Jessica's desk. "Harriet is at work. She works a lot," Sophie began.

"Yeah, it sucks. She's on a scholarship where she has to work to help pay for the school," Nia replied. "It's a lot of pressure for her."

"I'm sure it is," Charlie said. "Nia, how have you been? I don't think we've been able to reach out to you since we initially talked."

"I'm coping. You know, like the rest of us. It's hard."

"Sure. Well, I suppose we should get down to the reason why we're here."

"Okay," Sophie replied.

Charlie perched on the edge of Sophie's desk. "We'd like a little more detail on what you four did after Jessica left that day.

We know you were all at the beach when the call came in. And you helped her pack up to leave. But what about afterwards?"

Sophie glanced at her friends. "I guess I can answer for all of us. So, like, we were super worried for Jess, you know? She was so upset about what happened to her dad. We were like, 'is she going to get home okay,' because she was really, like, frantic."

"I offered to drive back with her," Nia said. "None of us thought that she should be alone."

Charlie grunted. "But she refused?"

"Totally," Madison began. "She didn't want to ruin our Spring Break, which was so stupid because, of course, we wanted to be with her."

"So, after she left," Lucy began. "What did you guys do?"

They traded glances before Sophie spoke. "Honestly? We packed up our things and walked to the nearest bar. They're all along the beach. We were super stressed out by what happened, and I think none of us really wanted to think about what could happen."

"That Mr. Healey could die?" Charlie asked.

"Yeah. And Jess, well, she was not herself. I mean, who would be, right?" Nia asked.

"Where did you guys go? What bar was it?" Lucy asked.

They traded glances again and this time, Charlie and Lucy seemed to take notice.

It took a few more moments before Nia spoke up. "I can't really remember the name. Can either of you guys?"

Sophie tucked her long brunette hair behind her ears. "Not really. We went to, like, three or four and I guess we got pretty slammed."

"I know, Sophie, that you messaged Jessica shortly after she left," Charlie began. "But you didn't follow up to make sure she arrived home safely?"

Her cheeks reddened as she gazed down at her feet. "I was pretty wasted by then. I didn't think to do that. No."

"According to the phone records the detective obtained during his investigation, it looked like Jessica had replied to you. I'm not sure we knew that before." Charlie held Sophie's gaze. "What did she say?"

"Oh, that's right. It was nothing. Like, just saying 'ok' or something."

LUCY CUT IN. "Nia, Madison, you both went bar hopping too? Were all of you together the entire time, including Harriet?"

"What are you trying to say?" Nia asked.

"I'm just trying to get a good timeline, so we understand everything that happened that day," Lucy replied. "I'm not suggesting any of you did anything wrong."

Sophie folded her arms and peered at Lucy. "Do you go to school?"

"Not anymore. I lost my mother a few years ago and last year, my dad died from a heart attack. Charlie and Allison took me under their wings and offered me a job."

"She's being modest," Charlie began. "Her father was one of the best P.I.s in the city. Lucy knew people who helped us set up our agency. She's had to change her life quite a bit. And would probably have preferred to be living a life that you three have."

"I'm sorry. I didn't realize," Sophie said.

"No need to be sorry. I'm happy with what I'm doing. We should get back to my question." She held up her palms. "And it's just a question. I'm not accusing anyone of anything. Were all of you together the rest of that day?"

Sophie shifted her gaze again and looked at Madison. "My

memory is a little fuzzy, but I remember Maddie and me hanging out with some guys we met later that night."

"And where were you, Nia?" Charlie asked.

"Probably back in the room. I don't remember. I'd had a lot to drink too."

"Did you guys post anything online during that time? Call or text anyone?" Charlie asked. "Just to piece together where you were."

Sophie pulled out her phone. "You can check my phone. I didn't contact anyone. I didn't post anything either. I'm not stupid enough to drunk post. Schools crack down on that. You can get suspended."

"I imagine so, especially if you're underaged," Charlie said under her breath. "I believe you. I don't need to see your phone."

"Did the police ask for your phones?" Lucy asked.

"No. They hardly asked us anything," Nia replied. "Nothing about phones or where we were. I mean, they didn't ask me any of that." She turned to her friends. "You guys?"

"Nope," Madison replied.

"Just me, I guess," Sophie began. "Because of that first text to Jessica. The detective said it was no big deal, just procedure or something like that."

"So then what about Harriet?" Lucy continued. "She was with you three, right?"

"Harriet came with us, sure," Madison said. "She's legal, same as me. But, honestly, I don't remember seeing her the whole time."

"Yeah, I don't either." Sophie cast her gaze to the ceiling. "She might've gone back to the room."

"I would've seen her because that's where I was, remember?" Nia replied. "She wasn't in the room with me. Unless I was asleep or something."

"When you all got up the next morning, was Harriet there with you?" Charlie asked.

"Yeah. We were all there. Woke up like no big deal. It wasn't until later that morning that Sophie got the call from Mrs. Healey," Nia replied.

"Then we all freaked out," Sophie added. "Came right back to Tampa after that."

"Okay. Listen, we really appreciate you girls talking to us. It means a lot to the family that we learn as much as possible about the facts surrounding Jessica's death," Charlie said. "I think that's all we have for now, but again, if you guys think of anything that could help..."

Sophie stood from the bed. "We'll call you. I promise."

————

HARRIET TORRES WALKED to her car carrying her folded apron in one hand and her phone in the other, gazing down at it.

Allison had parked near enough to spot her leave from the employee exit and stepped out of her car to catch up.

Harriet jumped back a step. "Ms. Hart? Oh, my gosh, you scared me. What are you doing here?"

"I'm so sorry to have startled you, Harriet." Allison placed a comforting hand on the young woman's arm. "I was hesitant to go inside again in case your bosses were watching you. Didn't want to get you into any trouble interrupting you at work again."

"That's okay. I was just going home. What can I do for you?"

"We're still working to piece together exactly what happened the day Jessica died. And, well, we'd like to ask where you and your friends were when it happened," Allison replied. "No one's in trouble. No one's done anything, in fact. It's just a process."

"Sure, I get it. So, you've talked to the other girls already?" Harriet asked.

"My partners are doing that now, actually."

"Together? My friends. Are they talking to them together?" Harriet's face wore concern.

"Honestly, I don't know. Is that important?"

"No. I guess not. It's just that sometimes I feel like I'm not part of their group."

Harriet's use of air quotes around the word 'group' was a particular point of concern for Allison. Was there a rift between them and if so, when did it happen? "Has it always felt that way for you? Like you were an outsider?"

"Not when Jess was here. She worked a lot too, like me. Both of us are on scholarship and we need the money. *Were*, I guess. Our parents aren't rich, you know?" She looked away for a moment. "It's just that since all this happened, I feel like they don't think this has bothered me like it has them. But Jess was one of my best friends. I miss her as much as they do, maybe more." Her large brown eyes reddened, and a tear fell down her smooth, full cheek.

It was all Allison could do to stop herself from pulling that girl in a tight embrace. Harriet was different from the others, more sensitive, like she'd been through more than a girl her age should have. "Of course you do. I know this is hard to discuss and you'll forgive me, but I need to know what that day looked like for you four girls. I know you were at the beach when Jessica got the call. What happened after that?"

"After we saw her off, we walked to the nearest bar. There's tons of them around there. And it was crazy packed. We decided to get a drink to toast to Jess and her family. To pray that her dad was going to be okay."

"And after that?" Allison pressed on.

Harriet shrugged. "Honestly, I'm embarrassed to admit it, but we got kind of drunk. I mean, I'm 21 and so is Maddie, but Sophie and Nia are only 20. So, we helped them, you know…"

"Sure." Allison smiled. "I was 21 once. Go on. You all got kind of drunk?"

"Yeah. Then, like, I don't remember much after that, except for later, like a couple hours later, I remember going back to the room. I had to lay down, although, that was a mistake. Laying down is not good when the room is spinning."

Allison chuckled. "You went back alone?"

Harriet cast up her gaze as if thinking about it. "Actually, yeah. I sort of remember Sophie and Maddie talking to these hot guys. But I don't remember seeing Nia. I thought she might be back at the room, but I don't remember seeing her there either. Probably got there after I did. And then, I remember we were all there the next morning."

"Okay. Did you happen to post anything on social media that night that you can remember?"

Harriet flushed with mild embarrassment. "I deleted a few things the next morning, but I left the post about us toasting to Jess and her family. I guess I'm really glad I left that there now."

"Do you remember the names of the bars you went to that day?" Allison asked.

"No. I really don't. There's so many. They all start to look alike after you've had a few."

"I'm sure they do. Listen, Harriet, thank you. And I'm sure you and your friends will be close again. I don't think anyone's trying to ignore you. I think it's a big thing to go through and everyone handles it differently."

"I guess so," Harriet replied. "Ms. Hart, I know you're trying to find out what happened, but, like, do you think Jess might've been, you know—killed?"

"I don't know, Harriet, I truly don't. But I intend to find out.

Thank you again and of course, please contact me if you think of anything else."

"I will, Ms. Hart. I'm glad Jess has you on her side." Harriet stepped into her car and drove away.

Allison walked back to her car and called Charlie. "Hey, I just finished talking to Harriet Torres. Where are you guys?"

"On our way back to the office. How did it go?" Charlie asked.

"It was heartbreaking, but we'll need to get hold of a tech guy," Allison said. "I'm sure Lucy knows someone who could retrieve deleted social media posts."

"I'll ask, but what for?"

"Harriet said she posted things when they were all drunk, but deleted them the next morning, well, except for one. I want to know what she deleted."

"Got it. We didn't get much on our end. The girls were together until Nia went back to the room later that night."

"Wait. She did?" Allison started up her car. "Harriet said she went back to the room and was alone there for a while. Apparently, they all were there the next morning."

"That's interesting. Nia insisted that Harriet was nowhere to be found. She was alone. Sounds like someone's having trouble recalling their whereabouts."

"Harriet also feels like they're leaving her out since all this happened," Allison replied.

"We might have found ourselves a little situation among these young girls," Charlie added.

"We'll talk more at the office. I'm not sure what was going on with them, but someone feels the need to keep the truth from us."

9

The investigation had taken an interesting turn; however, it was unclear if that turn would be enough to convince Detective Brenner to reopen it and call it a homicide. No concrete evidence had presented itself, but questions arose as to the validity of the girls' stories.

Allison was on her way to the office to discuss the recent findings when a call came in on her drive back. She pressed the speaker on her phone to answer. "This is Allison."

"It's Brenner. I convinced Dr. Lyman to come into the station to answer a few questions. I figured you might like to be here for that."

"Absolutely. When? I'm heading back to the office now," she replied.

"Thirty minutes. Can you be here?"

"I'll turn around right now. Detective, what did you tell him?"

"That I wanted him to clear up some rumors. He was more than happy to oblige. I'll see you in 30, Ms. Hart." Brenner ended the call.

Allison couldn't figure out if Brenner was simply humoring her or if he believed there could be something to the small trinket in Jessica's bedroom with a note attached to it. She understood that it was in no way conclusive, but it was a step forward in confirming whether Jessica was murdered, as her mother suspected, or was a troubled young woman who saw no way out.

She picked up her phone. "Charlie, it's me again. I just got a call from Detective Brenner. Lyman agreed to come in and talk. Brenner asked if I wanted to be there."

"Holy cow. That's good news," Charlie replied.

"I agree. I'm headed there now. Why don't you and Lucy move forward with getting someone on board to uncover those deleted posts. That could offer a lot of information about what those girls were doing that night. I'll head back as soon as I'm finished at the station. Hopefully, with some news that will help us."

"See you soon, Alli. We'll handle things on our end."

"I know you will." Allison ended the call and was only a few miles from the stationhouse. Shane deserved credit for once again coming to her aid and digging up surveillance footage from the university. It provided ammunition to present to Brenner to open up the possibility that Professor Lyman had some sort of relationship with Jessica Healey.

Allison walked inside and headed up the flight of stairs to the Major Crimes Division. Shane's desk was just ahead, and she spotted him.

He noticed her arrival and wore a grin. "Allison. Isn't this a happy surprise? What brings you here today?"

"Hi, Shane. I don't have long but I wanted to stop in before my meeting with Detective Brenner. Because of the information you offered, I was able to convince him to ask Dr. Lyman to come in and answer some questions." She held up her hands. "I didn't say where I got the information from."

"I'm glad to hear that, Allison. I hope it helps." He studied her a moment. "Thanks for stopping by first. I appreciate it."

"I'm here because of you, once again, so how could I not?" She returned a grateful smile. "Listen, I'd better run, but I'll keep you posted, okay?"

"Definitely."

Allison headed toward the senior detectives' offices. Brenner's was just ahead, and she knocked on his door that was already open. "Detective Brenner?"

"Ms. Hart. Please, come in." Brenner stood from his desk and extended his hand. "Thanks for coming down on short notice. Lyman is due here any minute. We'll be talking to him down-stairs." He started toward the hall. "Follow me."

She passed Shane again and offered a nod as she continued to follow Brenner.

Brenner appeared to notice the exchange and shot a sideways glance at her. When they reached the stairs, he began. "You and Sully have a pretty good relationship, huh?"

"We do. He's a good detective."

"I haven't had the pleasure of working with him yet, but I look forward to it." Brenner arrived at the interview room. "Go on inside. I'll see if he's here."

Allison walked inside the room where a table and four chairs lay in the center. A video camera in the top corner flashed a red light and there were no windows in the room. It was grey, cold, and she wondered how Lyman would feel about it. This was a room where interrogations took place and any assumption of innocence waited outside. It was as if Brenner was trying to intimidate him. A risky move, but time would tell if it would pay off.

The door opened and Brenner arrived. "Dr. Lyman, I don't know if you've met Allison Hart."

Lyman smoothed back his wavy brown hair and offered his hand. "I've met your partners. You're the private investigator."

"Nice to meet you, sir. Thank you for coming in." Allison accepted his hand.

"Like I told the detective, I'm not sure what I can offer that will help you, but I'm willing to try to clear up any confusion as to my relationship with Ms. Healey."

"Take a seat, Doctor, and we'll get started." Brenner pulled up a chair. "Ms. Hart, if you'd like to sit down."

Allison nodded and sat across from Lyman. He appeared pokerfaced. Clear eyes, not a hint of nerves behind them. To look at him would suggest he had nothing to hide.

"Dr. Lyman, I don't know if you're aware." Brenner sat down beside Allison, unleashing a low grunt in the process. "But a gift, of sorts, was discovered by the mother of Jessica Healey, a student of yours who was found dead on the side of the road roughly two weeks ago."

"I'm aware of what happened to Jessica. As I told you before and Ms. Hart's colleagues, I knew Jessica to be a very good student, but that was the extent of my relationship with her."

"This is why I've asked Ms. Hart to sit in on our conversation. Mrs. Healey is having difficulty coming to terms with the manner of her daughter's death. And rightly so. That said, I'd like to discuss something that Mrs. Healey discovered."

"The glass mermaid. That was what you mentioned on your call to me," Lyman said.

"Yes, sir." Brenner glanced at Allison. "It seems that the note attached to the trinket appears to match your handwriting."

"And how did you make that determination?" Lyman asked.

"I had a sample analyzed from comments on Jessica's papers from your class," Allison replied.

"Jesus." Lyman rolled his eyes. "What exactly am I here for, Detective? Should I get myself a lawyer?"

"We're just looking for the truth, Dr. Lyman. Were you seeing Jessica Healey?"

"I didn't have anything to do with what Jess did," Lyman replied.

"That wasn't his question," Allison cut in. "Were you dating Jessica Healey, Dr. Lyman?"

"So what if I was? She was of age. I did nothing illegal."

Still cool to any sentiment that his student had died, Allison regarded him. "No. You just committed adultery and probably created an ethics violation with the university. But no, you did nothing illegal, assuming Jessica died by her own hand."

"Oh, so now I'm a murderer?" Lyman peered at Brenner. "You're the detective here. What the hell is this? I came here voluntarily. I've answered your question. What more do you want from me because I won't sit here and be judged by her."

"Why don't you just calm down, Dr. Lyman. No one's accusing you of anything." Brenner shot a sideways glance to Allison. "Despite what the private investigator has to say on the matter, we're simply here to understand why you misled her partners in suggesting you hadn't known Jessica when clearly, you'd presented her with gifts and whisked her away for romantic weekends."

His mien hardened. "Why do you think? I'm a married man. I have a lot to lose. I wasn't going to willingly open myself up to a nasty divorce that will cost me half my net worth over some piece of ass."

The luster was gone. Lyman showed his true colors and Allison seethed. No matter how attractive this man was on the outside, he was ugly on the inside. "She was 20 years old. A kid.

And you took advantage of her. Did you attempt to break it off with her? Is that why she did what she did?"

Lyman appeared to soften his stance and sighed heavily. "No. I didn't want to break it off. I swear I had no idea what she was planning on doing. I cared for her, despite what you might think."

"Well, that's a sharp 180 you just made," Brenner added. "From a piece of ass to someone you cared for."

"I didn't mean what I said before. I was angry. I feel like this is nothing more than a trap. And I swear to God, I had nothing to do with what happened to Jessica."

"Where were you when she killed herself?" Allison asked.

"Here, in Tampa. I was at the school picking up some papers to grade over the break. It was the only chance I was going to get."

Brenner proceeded to swipe on his tablet and turn the screen toward Lyman. "Where were you going here."

"What the hell is this?" Lyman eyed them. "Have you been following me?"

"No. This is from the school's surveillance system," Brenner replied. "This was the day of Jessica's death. In fact, it was about an hour before we believe she died. This is really important, Professor, because whatever comes out of your mouth next will determine whether I'd suggest you get yourself a lawyer."

"Well, for God's sake, it sounds like I'd better get one now by what I see happening here. This is entrapment."

"No, it isn't. I promise you that," Brenner replied. "If you have an alibi, then so be it. You'll be free to go and neither I, nor Ms. Hart will bother you again. So if you want to put an end to this, tell me where you were going."

———

CHARLIE RAKED over her notes as she sat at her desk. "Alli already viewed the hotel video and didn't see anything out of the ordinary."

"Right, but she didn't know what we were looking for." Lucy paced the office floor with folded arms. "Nia says she was in the room from around midnight and didn't see Harriet, who says she went back to the room around 11pm."

"Either they were both too drunk, which is possible, or one of them is lying. But why? And how do we go about finding out?"

Lucy stopped at Charlie's desk. "We could put in a call to the hotel manager and ask for specific footage of the hall out front of the girls' room. We can find out pretty fast who was being honest, or just plain drunk."

"What if they were just drunk?" Charlie asked.

"We should know when they returned to the room. If they were alone at the time. Harriet said that Sophie and Madison met some guys. When did they return?" Lucy asked.

"I'm not sure, though, how this helps us figure out what happened to Jessica." Charlie leaned back in her chair, appearing resigned. "Okay, so maybe one of them was lying about what they were doing. Jessica was already dead at that point."

Lucy perched on Charlie's desk. "True. No, I still think it's important. Allison didn't know at the time what to look for. She was trying to find someone who might've been following Jessica before she left. Never checked the footage after Jessica was already gone. What if." She held up her index finger. "And this is a big 'if.' But say we assume Jessica was murdered. Could the murderer have known these girls? Could the murderer have joined up with them later at their hotel? We're talking an hour from Daytona. Who's to say the killer wasn't familiar to any of these girls and decided to drive back and party with them?"

Charlie raised her brow. "That's one hell of an assumption. You're saying the girls set out to murder their friend."

"That's not what I'm saying. I'm saying if Jessica was murdered, the murderer might've gone back to Daytona to hang out with the girls. They could've had no idea about any of it." She held Charlie's gaze. "I get that it's a stretch, but I think it's worth taking a look at when the girls, each of them, returned to their room that night. You said we had to cover all the bases. I think this is part of that."

Charlie nodded. "It can't hurt. Allison's trying to get the truth out of Dr. Lyman. She asked us to follow up on whatever the girls were doing that night. And to retrieve the deleted posts made my Harriet."

Lucy stood again and returned to her desk. "Right. I have just the person for that."

"I figured you would, kiddo. I'll contact the hotel manager and see if she can send us specific footage. You get in touch with your friend. We could still get some answers today."

———

Lyman's face drained of color. "I didn't do anything to Jess."

"Then where were you?" Brenner asked again. "It's a simple question, Doctor. And the longer you take to answer, the worse it makes you look."

Allison's heart beat just a little faster. His hesitation spoke volumes and she wondered if this was it. She was going to learn the truth about Jessica.

"We'd been texting back and forth that day, before she learned what happened to her dad. In fact, we'd been texting since she arrived in Daytona. Jess was beautiful, young. I guess you could say I was a little jealous. She asked me to come and meet her there.

She said she could sneak away from her friends because they were just going to get drunk anyway and no one would notice if she slipped away for a few hours."

"So you left from the school to drive to Daytona?" Allison asked.

"I started to, then she sent me a message."

"We didn't see your number on her phone records," Brenner said.

Lyman turned down his gaze. "We used an encrypted messaging app."

Allison scoffed. "Right. You couldn't risk leaving a trail of phone records. The wife might just check."

Brenner sighed, appearing to regret inviting the P.I. "She sent a message. Was it about the call from her mom?"

"Yeah." Lyman peered at him again. "She told me what happened and that she was coming home. I sent a reply saying that when she had time, if she wanted, I'd meet up with her afterwards. But..." He shook his head. "I never heard back from her."

"Where did you go after leaving the school, Professor?" Allison pressed on. "After you learned Jessica was coming home. Where did you go?"

"I went to a bar and had a beer. Then I went home to my wife."

Allison quietly sighed. She didn't know what to expect, but it wasn't this. A confession, maybe? But not a simple answer that offered no solutions to her investigation. "Can you prove that, Dr. Lyman? Did anyone see you at the bar?"

"I don't know. It's not like I go there every day, and everyone knows me." He pushed his fingers through his hair and appeared to grow impatient.

"What about your wife?" Brenner began. "Will she corroborate your story?"

"Corroborate? This isn't some conspiracy, Detective. My wife will say that I was home with her because I was."

"And at what time did you arrive home?" Brenner pressed on.

Lyman shook his head. "I don't know exactly. My wife might remember. I'd had a couple."

"What was the name of the bar?" Allison asked.

He peered up as if considering the question. "Shuckers Raw Bar. I had beer and some oysters. Didn't think that was illegal."

"It isn't, Professor. But I will need to see a receipt for your purchase," Brenner said.

"Fine. If I give that to you, are we done?"

"These messages you and Jessica exchanged," Allison began. "It might be a good idea for you to show them to the detective."

"First of all, not without a warrant, I won't. And secondly, I was having an affair, Ms. Hart. Are you out to destroy me and my family? Is that what this is about? You know I had nothing to do with Jessica's death."

"I don't know that, actually. Not until I see what you two discussed. We need to understand her state of mind, Professor," Allison replied. "And I'm not the one looking to destroy your marriage. You seemed to be doing a pretty good job of self-destructing."

"I'll get a warrant, if that's the route you want to go, Dr. Lyman," Brenner jumped in. "You were having an affair with the decedent and kept that information from Ms. Hart. If I do have to get a warrant, I will have to reopen this investigation and consider the case a possible homicide until proven otherwise. You said yourself, you've done nothing illegal. I agree with you. But the more resistance I get, the more I think you might be lying about that too."

"I think I'd like to get my lawyer in here before we go any further."

Brenner pushed up from the chair. "Fair enough. Make the call. We'll be waiting outside." He waved for Allison to follow him.

She stood with the detective in the hall. "Were you serious about reopening this as a suspected homicide?"

"I have no grounds for that right now. I need to see the messages exchanged between Jessica Healey and Jacob Lyman. It'll offer up a lot more detail as to her state of mind before she took her life. I was hoping he would cooperate, but we're dealing with a wealthy man who has a lot to lose. He's going to shield himself now. We may have lost our advantage."

10

A clattering rang out when the black rolling metal door ascended to the high ceiling of the warehouse-style office of Kendall Murray. Lucy waited on the other side as his shoes appeared, then his legs and finally all 5 feet 10 inches of him stood before her. "Lucy Boyce. I'm so glad you called. Come in."

"Nice office. New?" Lucy followed him inside.

"Yep. Just signed the lease on this. No turning back now. The view of the bay was what sold me. And the space," Kendall replied.

"It looks great. I'm happy for you."

"Working a new case then, huh?" He continued inside the loft-area workspace where a few stations were set up. "Please forgive the sparse nature. I'm in a hiring mode and trying to buy some furniture."

"I am working on something right now and I could really use your expertise," Lucy replied. "After what you did for us on the

Logan Carr investigation, I thought I could call on you again. I hope that's okay?"

"Like I said before, you need anything, I'm here." Kendall reached his office. "This is my little spot here. Come on in. Can I get you anything?" He gestured to a coffee bar. "I have water too, if you'd prefer."

"I'm actually okay but thank you." She let her gaze float around the space. "Wow. I can't believe how much your company has grown since the last time we talked."

He started toward his desk. "Well, it helped a lot getting the stamp of approval from the Tampa PD. Landed me a couple of nice contracts. And an angel investor."

"That's great, Kendall. I'm really happy for you."

"So, Lucy, you seeing anyone?" Kendall wasn't one for mincing words and had already asked her out once before.

"I am, actually."

"Ah." He nodded but couldn't quite hide the disappointment on his face. "Well, he must be a lucky guy."

"Kendall, I'm here because we really could use your help."

"I'm all ears. What's going on?" He sat at his ultra-modern black desk.

She filled him in on the general aspects of the investigation and the specific requirements she needed. "I thought that if anyone could recover deleted data, it'd be you. What do you think?"

The 22-year-old with the trimmed 5 o'clock shadow and dark hair pushed the glasses higher on the bridge of his nose. "I can handle that in my sleep. I didn't just happen into the drone industry without understanding a thing or two about computer tech. That was where I started *before* I started."

"Hacking?" she asked.

"No. Retrieving data. It's not as hard as you might think.

People think that when they delete stuff online that it goes away." He laughed. "That doesn't happen. It's there. Forever and always. And I know how to find it."

"I knew I came to the right person," Lucy replied. "Uh, does this mean I have to have dinner with you now?"

"Gee, don't sound so disappointed." He grinned with a hint of pink rising in his cheeks. "And no. Not unless you want to and with your boyfriend's permission. Look, I remember what you did with that last case. What you did for that ex-con who your dad helped out a long time ago. You're doing good things, Lucy. I want to help." Kendall retrieved his laptop. "Give me the deets, and we'll get started."

She handed over the details of the girls' social media accounts. "Harriet Torres, in particular, said she deleted some posts from the night in question. I'd like to start there."

Kendall keyed in commands and typed feverishly. "So, basically, what I'm doing is looking at Harriet's friends. This is through Instagram, which most people our age use now. None of them use Facebook anymore, or really ever did. So I'm going to search the easiest hashtags to find posts relating to them. In this case, hashtag, Daytona Spring Break, should do it. See, third party sites mirror user's content even when they delete something. It'll stay there."

"Their posts?" Lucy asked.

"Their posts, yes. But also posts they liked or commented on. If Harriet Torres had those drunk posts up for a few hours, which is what it sounds like, then I'm sure she had likes or comments. I'll be able to see those posts and the hashtag. It's kind of easy with both Twitter and Instagram to find content even when the user changes their privacy settings or deletes old posts."

"I'll have to remember that," Lucy replied.

"You should. It's no joke," Kendall added. "Okay, so here's

what I'm seeing right now with just a basic hashtag search." He turned the screen toward Lucy. "These are from the day they arrived, and I'll bet if I keep looking, we'll find the ones from that night."

Lucy peered at the photo of the friends standing in front of their hotel. "They look like a lot of fun."

"Sure. If you're into that kind of thing."

She cocked her head and gazed at him. "Having fun? You're not into that?"

"I mean, going to Daytona, getting wasted, hooking up. That's all they do there. I never really fit into college when I went, which was why I dropped out. Who needs that massive debt and then instructors telling me crap I either don't need to know or don't care to know."

"You just happen to be a lot smarter than the rest of us, Kendall. Some people don't drop out to start a tech company and become wildly successful," she replied.

Kendall turned to her and wore a grin. "You think I'm wildly successful?"

"Okay, okay, I think we're getting off track here. Can you see what Harriet posted the night Jessica died?"

"Got it." He returned to his computer and keyed in the parameters. "Right. I think I got something here. Take a look at this." Kendall pointed to the screen. "This is from that night. You mentioned Harriet said she was drunk, well, it sure looks like it here."

Lucy examined the Instagram posts. "Madison, Sophie and Nia are in the photo, so it was taken by Harriet. What time was this?"

Kendall looked at the screen again. "Looks like it was about 11:30pm."

Lucy pulled back and folded her arms. "I'm sure Allison said Harriet had returned to the hotel room by 11pm."

"She was probably too drunk to know the exact time."

Lucy nodded. "Probably. So we see they were out drinking. No one thinking anything about Jessica, which of course, they hadn't known what happened at that point. What else is there?"

Kendall searched the site again. "Hang on. Here's a twitter post." He turned to her. "Uh, this could be something."

Lucy peered again at the screen. "This is from Harriet?"

"Yep."

She leaned closer and viewed the tweet. "Oh my God. Hey, can you screenshot that for me?"

"Yeah, sure."

"Is that it? Are there any more posts from that night?" Lucy asked.

"I don't see any. There are a few from the next morning and as you can see, it's nothing out of the ordinary. Just hangover comments and stuff."

"Right. Okay. Well, clearly I can see why Harriet deleted this tweet."

"Yeah. Not cool looking at someone's phone like that."

"She saw the messages from Nia to Tony Cruz talking about Jessica, then posted about it. No wonder why she deleted it." Lucy turned to him. "Thank you so much for this. Text me that screenshot?" She grabbed her things.

"You got it, Lucy. Hey, if you need anything else, I'm here."

"Thanks, Kendall. It means a lot. I gotta run."

———

DR. JACOB LYMAN emerged from the private room where he and his attorney had been in conference for the better part of an hour.

Allison waited with Detective Brenner to learn if this case would be reopened.

"Detective Brenner?" Attorney Will Harris summoned him. "My client would like to willingly submit the messages contained in the phone app regarding communications with the decedent, Jessica Healey."

"No warrant then?" Brenner asked with Allison next to him.

"My client wishes to keep this out of the public eye and has decided to cooperate so that his association with Ms. Healey can be cleared up once and for all."

"Fine. Thank you. I'd like to submit Dr. Lyman's phone to our Computer Forensics team to retrieve the messages as soon as possible."

The highly polished attorney raised his index finger. "There's just one thing. Because this is not an active investigation and has been deemed a suicide, my client wishes for it to be known that he is offering this information of his own volition to provide answers for the grieving family. Given that, he will provide the messages through screenshots only."

Brenner unleashed a cockeyed smile as he glanced at Allison. "Let me get this straight. Dr. Lyman will give us the messages that he, himself, has chosen to reveal?" He scoffed. "You can't see that as cooperation, Mr. Harris. It's cherry-picking is what it is."

"We're only trying to assess Jessica's state of mind, Mr. Harris," Allison began. "Clearly, she was troubled. We'd like to understand the root causes of that."

"You think my client was the root cause?" Harris asked.

"We won't know until we understand the nature of their relationship. Detective Brenner is right. Dr. Lyman providing information of his choosing will serve no purpose in helping the Healey family at all."

"Ms. Hart, this is what my client would like to offer. And

without an official investigation, a warrant, without even a hint of evidence to suggest this was anything other than an unfortunate suicide, you have no standing to ask for anything more. Dr. Lyman is being more than generous."

Allison peered at Lyman who remained stone-faced and said nothing while his lawyer spoke on his behalf. "Do you not care to know what happened to Jessica, Dr. Lyman? Did she mean so little to you?"

"Of course she did." Brenner locked eyes with Lyman. "Okay, Mr. Harris, here's the deal. Your client can hand over his phone willingly, or I will get a warrant. And if that happens, I will reopen this investigation as a homicide."

Harris turned away with incredulity, placing his hands on his square hips. "On what grounds do you have to consider this a homicide? The forensics is against you, Detective."

"Dr. Lyman's resistance to cooperate is enough for me. What will it be Mr. Harris? A warrant or voluntary cooperation?"

———

SOMETHING THAT STRUCK Charlie as odd was that when she and Lucy questioned Jessica's friends, they were all there together. The occasional glances at one another also struck a suspicious note. The word "conspiracy" was often thrown around and rarely proven, however, in this instance, Charlie's hair, as stiff and spikey as it was, still stood on the back of her neck during the questioning. It felt as though the girls conspired to ensure their stories matched.

Shaking the idea had proven difficult as she waited at the office for Lucy and Allison to return with news. Not one to let things slide, Charlie decided it was time to dig deeper. What was the nature of the relationships between the young women? Had

Jessica been an insider or an outsider? That could certainly influence her actions. Going about determining this was another story.

Charlie grabbed her things and started out the door. Just as she turned to lock it, she spotted Lucy approach.

"Where are you going?" Lucy asked.

"I have a wild hair up my backside and wanted to follow up on a hunch. How did it go with your computer whiz friend?"

"Can we talk inside? Unless you need to go now," Lucy said.

"Sure, let's see what you got and that'll probably determine which direction I should take anyway." Charlie unlocked the door and returned inside.

Lucy set down her things and walked to Charlie's desk with her phone in hand. "Kendall sent me a screenshot of the deleted posts Harriet Torres made the night of Jessica's death."

"He found them?" Charlie asked wearing surprise.

"I told you he was good."

"I suppose I knew that from the last time we worked with him. But go on. Let's see the posts."

Lucy opened the message and handed her phone to Charlie. "Here you go."

Charlie pinched the screen to zoom in on the images and peered at Lucy. "Hey, my eyes aren't what they used to be, kiddo. You'll find out." Her smile quickly faded as she examined the posts and her eyes slowly turned to Lucy. "It's no wonder why she deleted at least this one."

Lucy nodded. "My thoughts exactly. Nia's been keeping something this critical from us, but why? Why would it matter if she was seeing Tony, who I'm sure his current girlfriend knows nothing about? He and Jessica broke up months earlier."

"What woman would be happy to learn that her close friend was dating her ex? I sure as hell wouldn't be. And my ex is a pile of crap on a hot paper plate. Maybe Jessica found out and that was what the argument Allison picked up on was about," Charlie continued. "Maybe it had everything to do with Tony Cruz."

"Why didn't any of them say anything about it when we talked to them earlier?" Lucy pressed on. "They must know it could've contributed to Jessica's state of mind."

"Maybe Sophie knew it contributed and she and Jessica communicated that day on the drive back to Tampa. We still don't know the contents of those messages."

Lucy sat down on the edge of Charlie's desk. "I don't know. What if none of this matters? We have a girl who was obviously dealing with a lot of drama in her life. School weighed on her mind. Tony..."

"Don't dismiss the possibility that she was involved with her professor, too," Charlie added.

"And then there's that. But does any of it amount to murder? The girls have an alibi. We know where they were that day. Allison's working with Brenner on Dr. Lyman. That only leaves Tony Cruz and his alibi."

"There are a lot of things about this case that don't sit right with me, Lucy." Charlie meandered around the office. "Too many hidden truths. Too much deceit." She grunted. "It doesn't amount to murder, yet. But given what we know right now? I want to start looking for forensic evidence that this girl was shot dead on the side of the road and it was made to look like suicide."

"How do we find evidence to that effect when the police didn't?"

"You and me?" Charlie grabbed her things. "We're going to the spot where it happened."

"The cops have been all over that place," Lucy replied.

"Have they? Because Brenner was all but assured that this was a suicide. Do you think he looked at other possibilities? Tire tracks from other vehicles? Do you think he has Jessica's car and is running forensics on it?"

"Not if the case is closed," Lucy replied.

"Exactly." Charlie checked the time. "We'll call Allison from the car. But you and me? We're going to that spot right now."

———

DETECTIVE BRENNER MARCHED AWAY in a huff with Allison trying to keep up with him. "Son of a bitch is hiding something."

"But you still don't have enough to reopen the investigation," Allison said. "Is there no way to compel a warrant for the messages contained in that phone app?"

"Not without an open investigation. It's the ol' Catch 22." He stopped as he stood at the bottom of the stairs. "Lyman may not have done anything to Jessica Healey, but I'll be damned if I'm going to let that rich son of a bitch think he can best the Tampa Police. I'm going to my lieutenant and discuss our options. You and your team press on. Find me something, Ms. Hart. If you don't, that little prick won't be held accountable for shit."

"And if he truly had nothing to do with Jessica's death?" she asked.

"He might not have, but he ain't getting off the hook that easy." Brenner walked up the stairs.

Allison remained at the bottom of the steps and considered her options. Her phone buzzed with an incoming text from Charlie. *"Lucy and I are driving to the location where they found Jessica's car. Need to find evidence."*

A moment later, she marched up the stairs and walked to Shane's desk. "Hi."

"Hey." He peered up at her. "I just saw Brenner storm back to his office. I take it the talk with the professor didn't go well."

"Not really. Listen, I'd like your help with something. Do you have some time?"

"When? Now?" he asked.

"Yeah. This has to happen now," she replied.

"Okay, sure. What do you need?"

"I want to meet Charlie and Lucy at the spot where they found Jessica's car. Charlie said they needed to find evidence. I agree, and especially now. We're running in circles and everyone is starting to look suspicious. It's time we see for ourselves what's out there. You game?"

He was already on his feet. "You know I am."

"Then grab a kit and let's go," Allison replied.

Shane snatched his keys from his desk. "You drive."

Allison started down the stairs again and walked outside. The afternoon hours slipped by and it was already 3pm. Still more than enough daylight, but the journey would take an hour.

She started through downtown and toward the highway. "Thanks for doing this. The girls and I are good at what we do, but you're still the detective and I'll defer to you in spotting evidence."

"Make no mistake, it'll take all of us, but I appreciate the compliment." Shane peered at her from the passenger seat. "I thought you were going to get rid of this old clunker?"

She laughed. "Maybe after this case."

"You realize that you say that every time I ask." He smiled and peered through the windshield. "Do you think this professor had anything to do with Jessica's death?"

"I honestly don't know. I wish I had a clear answer. I think that was what I had hoped for in this questioning. But as soon as Lyman asked for his lawyer, Brenner knew the door just slammed in our faces."

"But you think he's hiding something?"

"Oh yeah. The guy's been cheating on his wife with that girl."

Allison glanced to him. "And if he's cheated once, I guarantee there are others."

Shane nodded. "That only makes him an asshole, not a killer."

"It does. But when a girl is dead and you still won't cooperate, it starts to make you look a little guilty."

"The only thing he's guilty of is not wanting his wife to find out," Shane replied.

Allison raised the corner of her mouth. "For now. We'll see what happens. But Brenner said he can't do much without some kind of proof that this was murder."

"And that's what we'll be looking for now?"

She turned to him with a wry smile. "With everything I have, we'll be looking for something to point us in the right direction."

"What if we don't find anything, Allison?"

"Then I'm out of runway."

11

Charlie's white Chevy SUV was parked alongside the shoulder of the stretch of highway where Jessica's car was found. She waited inside with Lucy for Allison's arrival and peered through the rearview mirror. "That's them."

Lucy glanced over her shoulder. "Yep. That's Allison's Honda." She turned back. "What do you think about her bringing Shane?"

"Hey, I got no issue with that. He's a good detective. Not to mention he has all the fun forensics stuff, which we're going to need here." Charlie opened her door and stepped outside, offering a wave to Allison amid the bright sunshine and cloudless sky.

Allison started ahead. "Are we back far enough from the exact location? Last thing we want to do is destroy evidence."

"We're about 300 feet behind, according to the markers ahead. But it has rained a few times since it happened. We might already be shit out of luck," Charlie replied.

Shane approached with his kit in hand. "All we can do is try.

Nice to see you, Charlie. Lucy. Let's see what we can find." He started on and walked the several feet where a police marker remained in place. The others quickly caught up to him. "X marks the spot. This is where she was. You can see tire tracks here." He pulled out his phone and snapped photos. "What I'd like to see is another set. And not the ones the patrol cars left."

"Like these here?" Allison squatted and peered at the ground. "It's a little hard to tell because it's grassy here, but what do you think of this?"

Shane joined her while Charlie and Lucy hovered over them. "I can see tracks, but it's hard to find the tire pattern. I'll take pictures. It can't hurt."

"What else should we be looking for?" Lucy peered around. "Was there any damage to her vehicle?"

"No. That's the kicker. No evidence to suggest an accident," Charlie replied. She joined Lucy to survey the nearby grounds. "Footprints. We might get lucky and find some of those, but like Shane said, we'd have to rule out that they're from the cops."

Allison returned upright. "Is this a fool's errand, Shane?"

"Not a chance. If you don't do everything you can to get to the truth, then what's the point of doing anything?"

"You're right." Allison continued to study the area, carefully considering anything of interest. But when she stopped for a moment, she walked to the edge of the shoulder, near the road. "Why here?"

Charlie approached her. "What's that?"

"Why this place? This spot. It's open. Another mile that way," she turned east. "There's a few fast-food places and a gas station. Another, what, two miles that way," she turned in the opposite direction. "There are more stores. So, what made this 20-year-old girl stop right here and put a gun to her temple?"

"She had plenty of other places she could've stopped. Probably more discreet than this. I guess this spot seemed the best for her," Charlie said.

Allison pressed her lips together creating a thin white line. "It doesn't make sense that this girl, who was obviously excited to go on Spring Break with her friends only 2 days earlier, would then somehow decide on her drive back to see her ailing father to just off herself."

"What are you getting at, Alli?" Charlie pressed on.

Allison turned to her. "That's just not the behavior of a suicidal girl."

"I hate to break it to you, Alli, but it is. These kids, they try hard to show everyone that they're doing just fine when they're not."

"But the dad. She had a great relationship with her parents," Allison added.

"That's what Mary Ann said, but is that true? We don't really know other than what her friends have said, which frankly, wasn't much as far as that was concerned," Charlie replied.

Allison nodded. "We need to see the messages the professor exchanged with Jessica. That will tell us a lot. But we need to find something to show Brenner this case is not what it seems."

"Then I say we'd better look damn hard." Charlie placed her hand on Allison's shoulder. "Come on, Alli. We'll find something, no matter how long it takes."

"Uh, hey guys." Lucy stood about one hundred yards back and near the retention area where water ran during the rains. It was nearly empty with only a few inches at the bottom, which was about 5 feet deep.

The three of them walked toward her when Allison began, "What is it, Lucy?"

She pointed to the ground just inches from her feet. "I think that's a cell phone. It's embedded in the grass and mud a little, but it looks like a cell phone to me."

Shane stepped closer and squatted in front of it. "It's a phone." He peered back up at her. "Jeez, Lucy. Good eye."

A broad smile rose on Allison's face. "What are the odds that phone belongs to either Jessica or someone Jessica knew?"

"A second phone?" Charlie asked. "Mary Ann has Jessica's phone."

Allison nodded. "Sure. But there could be another."

EVENING HAD ARRIVED while the team returned to the ACL office. Shane accompanied them and so did the cell phone that had been carefully placed in an evidence bag. Detective Brenner was on his way to view the new and potentially invaluable evidence uncovered near the location of Jessica's car.

Lucy peered through the office window at the parking lot below. "Brenner's here."

"He was skeptical when I called him, so we'll have to see how he wants to handle this," Allison replied.

"What's to handle?" Charlie asked. "We found a phone."

"I understand that, but the battery is dead. It's probably damaged from being in the elements for weeks, assuming it had something to do with Jessica. And we have no way to confirm it belonged to Jessica. I get where he's coming from, but my gut tells me this has everything to do with our investigation."

"It won't take long to confirm it," Shane added. "He takes that into Forensics, they'll be able to charge it up, getting it working again, most likely. Whether they can get into it is another story."

Their attention turned to the door as it opened, and Detective Brenner walked inside. The stocky man with dark hazel eyes and rugged features peered at them. "Don't you all look like the cat who ate the canary?"

"Thanks for coming down, Detective Brenner. We are excited about the find," Allison replied.

"Where is it?" He continued inside and cast a glance to Shane. "Sully. I hear you helped out these ladies."

"Not really. It was their idea to check out the site. I just brought a forensics kit. It was Lucy, here, who found the phone."

Brenner displayed a crooked smile as he peered at Lucy. "Maybe you should be working for us."

"Trying to poach my people?" Allison asked with a smile. "Here's the evidence bag. Come see for yourself. You asked us to find something and we did."

Brenner approached the conference table and spotted the bag. "You take a look at this yet, Sully?"

"Only insomuch as to get it properly bagged. You won't find any of our prints on it. I promise you that. Battery appears to be dead. That's as far as we got," Shane replied.

"Then I'll take it into the lab and see what they can do with it." He looked at Allison. "You feel pretty confident this belonged to Jessica Healey?"

"I'm pretty confident it belonged to either her or someone she knew. We also got photos of what appear to be tire tracks and shoeprints. But those could have been from anyone or any car. I saved them to a USB if you want them." She held out the flash drive.

"We did have cars on the scene, of course, and patrolmen walking around. But I'll still take a look and compare it to what we have. At this point, it can't hurt."

Charlie approached him. "You also might be interested to know that we've uncovered deleted social media posts from one of

Jessica's close friends." She gestured to Lucy. "You want to show him?"

Lucy pulled up the images on her phone. "I have a friend who's pretty good at this stuff. This one is what caught our eye."

Brenner peered at the screen. "Yeah, I'd say that's an interesting development." He turned back to Allison. "I can see you all have been doing your homework. Keep at it. I'll work on the phone and see if our guys can get into it. I still have Dr. Lyman to contend with. We'll take this one step at a time and see where it leads."

Allison regarded Brenner for a moment. "It's looking like we have a lot of moving parts right now. Jessica Healey's life was anything but ordinary. But the look of things right now, there seems to be some dissention among the group of friends. I need to understand why. The ex-boyfriend obviously comes into play here as well. But as it stands, this is looking less like a suicide to me. And I think that's how my partners see it as well."

Brenner nodded. "It certainly isn't as cut and dry as it seemed on its face, I'll give you that. Lyman's resistance proved that much. We'll keep in close contact." He picked up the evidence bag. "Thank you. All of you. This is good work." He looked at Shane. "Thanks for your help too, Sully."

Allison showed him out and as she returned to the group, she began. "While Brenner's working on the phone, we need to keep tabs on the friends. I'm especially interested in Nia and her relationship with Tony Cruz."

"As far as I knew, Tony was dating Hailey. Maybe I'll see what more I can find on that front," Lucy said.

"Good," Allison replied. "Then Charlie and I will focus on the other three. We're missing something about those kids."

"I agree. The way they seemed to collude with one another in regard to talking to Lucy and me. Something's up," Charlie said.

Allison returned to her desk. "Then let's find out what that is."

———

On the other side of Allison's front door stood Leo Hart with thinning hair, a lined face, and a slight paunch. Still, he held onto his baby-faced good looks, even if they appeared middle-aged. Shielded from the rain beneath Allison's front porch, he waited for her. A quiet knock again, and a moment later, she appeared. "Hi."

"Hi. Come in." Allison stood in capri yoga pants with a long t-shirt and let in her ex-husband. It had been almost six years now since the divorce, but their cordial relationship endured mostly due to the children, though they were no longer children.

It wasn't until Leo's recent engagement announcement that their connection grew strained. Allison held no ill-will toward him anymore. She didn't love him. But that didn't mean the pain wasn't real when he said he was getting re-married and to a younger woman. Of course, she'd known Jenny, the soon-to-be new wife, and had known they lived together, but his engagement stung, nonetheless. Nolan and Micah did their best to accept it, but Allison didn't think they'd quite come around just yet. She was sure they would soon enough.

"You want a beer?" Allison closed the door and padded in bare feet into the kitchen.

"Sure. I'd love one. Thanks." Leo followed her. "I'm sorry to come by so late."

"That's okay. I only just got home about an hour ago. Busy day." She opened a bottle for him.

"Thanks." He took a long swig and sat down on the stool at the kitchen island. "Glad to see you're working a new case. I'm really proud of what you've been able to do with this, Alli."

"It isn't just me. I have great partners. So, what's going on,

Leo? Why are you here?" She brushed off his use of her nickname because he only used it when he wanted something. It was nothing more than a reminder of the relationship they once held.

"I always seem to show up on your doorstep, don't I?" He traced his index finger around the rim of the beer bottle.

She chuckled. "I'm still your friend, Leo. We shared a life. We share children. If you need to talk, I don't mind."

"You should," he replied. "After everything I did."

Hold up now. This wasn't like him at all. He never wanted to talk about his mistakes. "Leo, what's wrong? Is everything okay?"

He eyed her. "You remember when I told you Jenny and I were engaged. You remember asking me why I thought this marriage would be any different than ours?"

She smirked. "I believe I asked why it was you thought this one would work when ours didn't."

"Right." He peered at his bottle of beer. "I didn't have an answer for you then because, well, because I didn't know. I didn't know if it would work a second time around." He held her gaze. "Alli, I still don't."

While Allison didn't love Leo anymore, she did care about him. And there was something in his eyes. Something she hadn't seen since he admitted to his affair, which brought about the demise of their marriage and the new life Allison now enjoyed. "Leo, did you do something stupid? Please tell me you didn't screw things up with Jenny."

He smiled. "I can understand why you'd think that, all things considered. But, um, no I didn't do anything stupid. I don't think I did, anyway." Leo took in a long breath through his nose and closed his eyes. "I think she's cheating on me."

A tiny part of Allison, just a small fraction, wanted to remind him that karma was a bitch. She felt almost vindicated but kicking him while he was down wasn't who she was. No matter what had happened, she couldn't do that to him. There was a time when she absolutely would have, but it was water under the bridge. "I'm sorry to hear that, Leo. Are you sure?"

He shrugged. "No, but it feels like she is. You must know what that's like."

She turned away for a moment. "I have a vague recollection."

"Since we got engaged, Jenny's just sort of pulled away. I don't know why. I thought she wanted to get married. I thought if I didn't ask, then she'd leave me."

"That's the only reason you got engaged? You thought she might leave you?" Allison shook her head. "My God, Leo."

He raised his hands. "I know. I know how that sounds. But she's younger. I knew she wanted a baby and I told her I was past that stage in my life. She said she could accept that."

"Now you think that wasn't true?" Allison pressed on.

"Maybe it wasn't."

Allison walked around the island and sat down next to him. "Leo, you decided to live with this woman who is almost fifteen years younger than you. What did you expect?"

He returned a remorseful gaze and placed his hand on her thigh. "I expected her to be like you."

"Leo, don't." She gently removed it. "Look, I know we are one of the lucky ones. We survived a painful divorce and were able to maintain some sort of amicable relationship. I'm grateful for that, I truly am. It's what's best for the kids. But you can't come here and say these things to me. It's not fair. I have a life now, Leo. I'm happy. For the first time, in a long time, I'm happy. I have a purpose."

"You always had a purpose with me," Leo replied.

"Did I? I was your wife. I was a mother. Who was I to anyone else? Now, I'm Allison Hart, Private Investigator. Look, I'm sorry for what you're dealing with right now. I get no joy in seeing you this way. But this is something you're going to have to deal with. Confront her. Tell her your suspicions. Don't condemn her before you know for certain. Believe me, I begged for an excuse from you that could explain why you did what you did. I prayed for one. But I never could accept any of them. You need to learn the truth."

Leo nodded. "You're right. Jeez, Alli, I'm so sorry. I'm so sorry for putting you through what I put you through."

"It wasn't just me."

"I know. I put the kids through it too and that's something I'll have to live with for the rest of my life."

"But know this, Leo. Our kids? They'll be just fine. They love you. They've come to accept what happened. Even Micah, as hard as it was for her. As much as she blamed me. She's matured and she gets it. And Nolan. Well, you've been his biggest supporter. His newfound baseball career was in big part because of your persistence. You pushed him harder than anyone and that's why he is where he is now. And he'll only get better. One day, he'll play in the big leagues. I know he will."

Leo smiled. "I think so, too." He pushed up from the stool. "Thank you, Alli, for listening to me. You were always good at that."

"Not always, but you're welcome." She stood and joined him. "Go home, Leo. Sort this out with Jenny. It'll either work or it won't. But it's better to know now before you stand at the altar. I think we can both agree on that."

"Yeah." He started toward the door and stopped as she opened it. "Can I hug you?"

"Of course you can." Leo embraced her tighter than she could ever remember him doing before. "You'll be fine, Leo. You'll be just fine." She closed the door behind him and secured the dead bolt.

Allison gasped for breath and her eyes welled. Her heart

ached and not because of his suffering. It ached because a long time ago, she'd prayed he would go through what she had. That his heart would be broken into a million pieces, just as hers had been. Now she regretted it. Seeing him suffer didn't feel like what she thought it would. Could it be that Allison had finally recovered from the pain he'd inflicted on her? And she had been able to help him rather than relish in his suffering. It had been a long time coming.

12

Headlights shone through Allison's front window. She finished tying her shoes and snatched her keys from the side table. On opening her front door, Charlie stood outside. "Right on time."

"As always. You ready to hit the road?"

"Let's go. You want me to drive?" Allison asked.

"I got it." Charlie pressed the remote to unlock the doors of her SUV. "I'd rather take the trip knowing we won't break down."

Allison stepped in. "I'll have you know my car is just as reliable now as it ever was."

Charlie slipped inside and pressed the ignition. "Alli, it's time you put that old girl out to pasture. Don't you think?"

"Maybe after this case is finished." Allison clicked her seatbelt.

"I'm pretty sure that's what you always say." Charlie pulled out onto the road beneath a bright blue morning sky. "You sure you don't want to wait to see if Brenner gets something on the phone?"

"We need to push forward. It could be days before he's able to recover anything if at all. No, we're going back to Daytona and we're going to find out the truth about what those girls did that night," Allison replied.

As Charlie drove on, she glanced at Allison. "I hope you have a plan as to how to go about finding out. Or are we winging it?"

"Of course we're winging it. Since when do I ever have a plan?" Allison chuckled.

"That's what I thought. Business as usual."

Allison's laughter trailed off and she peered at Charlie. "Guess who stopped by last night?"

Charlie shot her a glance. "Shane?"

"No. Nice try, though. Leo. It was about 10:30, I think."

"What did he want?" Charlie continued.

"Apparently, he thinks Jenny is cheating on him."

"What? Are you serious?" Charlie's mouth fell agape. "Well, karma really is a bitch. But why on earth would he tell you that? Does he not see the irony?"

"Oh, he sees it. It's as big and bright as the sun and shining right down on his balding head," Allison replied.

"How do you feel about that?"

"I thought I'd feel validated." Allison peered through the windshield. "Instead, I just feel bad for him. It's a pain I wouldn't wish on anyone, not even him. He's not sure she is cheating, but when you feel it, you feel it."

"Yep. Well, despite it all, I feel for him. What's he going to do?" Charlie asked. "Please tell me he didn't get fresh with you?"

Allison tossed back her head in laughter. "Fresh? No, Mom, he didn't get fresh with me. I told him to go home and ask her. Be honest and upfront. That's all anyone can do in that situation."

Charlie nodded. "Good for you, Alli. Looks like you really have closed the book on that part of your life."

"Thanks. I think I have too."

"Which leaves a place on the old shelf for someone new, right?" Charlie raised her lips in a cockeyed smile.

"Someday."

"Alli, you aren't 30 anymore. Hell, you aren't 40 anymore either. Clock's ticking, my friend. Time waits for no woman."

"Appreciate the support," Allison replied. "Like I said, someday."

"Fine. Fine. I'll let it go, for now. We do have more pressing matters than your love life, or my lack of one. You've already talked to the hotel manager and looked at their surveillance. How do we plan on handling this from here? I know you well enough to know we aren't completely winging it."

"Okay, so I had a few thoughts. Those girls gave you and Lucy alibis."

"That's right. They were practically recited in unison," Charlie added. "Which I thought was..."

"Planned. Yeah. So we need to find out why. In my opinion, Harriet Torres is different than the others. She seems a little bit like an outsider. I assume part of that is because she works a lot and doesn't have as much free time to spend with the others."

"Or it's because she knows the truth and has been keeping her distance," Charlie replied.

"Uh-huh. But before I go to her again, I need to have something. Something that will get her to talk. If we're going to uncover whatever it is those girls buried, we need a crack in the façade." She paused for a moment. "Last night, after Leo left, I called Lucy. I asked her to reach out again to her friend, Kendall, and see if there was a way he could find out the location of Harriet's post. Where they were at the time."

"And?" Charlie asked.

"And a few hours later, Lucy called me back. Neither one of us could sleep. Anyway, Kendall said her Instagram account's locator was set to public. So wherever she posted from, it would indicate where she was at the time. Most of the social media apps do that."

"That's scary," Charlie replied.

"Yeah, it is. So at any given time, anyone who might be a friend on your social media knows where you are whenever you post something." Allison shook her head. "These kids leave themselves completely exposed."

"And the social media giants don't give a damn," Charlie added.

"Not as long as they're making money. But my point in all this was to determine where exactly the girls had gone that night because as we know, they were all too drunk to remember. Just that it was somewhere along the beach."

"Which spans about 25 miles," Charlie said.

"Except now we know, because of Lucy's work with Kendall, we know the name of that bar and that's where we're going first," Allison replied.

———

Mary Ann Healey put away the breakfast dishes when a knock sounded on her front door. She wiped her hands dry and started toward the foyer.

"Honey, someone's at the door," Jim said.

"I heard the bell. I'm coming." She peered into the living room where her husband lay until reaching the front door. "Tony, good morning. Come in, please."

"Thanks Mrs. Healey." He walked inside.

"This is an unexpected surprise. How are you? I haven't seen you since..."

"I know and I'm sorry for that. I wanted to ask you, first of all, when Jessica's funeral is going to be."

Mary Ann took in a long breath. "I'm waiting on the delivery of the casket I selected, which should be any day now. I hope to get the service scheduled for next week. You'll be there, yes?"

"Of course." Tony reached for her hands. "You and Mr. Healey have always been kind to me. Even after me and Jess broke up. I want to be there."

"We wouldn't have it any other way. I'll send the details as soon as I have them." She waited for a moment as he went silent. "Was that the reason you came over? Don't you have school this morning?"

"In a little while, yes. I was actually wondering if I might." He looked down. "I don't want to impose."

"What is it, sweetheart?" she asked.

"Would it be okay if I went into Jess's bedroom? I feel like I need to say goodbye, you know? There's the funeral of course, but I feel like this would be more private. I promise not to touch anything."

"Of course you can. Please, go ahead. There's no rush. Take as long as you need," Mary Ann replied.

Tony nodded and started inside, but before he walked up the stairs, he turned to see Jessica's father on the sofa. "Mr. Healey, how are you feeling, sir?"

"Tony. I'm well on the way to recovery. It's good to see you, son."

"And you, sir. I was just going..."

"I heard. Please, don't mind me. You do what you need to do. We all have our own way of dealing with things."

"Thank you, sir." Tony climbed the stairs and stood on the landing. Jessica's room was down the hall and to the left. He swallowed hard and started along the corridor.

Her bedroom door was slightly ajar, and a sliver of morning light peeked through. Tony pushed it open with a gentle touch and stepped inside. A hint of a smile rose on his lips as he looked at the room. It was exactly as he remembered, though he hadn't been inside it in months.

The walls were still a golden rose and her bedding was ruffled and white. He recalled being in here for the first time when they met in high school. The sickly-sweet floral perfume she used to wear lingered then but was long gone now. At the time, he thought it was the best smell ever. Tony walked to her bed and sat down, taking great care not to disturb it more than necessary.

This was also the place where he lost his virginity. A lump caught in his throat and he swallowed it down. He had loved her.

Tony stood again and set down his backpack, unzipping the top of it. He slipped his hand inside and retrieved a box about 6 inches square. It was pink with a white ribbon and he studied it for a moment, then slid it under Jessica's bed. "Goodbye, Jess." He walked out of her room and closed the door behind him.

———

THE BAR WAS JUST AHEAD, and Allison spotted it in the distance. "That's it up there."

"The Tiki Bar," Charlie began. "How original." She turned to Allison. "Do you really think the manager will let you look at video?"

"If he doesn't want me to look into his establishment serving underage kids, I think he'll cooperate," she replied. "Remember, Sophie's only 20. So was Jessica."

"I see you do have a plan." Charlie patted her on the back. "I like it. Oh, hey, unbutton your top button."

"What?" Allison shot her a look.

"You got the rack, and the looks. Time to put them to good use for once so we can get what we need."

Allison laughed. "Right. Sure, I'll jump right on that." She shoved Charlie in the arm.

"Hey, I'm just saying..."

"Whatever. Let's just go inside." Allison removed her sunglasses and entered the bar that appeared to have just opened. Only a few customers were inside. "Morning." She approached the bar and retrieved her credentials. "I'm a private investigator, Allison Hart. This is my partner, Charlie Wells. We'd like to talk to your manager, if he or she is around."

"She is around." The bartender peered at Allison's card. "What's this about?" he asked.

"I'm verifying alibis."

He nodded. "I'll go get her. Hang on a minute."

Allison surveyed the bar. "Small place. Bet it gets pretty packed."

"Especially over Spring Break," Charlie added. "You know, even if they do agree to show you their security footage, assuming they still have it, you might not see anything you want to see."

"I just need to know if all four girls were here and at what time Nia left as well as Harriet. If we can find that it isn't when they said, then we'll go from there."

"Excuse me?" A woman in her late 20s appeared. "You're the private investigator?"

"Allison Hart." She extended her hand. "Thank you for coming out. This is my partner..."

"Charlie Wells." Charlie shook the woman's hand. "Nice to meet you."

"Same. I'm Gillian." The woman wore a yellow t-shirt and khaki shorts with her blonde curly hair resting just above her shoulders. "What can I do for you both?"

"A couple of weeks ago, over Spring Break, a group of girls were here."

Gillian laughed. "Sorry, I don't mean to be rude, but you just described half of the people who were here over Spring Break. This is Daytona Beach."

"I know, and I'm sure there were a lot of people during that time," Allison continued. "But I need to know about these girls, in particular." She retrieved a copy of Jessica's social media post from the day they left the school.

Gillian took the paper and examined it. "Well, do you happen to know the exact date? We keep security footage here onsite for 30 days. After that, it's archived and sent to corporate. I don't know what they do with it."

"I do know the date. April 19th," Allison began. "It was the day one of those girls in that picture died."

"Oh. I'm sorry. I didn't realize…"

"That's okay. I'm here on behalf of the family of that girl. We're trying to piece together what happened that night when four of them were here."

"Of course. Follow me." Gillian turned back and started toward a back room. "What happened to her? Was it here in Daytona?"

"No. Her name was Jessica Healey. She pulled off the side of the road on her way home to Tampa and put a gun to her head."

"Oh my God." Gillian turned on a light inside the storage room at the back. "That's awful. And her friends just went out that night like it was no big deal?"

"They didn't know until the next morning. After that, the girls came home," Allison replied.

"Jeez." Gillian sat down on a folding chair at a table. "This isn't sophisticated or anything, but it does the trick. Take a seat."

Charlie gestured for Allison to take the seat next to Gillian. "I'll stand."

"I can grab another chair..."

"It's fine. I'm okay," Charlie replied.

Gillian keyed in a few commands on the desktop computer and the screen flashed before opening a program. "This is the recorded data. I just need to enter the date in question and pull the files." She keyed in April 19th. "This is it, here. You say it was that night?"

"Yes. I don't know what time and the girls don't remember. Apparently, there was quite a bit of alcohol involved."

"I'm sure there was. There always is. Okay, I'll start from nightfall and go from there." It took a few moments before the files loaded. "This could take a while."

Charlie folded her arms. "We're in no rush."

———

Dr. Jacob Lyman peered through the window of his lawyer's office. "What are you going to do about this, Will? I can't afford for this to come out. You know that. Not when I have that deal so close to completion."

Harris turned to his client and handed him a glass of scotch. "Maybe you should have thought about that before you screwed one of your students."

Lyman took the glass. "I don't need a lecture from you, Will. I need answers. I pay you a lot for answers, so let's hear it."

"Okay, look." Harris shoved his hand into the pocket of his black dress pants. "That detective has no standing right now. Hell, he doesn't even have an active case. He's puffing out his chest to scare you."

"He's doing a pretty good job of that." Lyman tossed back the drink.

"That's what he wants. You went against the university rules. You slept with one of your students. But." He held up his index finger. "You didn't kill her. And I think Brenner knows that. The forensics show it already."

"Then why is he pushing this?"

"Because the family can't come to terms with the fact their daughter put a gun to her head. They're looking for any other reason they can find and so they hired a private investigator. From what I understand, that P.I. has a decent reputation at the station."

"So this private investigator is just grasping at straws, right?" Lyman asked.

"Right. So I say, give them what they want," Harris replied.

"My phone. You want me to hand over my phone?"

"Why not? So you were screwing her. So what. You think you're the only professor to take advantage of a student? Come on, man. It is what it is. But here's the deal. You agree to hand over your phone and even show them the app you used to communicate with this girl but only if they keep it out of the press. No leaks or we sue. Plain and simple. No way this Detective Brenner will want to have to explain a lawsuit against the city."

"Can I go through it first?" Lyman asked.

"I can't stop you from deleting messages, but I will tell you this, if Brenner gets a whiff that you've deleted a bunch of stuff, and it wouldn't be that hard for him to figure out, he'll ride your ass, of that I'm sure. You don't want that, Jake. Not now. This is the best way to keep your private affairs out of the public eye and out of your wife's purview. Let them see what you did and move on. They'll see you had absolutely nothing to do with that girl taking her own life." He peered at Lyman. "Unless you're not telling me something."

13

Allison's college years were not at all dissimilar to those girls who she now watched on security footage. Although it was hard to separate the fact that she was the mother of a college-aged woman now, she wasn't naïve enough to think Micah never did anything like what she now witnessed. She glanced over her shoulder at Charlie. "See what you get to look forward to?"

"Not my boys, I'll tell you that," she replied.

"Uh-huh. Come tell me that in five years," Allison added. "What time are we looking at right now?"

Gillian, the bar manager, peered at the timestamp. "This shows 10:35pm on the night of April 19th. Looks pretty typical so far."

"The four of them are all still together," Charlie said. "I thought Harriet mentioned that Sophie and Madison went off with a couple of guys?"

"I can fast forward a little if you'd like," Gillian said.

"Well, if what Harriet said was true, then we should see her

147

leaving in the next few minutes. I can always corroborate that with the hotel footage as well," Allison continued. "But let's let this play out and see what happens."

Charlie pulled up a chair. "Then I'd better sit."

"Wait a minute." Allison leaned closer to the screen and slipped on her reading glasses. "I think this is it. Two young men are approaching Sophie and Madison."

"Yeah, and look at Harriet and Nia," Charlie said. "They're standing at the bar ordering drinks and haven't taken notice of their friends yet."

"Harriet's walking toward them now with Nia behind her. Both are carrying drinks." Allison turned to Gillian. "We can't get any sound?"

"I'm afraid not. We have CCTV mostly to prevent overserving and determine responsible parties when fights break out. Things like that. Conversations aren't recorded."

"Look at Harriet now," Allison added. "She handed Madison a drink before being squeezed out of the conversation. Do you see this?"

"I see it," Charlie said. "Sophie and Madison are huddled around those boys. This must be why Nia and Harriet left."

"Right, but neither one is leaving right now." Allison peered at the timestamp again. "It's almost 11 o'clock. That was when Nia said she left."

"She's looking at her phone," Charlie added. "Like she just got a message."

"Yep. And now she's looking around, expecting someone." Allison was glued to the screen, waiting for what would happen next.

"She's leaving." Charlie thrust back her shoulders. "She didn't even tell the others. Just walked right out."

Allison turned to her. "She was meeting someone, but it was clearly outside. Who the hell did she meet?"

"Gotta be the ex-boyfriend," Charlie continued. "Tony Cruz. We know only a few hours later when Harriet returned to the room, she spotted Nia texting Tony."

"But if that was the case, then that implies he wasn't there after all. That she must've been meeting someone else." Allison took in a breath. "Charlie, why don't you call Lucy and have her track down Tony Cruz. Let's find out where he was the night Jessica didn't come home."

Charlie stepped out to make the call while Allison continued to view the screen. "It looks like Harriet was telling the truth. Nia said she went straight back to the room. That doesn't appear to be the case."

"Sounds like you're dealing with something that turned bad," Gillian replied. "Is there anything else you need from me?"

"Don't suppose you have security footage outside your property?"

"Just for the immediate perimeter. Would you like to see it?"

"Let's take a look. Whoever Nia was trying to find might be right outside that door," Allison replied.

"I'll pull it up." Gillian keyed in a few more commands.

Charlie walked back inside. "Lucy's going to the school."

"She knows for sure that he's there?" Allison asked.

"Yep. Apparently, she has an 'in' with the new girlfriend who told her Tony had practice in two hours. And, the girlfriend wants to arrange a little interview."

"Lucy's good with that? How is she going to play it?"

"Like she did before. Pretend to work for the school's paper."

Allison nodded. "It's risky. I don't know. It sure does seem like Tony Cruz is putting on an act when it comes to Jessica. Between this new girlfriend and the fact that he appears to be dating Jessica's friend, Nia, it's putting him in the spotlight and not in a good way."

"You want me to pull Lucy?" Charlie asked.

"No. She's smart enough to handle this on her own. Gillian's pulling up footage from the bar's perimeter to see if we can spot Nia and whoever it was she was trying to meet up with."

"Ms. Hart, I think I have it right here," Gillian said. "This might help."

Allison and Charlie pulled in to see the slightly grainier video.

"Sorry it's not the best quality. Light is lower outside."

"That's okay." Allison checked the timestamp. "This is right about the time she walked away from the girls."

"Yep," Charlie replied. "I don't see her yet. Oh, wait. There she is."

"That's her. She's looking around. Do you see anyone approaching her?" Allison asked.

"Not yet." Charlie pushed her glasses farther up on her nose. "Come on, kid. Who you looking for?"

Nia picked up her pace and looked ahead, wearing a smile.

"She sees someone," Allison said. "Damn it. Damn it."

"I'm sorry, Ms. Hart. She's walked out of the frame," Gillian replied. "That's all I have."

Allison sighed. "That's okay. This is still good. Thank you for your help. At least we know she didn't go straight back to the room like she said."

"Now we just need to find out who she was with," Charlie added. "Thank you, Gillian."

They started into the bar again that had begun to fill up as it neared lunchtime.

"We didn't get what we wanted, but it cleared up a few things for us," Allison began. "Maybe Lucy will have better luck. If Nia was meeting Tony, that'll change things."

"Are you saying he would've known about Jessica? That she was already gone?" Charlie asked

"We can't rule it out. If he didn't know, maybe Nia planned to tell Jessica about the two of them with him by her side."

"What kind of friend would do that?" Charlie asked.

"Not any kind of friend I would want." Allison started down the boardwalk toward the parking lot. She glanced over her shoulder and turned back. "Don't look but I saw that guy inside the bar a couple of times."

"What guy?" Charlie shot around.

Allison closed her eyes. "I told you not to look. Let's just get to the car."

"Are we being followed?"

"I don't know. I know I can be paranoid about these things, but I'm trying to stay grounded here. We'll find out pretty quickly," Allison replied.

Charlie pressed the remote to unlock her SUV. "Just get in." She slipped onto the driver's seat.

Allison walked around to the passenger side and as she opened the door, she locked eyes with the man before quickly stepping in. "Yeah, we're being followed."

———

BASEBALL PRACTICE HAD ALREADY BEGUN when Lucy arrived and found Hailey Buford sitting on the bleachers.

"Lucy! Oh, my gosh. How are you?" Hailey stood to offer an overly friendly embrace.

"I'm good. Nice to see you." Lucy sat down next to her. "Sorry I'm a little late. Did I miss anything?"

"Nope. Tony's at bat soon, though. So, I'm thrilled you

decided to come back. I thought maybe I scared you off or something."

Lucy waved off her concerns. "Not at all. I just got a little busy with essays, actually. But I'm here now and I'd really love to talk to Tony. He said it would be okay?"

"Of course. He's super excited to speak to you," Hailey replied.

"That's great. I think it'll help get him exposure and help me, too," Lucy said. "I need a feel-good article and with what just happened to his ex-girlfriend, well, it'll be good for people to see that he's moving on with his life despite the pain."

Hailey's face changed. Her smile faded and the spark in her eyes disappeared. "How did you know about that?"

"Oh, I'm sorry. I—I thought everyone knew. It's been on the news and his name was mentioned in connection with it." That was a lie.

Hailey tossed back her brown hair. "Is that the only reason you want to talk to him, because he won't go for that."

"No. No, it's not. I promise you. I really thought it would be a touching story about him and his achievements even with the grief I'm sure he feels. Hailey, I didn't mean to upset you. I'm so sorry." Lucy wondered if this was about to be called off right now without her having a chance to even see Tony. Charlie had asked her to find out where he was that night, and it would take time to build trust with him. Maybe it was time they didn't have.

Hailey turned toward the field, appearing to consider whether to forgive Lucy. She finally turned back. "Maybe you're right. But just so you know, Tony and Jessica Healey broke up months ago. It's not like he was dating her when she decided to... whatever." She rolled her eyes.

"I know. I was wondering, over the Spring Break, did you and

Tony do anything? Spend time away together or go with a group of friends or whatever?"

"No. He was busy with practice. I went with some of my friends to Ft. Lauderdale. I hate Daytona Beach. It's way too crazy there."

"Did he call you when he found out? I'm sure it must've been a total shock for him. And that was, what, like a couple of days into Spring Break?"

"Something like that. No, he didn't call me. He was super upset and just, like, vegged out with his parents trying to understand it all. And he said he didn't want me to feel like I had to come home and be with him."

"Sure, I totally get that," Lucy replied. "I can't imagine what that must've felt like for him."

"Honestly, he was totally over her a long time ago. I know he was sad and all because they were together through high school, but...

"Well, he's very lucky to have someone like you by his side to help see him through it all. I really do appreciate you setting this up." Lucy glanced at the field. "That's him there, isn't it? You said he was number 12?"

"Yep. That's my Tony." Hailey cupped her hands around her mouth and yelled out. "Go get 'em, Tone!" She turned back to Lucy. "You'll see when you talk to him. I'm okay with your story angle, but you'll see he's doing just fine."

Lucy began to feel as though this entire interview was going to be monitored by Hailey. *Overbearing much?* She needed a way to get him alone. Find out how he really felt about Jessica's death. Right now, that seemed an impossibility.

———

ALLISON GLANCED through the sideview mirror with her phone in her hand. "Shane, it's me. Hey, can you run a plate for me?"

"Why? Where are you?" he asked.

"I'm with Charlie. We're driving back to Tampa."

"Where did you two go, Allison?" he pressed on.

"I needed to find out who was lying to us. Turned out, it was Nia. She was meeting someone and didn't go straight back to the hotel the night Jessica died. Anyway, we were able to take a look at CCTV from the bar where they were. By the time we left, we noticed someone who appeared to be trailing us. He's two cars behind us now but I had a chance to see his plate number."

"What is it?"

Allison glanced at the scrap receipt she scribbled the number on. "TW4 0J7."

"Got it. Stay on the line. I'll run it now."

Allison lowered her phone and looked at Charlie. "He's running it now."

"Good boy," Charlie replied.

"Okay, I got something," Shane said on the other end of the line. "The car is registered to Chuck Meisner. St. Pete's."

"That doesn't help much," Allison began. "Any record? Arrests, tickets. Anything?"

"No. He's clean." Shane typed on his keyboard. "Hold on. Okay, I got something else here."

Allison picked up on the long pause. "Shane, what is it? What did you find?"

"Guess who this guy works for?" He didn't wait for her to respond. "One Will Harris, Esquire."

"The lawyer. He works for Lyman's lawyer," Allison replied.

Charlie shot her a look. "Are you serious?"

Allison pursed her lips and nodded. "What the hell is he trying to prove?"

"I have a feeling he's building a case against you. A harassment case, defamation, you name it. At least, that's what he wants it to look like," Shane replied.

"And if we find something on his client?" Allison pressed on.

"Then he'll use your actions in a lawsuit. Look, Allison, you and Charlie are on the right track. Keep an eye on this guy, but he's harmless. Lyman's attorney is looking to intimidate you. He can't go after the cops, not yet anyway, so that just leaves you. As soon as you decided Lyman could have had anything to do with Jessica's death, they went into protective mode."

"Doesn't this guy realize all he's doing is making himself look guiltier?" she added.

"Looks don't matter. Evidence does. If you want, I can run over to Brenner's office and let him know what's going on. It might get him to spur on the computer lab concerning that phone."

"No. I appreciate it, but I'll reach out to him when we return. Like you said, we're not in any danger. I don't want Brenner flying off the handle at this lawyer and making things worse for my investigation. Thanks, Shane. I appreciate the backup. I'll be in contact soon." Allison ended the call. "You get the gist of that conversation?"

"The lawyer's trying to scare us off, I'm guessing," Charlie replied.

"Yep."

"Boy, is that a mistake. After what we've been through? Drug runners, crooked politicians. They think they can scare us by having some guy..." Charlie lurched forward. "What the?"

Allison shot around to peer through the rear window. "Oh my God. He just hit us! Charlie, go!"

She slammed her foot on the gas pedal and picked up speed. "What the hell is going on? Is he trying to kill us?"

"I don't know what he's trying to do, just keep going. We're near the exit. He won't follow us." Allison kept her eyes on the sideview mirror.

"You sure about that? Cripes, Alli, what the hell did we just walk into?" She gripped the wheel with white knuckles and her steely eyes peered at the road ahead. "A quarter-mile. Hang on, because I ain't slowing down." She sped up again as another tap hit their bumper. She let out a small scream.

"It's okay." Allison reached for her phone. "I'm calling for help."

"911, what's your emergency?"

"A car is trying to run us off the road. We need help," Allison began. "License plate TW4." Allison tried to continue, but she let out a yelp. "He hit us again."

"Is there a place you can safely pull off the road? A public place?" the operator asked.

"Not yet, we're.... Jesus!" Allison dropped the phone as another bump hit harder. "Charlie get off here. Now!"

Charlie made a hard right off the highway and onto the exit ramp. "Is he following? Alli, is he following us?"

She watched as he sped past them and caught sight of his gaze again. With dark brown eyes, he peered at her. "No. No, he just went by." Allison pressed her hand on her chest. "Are you okay?"

"Hell no." Charlie made her way to a nearby strip mall and pulled into the parking lot, slamming the gearshift into Park. She took a moment to catch her breath. They both did. "What the hell was that?"

Allison heard a voice still coming from her phone that had fallen to the floorboard. She reached down and picked it up. "Hello?"

"Ma'am, are you okay?" Are you hurt?"

"No. We're fine. We got off the road and he left."

"Ma'am, please repeat that license plate number. We'll find him," the operator continued.

She pressed the mute button on her phone. "She wants the plate number, but I don't know if we should..."

"Are you crazy? Of course we should. Alli, that guy tried to run us off the road."

"I know, but if we do, it could put us at risk. The worst that will happen is that guy will get a ticket for road rage. He won't go to jail or if he does, they'll post bond. No. I think we have to deal with this. We'll tell Brenner, of course, but anyone outside the investigation... no one else can be involved. Not until we learn what Lyman is hiding."

"He sure as hell didn't do himself any favors just now," Charlie said. "Fine. Tell her you didn't get the full plate number. Then we get on the horn with Brenner and tell him what happened." Charlie glanced over her shoulder and the highway again. "I don't know what Dr. Lyman is hiding, but if we didn't think Jessica's death was a murder before, we sure as hell should now."

14

———

Hailey Buford leapt to her feet and hurried down the bleachers when her boyfriend and rising star on the community college baseball team made his way toward her. "Lucy, come on. I'll introduce you."

Lucy navigated through the other spectators and walked down the shaky metal steps until reaching Hailey and Tony at the bottom.

"Lucy, this is my boyfriend, Tony Cruz. Tony, this is the girl I was telling you about. The one who writes for the school paper, Lucy... You know what, I didn't get your last name." Hailey peered at her.

"Boyce. Lucy Boyce. It's nice to finally meet you, Tony. Hailey has said great things about you."

Tony smiled at Hailey. "Well, she is a little biased." He offered his hand. "Nice to meet you, Lucy."

"I was hoping you might have a few minutes to talk? I'd like to, first of all, see how you're doing with the news of your ex-girlfriend's suicide, and secondly, on a lighter note, talk a little bit about your plans for a future in baseball."

Tony shot Hailey a scornful gaze before she spoke up to defend herself against the tacit allegation. "Lucy knew about Jessica Healey. I didn't say..."

He turned back to Lucy wearing a smile. "No, it's fine. I'm happy to talk to you."

"Great." Lucy peered around. "Well, I suppose we could just have a seat on the bleachers if that's okay with you."

"Sure. Fine." Tony glanced at Hailey again. "Why don't I call you when we're finished? We'll go and grab something to eat. I still need to go home and get cleaned up."

Hailey appeared taken aback by the notion he hadn't wanted her there. "Oh, sure, yeah. I'll let you guys talk."

Tony kissed her forehead before she started away.

"Thanks, Hailey," Lucy called out. "Okay, Tony. Should we get started?"

After Hailey was out of earshot, Tony turned back to Lucy. "I know you work for that private investigator."

"Sorry?" Lucy scrambled to think of an explanation.

"You think I don't talk to Jess's friends?"

Lucy cleared her throat and regained her composure. "No, I'm sure you do talk to them. Well, one, in particular, considering you're dating Nia Brown. I met Nia several days ago. Nice girl. I wonder, though, does Hailey know about her?"

"What do you want from me, huh? I told your boss everything I know. So I'm going out with Nia too. Big deal. I'm not married to Hailey. And what does that have to do with what Jess did to herself?"

"We're just trying to figure out what happened to her."

"You already know," Tony added. "Jess was messed up. She

took her own life. Case closed. Look, I miss her, okay? But she was the one who broke up with me. Not the other way around."

"Is that why you're seeing Nia? To get back at Jessica?" Lucy asked.

"What does it matter now? She's gone. I'm still here trying to pick up the pieces from Jess's selfish behavior. Do you have any idea what this has done to her parents?"

"As a matter of fact, I do," Lucy replied. "And it matters because I'm wondering why Jessica wanted to come see you that day and her supposed best friend, Sophie, steered her away from that decision."

Tony's face fell. "Ms. Hart told me that, but I didn't know it at the time."

"The two exchanged text messages," Lucy continued. "Jessica was distraught and wanted you by her side while her father suffered the heart attack. Sophie warned her against it, suggesting that it wouldn't help her get over you."

"I didn't know about any of that." His tone softened. "She never liked me."

"Sophie?"

"Yeah, Sophie frickin Matthews. I don't know what I ever did to her, but I know it was her who convinced Jess to break up with me," Tony added.

"There's one thing I have to ask you, Tony, and we won't have to go through this again. I need to know where you were that day and into the evening when Jessica was on her way back home, but never made it."

He sat down on the edge of the shiny metal bench and cast his gaze to the sky. A long intake of breath, and it seemed Tony was ready to answer the question. "I drove to Daytona later in the day. Nia texted me and told me what happened with Jess, that she was coming home, not that she was dead. She said I could meet her up there and that we could hook up." He swallowed down the lump in his throat. "She said the girls wouldn't know and that she had some guy friends there who said I could crash in their room for the night if I wanted to."

"So you drove to Daytona that day?" Lucy pressed on. "What time was that?"

He appeared to think on the question. "I—I guess it was around 2pm when I left."

Lucy knew Jessica's time of death was between 3 and 3:30pm and the implications against Tony. "Did you drive there alone?"

"Yeah. It was just me."

She'd hoped this would eliminate Tony as a possible suspect, but all it did was confirm he was on the same route at Jessica going the opposite direction. Tony had just made himself a suspect.

———

DETECTIVE BRENNER PACED his office before turning back to Allison and Charlie. "You should've called me the moment you suspected you were being followed."

"There was nothing you could've done, Detective," Allison began. "And we do know how to handle things like this. Believe me, this isn't the first time we've been followed, and I guarantee you that it won't be the last. It wasn't until things turned ugly that we made the 911 call."

Brenner returned to his desk and sat down. "You two got lucky he didn't run you right off the damn road."

"Maybe so, but the problem now is, why the hell did Lyman's attorney have someone follow us? Lyman, so far, has done nothing wrong apart from sleeping with one of his students. Why risk scaring us this way?" Allison added.

"He had to know we wouldn't just roll over and let it happen," Charlie said. "That we'd intensify our efforts."

"Maybe not," Brenner started. "Lyman has money to get people to do what he wants them to do. It was a threat. That's how I see it. A threat to keep you from pursuing this."

"Well, he threatened the wrong people." Charlie peered at Allison. "What's our next move, Alli?"

Allison studied Brenner. "Do we have enough to charge Lyman with anything?"

"We can bring charges against the man who hit your car, but he works for Lyman's attorney. That was by design, I guarantee you that. Lyman wanted to be sure nothing stuck to him. So to answer your question, I still don't have enough on Lyman, unless Forensics can pull a rabbit out of a hat with that cell phone."

"When do you expect something to come of that?" Charlie pressed on.

"I'm hounding those guys daily. Thing is, these damn phone manufacturers don't like to help law enforcement. They don't make anything easy for us. Unless those guys can get into that phone, it's nothing more than a paper weight."

"What about Jessica's phone records?" Allison began. "You sent them to us, but we've been focused on alibis and haven't looked at them yet. It's time we cross-reference the numbers with her family and friends."

"Then that's what we should be doing right now." Charlie looked at Allison. "We can trace every number on Jessica's records and see if any of them are from that phone Lucy found. All we have to do is call the numbers we can't identify."

"Then problem solved." Brenner sighed. "Do me one favor, though?"

"What's that?" Allison asked.

"Next time you think you're being followed, call me for backup. I don't need any dead P.I.s on my watch."

———

MARY ANN HEALEY stood inside Jessica's room. With her hands on her hips, she surveyed the area. "I did it at the dorm. I can do it here. It's time." The funeral was in two days and she still needed to pick out a dress for Jessica. She turned at the sound of approaching footfalls. "Jim, sweetheart, what are you doing? You shouldn't be walking up those stairs, let alone by yourself."

"I couldn't let you do this alone too, Mary Ann. If it's time to lay our daughter to rest, then we do it together," he replied.

Tears welled in her eyes as she smiled tenderly. "Then at least come sit down. I don't want you to overdo it. You can keep me company." Mary Ann led him to Jessica's bed. "We'll get through this. I know we will."

Jim peered at his wife with admiration. "I don't know how you've managed to be so strong through this. Stronger than I ever thought any human being could be." He peered around at the room. "She was so much like you. I still can't believe she could..." He trailed off as he choked back tears.

Mary Ann opened her closet doors and peered inside. "Now, what dress should we choose?"

Jim's heel kicked something under the bed. "What was that?" He tried to bend down but grunted in pain.

Mary Ann turned to him. "Jim, what are you doing?"

"I felt something under the bed. My foot hit it. I was trying to see what it was."

"Let me, sweetheart." Mary Ann got down on her knees and raised the white bed skirt, peering into the darkness. "Oh, I see it."

She reached inside with some effort. "You must've kicked it back farther under the bed."

"Let me do that," he insisted.

"Don't be ridiculous. I just need to reach a little..." She stretched her arm as far as it could go. "Got it." She pulled out the box and sat on her knees. "Hmm. I don't recognize this."

"What's inside?" he asked.

Mary Ann opened the box. Her eyes widened as she retrieved the necklace. "It's Jessica's pendant. The one we got for her fifteenth birthday." She peered up at Jim with shock. "She never took this off. How did this end up here? Jim, how did this get here?"

"I—I don't know. Maybe it's always been here."

Mary Ann stood and marched downstairs without another word. A moment later, she returned with her phone in hand. "No. No, this isn't possible. Look here." She opened a text message. "Jessica sent this when they arrived in Daytona. Look. Look!"

Jim peered at the text and photo. "My God. She's wearing it here."

Mary Ann nodded. "Jessica sent this to say she and the girls arrived safely. It's a picture of them outside their hotel. Jim. My God, she was wearing this very necklace."

"I don't understand," he began. "Then how did it end up in a box under her bed?"

———

LUCY OPENED a bottle of water as she returned to her desk. "All I did was muddy the waters."

Allison pulled off her reading glasses. "You learned that Tony doesn't have an alibi. We now have two people who could have easily caught up to Jessica on her drive home. Neither have an alibi."

"There is one way that Tony could clear his name," Charlie began. "If he can show us his GPS location between the hours of 3 and 3:30pm that afternoon. He says he was driving. Okay, then I'll bet we can get Brenner to confirm his location via GPS."

"You could be onto something." Allison reached for her phone. "I'll call him now and ask about that."

Charlie walked over to Lucy's desk. "How did he seem to you?"

"Honestly? Like an innocent man," she replied. "He was clearly upset when I told him Jessica considered seeing him that evening. But I still can't believe that guy followed you two and bumped your car. It just doesn't make sense."

"It does. Like Brenner said, Lyman's trying to intimidate us. That doesn't bode well for a man with no alibi and who doesn't want to cooperate." Charlie's phone rang. "Oh, it's Mrs. Healey." She glanced at Allison, who was on the phone with Brenner. "This is Charlie. Yes, Mary Ann, hi. How are you?" She nodded and returned to her desk. "You found what?" She slowly sat down. "And you're sure about that?" Charlie nodded again. "Okay. No, I understand. It doesn't seem possible. Mary Ann, had anyone else besides you and your husband been in Jessica's room?"

Allison ended her call and appeared to pick up on Charlie's conversation.

"I see. That is a little strange." Charlie glanced at Allison. "Okay, can you send us a picture of the necklace and box? Great. Just text it to me. Thank you, Mary Ann. We're still working hard to narrow down the details, but this will help us a lot. I'll be in touch. Goodbye."

"What was that about?" Allison asked.

"I'll show you in a minute." Charlie peered at her phone while she walked to Allison's desk. "Here we are. Mary Ann said this necklace pictured here." She held up the phone's screen. "She insisted that Jessica never took this off and yet it was found under her bed today inside a small box." Charlie glanced at them. "And she says the only other person who's been inside Jessica's room was Tony Cruz. He came over the other day and wanted to supposedly say goodbye to her in his own way. Now we've got Tony possibly in possession of a necklace Jessica was wearing on her trip. On a drive to Daytona at around the same time as Jessica was coming back…"

"And a professor who was dating Jessica seen getting into his car going who knows where about an hour before she was said to have died," Lucy replied.

"Yep. That makes this phone we found all the more important," Charlie continued. "We need to check every number on Jessica's phone records to see if one of them might be the newly found phone."

Allison nodded. "I mentioned the GPS scenario with Brenner just now. I also told him to let his forensics team know that the phone in their possession might ring. They'll answer if it does. Let's get on that right now." Allison opened the file folder with pages of phone records. "We're going to split this up and start making some calls." She handed several sheets to Charlie and then to Lucy. "One way or another, we're going to determine whose phone that is. Because if it didn't belong to Jessica, then it belonged to someone who might have killed her."

"That's it then?" Charlie began. "You're convinced she didn't take her own life?"

"Based on Mary Ann finding the necklace and seeing that Jessica had been wearing it the day before she died…well, let's just say this, we'll find out as soon as that phone rings. Let's get to it." Allison sat back down at her desk and picked up her landline.

Lucy returned to her desk and so had Charlie. Within minutes, they were on the phone and making calls. "I keep getting voicemail." She looked to her partners. "Should I leave a message?"

"No. Just see if you can get a name on the message. I wouldn't be surprised if no one answers. Most people don't answer if they don't recognize the number," Allison said.

"And if these are all 20-somethings, they're even less likely to answer," Charlie began. "Most of them don't even know a phone is for talking."

"Right." Lucy returned her attention to the phone and jotted down the name on the voicemail.

As they continued at a diligent pace, they grew desperate for someone on the other line to answer, so that they might get some idea of the owner of that phone. Had it been Jessica's and she tossed it out the window before putting a gun to her head? Thanks to the arrival of the police and emergency services, tire tracks were everywhere on the scene and it was impossible to know if another car had been there. However, the more they delved into this investigation, the more likely it seemed that the men in Jessica's life could have been responsible for her death.

Nearly thirty minutes had passed while they continued to cross off each number on Jessica's phone records.

"That's it. That was my last one," Charlie said. "No one from Forensics answered."

Allison set down her receiver. "I'm done too. I didn't call the numbers I knew were her friends. But only two others answered. One was a retail clothing store, and the other was the Department of Motor Vehicles." She turned to Lucy. "That leaves you. Any luck?"

Lucy still held the phone in her hand and raised her index finger. "Hello?" Her eyes widened as she shot a look to Allison.

"This is Lucy with ACL Investigative Services. I'm calling from Jessica Healey's phone records. Okay. Great. We know now. Thank you, I'll let my boss know. Goodbye."

"You got a hit?" Charlie hurried toward her. "What was the number?"

Lucy highlighted the number. "It was the Tampa PD Forensics Department. There were two calls received only from that phone number."

Allison joined them. "No calls to it, just from it. So, someone called her. We've just eliminated the idea that the phone belonged to Jessica. What days were those calls made?"

Lucy checked the dates. "A day before they left for Spring Break and..." She slowly turned to them. "Just hours before she died."

"We know it wasn't her phone," Charlie shot back. "It was someone else's. Someone who was there and chucked the phone hoping no one would find it."

"It's got to be a Pay and Go—a burner," Allison replied. "We won't be able to trace an owner."

Charlie glanced at her partners. "This is it. This has to be enough for Brenner to consider this a murder."

15

Allison was never the "I told you so" type of person, but right now, she wished she had been. Once again, she waited for a response from Detective Brenner, who was in the process of re-examining Jessica Healey's phone records, double-checking her team's work. Her instincts to take on this case proved to be correct. More to the point, Mary Ann Healey's instincts appeared to be right about her daughter. The way things stood now, it sure looked as though someone had been with Jessica in the last moments of her life.

Brenner viewed the records. "The lead forensics inspector let me know about the calls on the phone you and your team found near Healey's car." He pulled off his reading glasses and peered at her. "I was doubtful we'd get this far, Ms. Hart."

"So that's it, right?" Allison anticipated his next words. "We have proof that someone else was there on the side of the road with her that day."

"It does appear to be the case. But by no means does that mean the girl wasn't the one who pulled the trigger. It just means she might not have been alone when it happened, or it happened after the unknown subject left."

Allison tried to hide her growing frustration, but suspected it was a futile effort. "Detective Brenner, I know you see it for what it is. Why the hesitation to re-open this case?"

"Forensic evidence carries a lot of weight. That evidence isn't wrong. Gunpowder residue was found on Jessica's fingers. The shot was taken at point-blank range. The gun was unregistered and still in her hand when she was found." Brenner sighed. "That is extremely compelling evidence that points to the fact that girl took her own life."

"What about this gun? Doesn't it strike you as odd that if it belonged to Jessica that would mean she carried it with her on the trip?" Allison continued. "Or better yet, what are the odds she slipped away from her friends in those two days and made the clearly illegal purchase in Daytona?"

"I'll grant you, the gun is a question mark. But as you know, it's hardly difficult to purchase a gun here, registered or not. That said, my people are doing what they can to track down the gun's origins. After you discovered the phone, I figured this was going to blow up one way or another, so I asked Mrs. Healey to grant access to Jessica's bank account and any credit cards to see if we can find the purchase. But look, when someone wants to harm themselves, they'll figure out a means by which to do it," Brenner replied.

Allison nodded in consideration. "I can accept that, but what if someone else was there and convinced her to do it? Cases have gone to trial for just such a scenario."

"You're absolutely right." Brenner peered again at the records. "Here's what I think our next move should be."

'We' was a good start as far as Allison was concerned. "Go on."

"I'll take up the professor's offer to hand over his phone, knowing full well he would have every opportunity to have deleted whatever might incriminate him. Then I think it's time to home in on her friends. If you want to run on the theory that someone might've had a part in convincing Jessica to take her life, then who better to start with than her immediate circle?"

"I think the most trustworthy of the bunch is Harriet Torres," Allison replied. "Sophie was the closest to her, but I get a feeling she's holding something back."

"And the other two?" he pressed on.

"Nia's been seeing Jessica's ex without her knowledge. That's a problem. The two had an argument the previous evening that was supposedly worked out. And then there's Madison. She definitely doesn't think it was suicide and has concerns about Dr. Lyman."

"Don't we all?" Brenner leaned back again. "While I'm working on Lyman's phone and the app he used to communicate with Jessica, I'd like you and your team to work on the underlying relationships these girls had with Jessica. You said yourself that surveillance video put those girls in Daytona but how hard would it have been for one of them to slip away? Who else drove there? Was there time to slip away? We have the phone, thanks to the hard work your people did. Now, it's time we find culpability either by Lyman or her friends. We do that, then I'll move forward with reopening this as an involuntary manslaughter case, much like the one you're referring to out of Massachusetts. But if that happens, be prepared for an onslaught of press. It's a whole new world when you try to convict someone for murder based on their words and influence."

———

ALLISON OPENED her front door at the knock, already knowing who waited on the other side. "Hi, come in."

Shane wore a subdued smile as he stepped inside. "Must be important for you to call this late. Anything later than 10 pm and you think the streets should be rolled up and lights out. You alone?"

"Funny." She returned a grin and started into the kitchen. "Nolan's on an away schedule. It's just us chickens here. You got my message, then?" She opened the refrigerator door and pulled out a couple bottles of beer, popping them open.

"I had to listen to it a couple of times to be sure I understood what you were asking, but yeah, you got my attention."

She set down a bottle in front of him. "I can't think of another way to cross any of those girls off the list. My two cents? It's a waste of time because I'm convinced Lyman had a hand in what happened to Jessica. She was young and he took advantage of her. I can't see any of those girls somehow trying to convince Jessica she should end it."

"So this is an exercise in futility. Is that what I'm hearing from you?" Allison asked.

"It's a stretch, is all I'm saying. You've done a lot of leg work already. I think your focus should be on proving to Brenner none of them influenced Jessica in that way. Because I don't believe you think they did. It's Lyman who should be wearing the target."

"You see right through me, Shane. What I need now to push Brenner's focus on Lyman is to get the phone carrier to show us the content of the messages Jessica received in those few days. It won't tell us the whole story because, as we know, Lyman used an encrypted internet-based app to communicate with Jess, but two messages were sent to Jessica's phone from the burner we found. We need to know what they say." She tossed back a swig of beer. "That's where you come in."

Shane pulled out a stool and sat down, taking hold of the bottle. "You have it all planned out. Only one problem."

Allison set down her beer and studied him. "I'm listening."

"Jessica was an adult, so unless her parents paid for that phone, I don't think they'll be able to request that information. And, it would also require a subpoena. If Brenner isn't willing to get one, then I sure as hell won't be able to. No active investigation, how does he justify a subpoena?"

Allison instantly deflated.

"There could be another way you can learn more." Shane reached for her hand on the counter. "Hey, there is something you can do."

She didn't pull away this time. "And what is that? Brenner won't reopen this case without a definitive lead that someone convinced Jessica to take her life. He won't take that chance, especially given the controversy surrounding cases like that. And if I go and ask those girls to hand over their cell phones, I have a feeling their parents will step in and shut it down, rightly so, I might add. I wouldn't allow it either."

"First of all, those kids, as you keep calling them, are adults. But that's beside the point. Hear me out. Mary Ann Healey came to you because she didn't believe her daughter could take her own life. So, you already have her cooperation. Allison, she collected Jessica's things already. My guess is, there's a laptop in there somewhere. That laptop is hers to hand over to whoever she wants. There's no law against that."

A cautious smile played on Allison's lips. "Jessica's laptop. It's not as good as her phone would be, but I'll bet there's some clue on there. And hopefully, it's more likely that her parents would know how to access it. No guarantees, but..."

"Her phone was an iPhone, right?" Shane asked.

"Yeah. No one's been able to get into it, though. No one knew the password, which is why we have no idea how she communicated really with anyone. Texts, according to her phone records, were few and far between."

"If she has a Mac, she could've used iMessage, which would link between her phone and her laptop. You might have some luck there," he added. "It would be the next best thing to her phone."

Allison's smile widened and the spark returned to her eyes. "This is why I love you, Shane. Just when I think I'm in a jam..." She stopped cold, realizing her choice of words and sputtered out a quick walk-back. "I mean, you always seem to know..."

He revealed a closed-lipped grin. "It's okay, Allison. I know what you meant. I'm here to help. I want to."

She glanced at his hand that still rested on top of hers before he was the one to pull it away. Allison turned a tenuous gaze at him. There was no mistaking the look in his eyes. While he accepted her rebuff of his feelings, they hadn't gone anywhere. Allison had tried hard to separate their professional relationship from their friendship and was determined to keep it that way. But it grew harder by the day to understand why she insisted on doing so. Maybe it was Leo's visit to her the other night, claiming his fiancé was cheating on him, that set her on this train of thought. She'd been Leo's sounding board since the divorce. It occurred to her that was what Shane had been and that wasn't fair to him.

Allison reached out for his hand again and took hold of it. "Sometimes I forget just how lucky I am to have you in my life, Shane. I'm sorry if I don't always make that clear." She let go of his hand and walked around the island to stand in front of him.

Confusion and trepidation masked his face. "Allison..."

She placed her hand on his cheek before leaning in to touch his lips with hers. Just a small kiss. Tender. Barely there. And when she pulled back, he looked more confused than ever. Allison didn't know what to say. The moment had been unexpected, unplanned, and now the aftermath of uncertainty swirled around them.

Shane cleared his throat. "Well, I should probably go. It's late. I'm sure you'd like to get some rest. You'll have your hands full tomorrow."

"Right. Sure. That's probably best." Allison stepped back while he stood. "Thanks again for running to my aid, as usual."

"You don't need me to do that. We all need help to see things in a new light. That's all I'm here to do for you, Allison. Get you to see things in a new light." He started toward the door offering no other words.

She opened the door for him. "I'll let you know how it goes with Mary Ann. Thank you, Shane, for everything. Good night."

He stood on the other side of the door for a moment as though half-expecting another kiss, an explanation, something. "Yeah, you have a good night too, Allison."

———

MARY ANN HEALEY walked into the ACL office with her daughter's laptop in hand. "Good morning."

"Mrs. Healey, how are you?" Lucy hurried to greet her. "Let me take that for you." She walked to the conference table and set it down. "Can I get you a cup of coffee?"

"No, thank you, sweetheart. I haven't been sleeping well as it is."

Allison approached her. "Thanks for coming down this morning. How's Mr. Healey doing?"

"Better. Recovering. Thank you for asking."

"Why don't you come and sit down." Allison glanced to Charlie. "Let's get started."

Charlie nodded and joined them at the table.

"There is something I wanted to mention." Mary Ann sat down. "Jessica's funeral is tomorrow afternoon."

"Sure, that's right. I remembered you mentioned that before," Allison said.

"I would be grateful to you three ladies if you'd attend. I have a feeling I'm going to need all the support I can get."

Charlie reached for Mary Ann's arm. "We'd be honored to attend. Thank you."

"We should take a look at what's on here." Allison opened the laptop. "You have the password?"

"We gave Jess this laptop when she left for school last year. At the time, her father helped her to set it up. It's kind of his thing—computers. Unless she'd changed the password, it should still be the same." Mary Ann typed on the laptop and waited.

When the desktop screen illuminated, Allison raised her lips into a half-smile. "Thank goodness for small miracles. And you picked this up the other day from Jessica's dorm room?"

"I did. Sophie and Madison had everything boxed up and ready for me. It was very sweet that they went through the trouble." She cast down her gaze. "Jessica was loved."

"Yes, she was," Allison replied. "Let's take a look at her messages first."

"Of course." Mary Ann swallowed down her emotions and keyed in the command. "Here we are." She turned the screen to Allison. "What do you think?"

Charlie stood, slipped on her readers and walked behind Allison. "These should coincide with her phone."

"Which is inaccessible. Unfortunately, the phone we found wasn't an iPhone, so this will just be communications with her friends, most likely," Allison pressed on. "But right now, something is better than nothing." She scrolled down the messages. "I'd like to track this back to Christmas when Jessica and Tony split up."

"See if it was as amicable as he made it seem," Charlie replied.

"Mrs. Healey," Lucy began. "Tony was the last one in Jessica's room before you found the box, isn't that right?"

"That's right. The necklace. I don't know how he came to have it in his possession."

"Can you prove he was the one who left it?" Allison asked.

"Prove it?" Mary Ann considered the question. "I don't know how I would do that, but I suppose not."

"Unless his prints are on it." Charlie pulled back and folded her arms. "We should hand it over to Brenner and see what his people can find."

Allison nodded. "Agreed. We still have the burner to consider. Let me put a call into Brenner and ask if his team has found out where the phone was purchased."

"How would they do that?" Charlie asked.

"By pulling the sim card. There's an identification number on the card. An IMEI number. Not only will it reveal where the phone was purchased, but it will identify the location of the last call connected. What tower, what city," Allison replied.

"So if data or a call was made and picked up on a tower in Daytona, we know the person who used it was in Daytona," Charlie began.

"I have no doubt Brenner's team is already on that, but let's find out if they have those details yet," Allison added. "In the meantime, we'll scour through these messages and note dates, times, and who was in communication with Jessica most frequently over the past four months, and what was said."

Mary Ann nodded. "Then I should leave you all to it." She pushed up from the chair. "I still have a few details to iron out before the funeral tomorrow. You all will be there, yes?"

"Yes." Allison reached for her hand. "You have our support, Mary Ann." As she ushered her to the door, a final thought emerged. "I know we haven't made the sort of progress you might've hoped for by this point, but I never dismiss a mother's intuition. Whatever happened to Jessica that afternoon, Mary Ann, we will learn the truth."

She smiled, though it didn't reach her eyes. "I know you will, Allison. I know all of you will."

———

NIA BROWN SAT in her car outside Tony's house. He stopped answering her messages two days ago. They had plans to go out last night and he never showed. Something had happened and Nia was about to find out what it was. After all they'd sacrificed, this was how he was going to treat her?

His car was in the driveway and she knew he had a class soon. If that chicken shit wasn't going to message her back, she wouldn't sit idly by and let him ghost her.

Nia perked up as Tony came into view. With a backpack slung over his right shoulder, he held his car keys and pressed the remote to unlock his car. She stepped out and walked across the street. "Tony."

Startled, he turned to her. "Nia?" He glanced around as if expecting to be on hidden camera. "What are you doing here?"

"What the hell, Tony?" She marched toward him and stopped just inches away. "We had plans last night. You haven't responded to my messages in two days."

Tony lowered his gaze. "I'm sorry, Nia. I guess with the funeral coming up. I don't know. I guess it's all starting to hit me now."

"Now? It's hitting you now?" She placed her hands on her hips. "This isn't about Jessica. This is about her, isn't it?"

"Who?"

"I'm not stupid, Tony. I know you're dating someone else. I mean, after everything. After Jess. This is how you want to be?"

He placed his hands on her shoulders. "Look, I'm sorry, okay? Hailey is just a friend. I swear it."

Nia reached for her phone in her back pocket. "Really?" She swiped open the photographs. "This looks like you're a lot more than friends."

"Where did you get this? Are you following me, or something?" Tony's eyes darkened as he peered at the photo. "What are you, a psycho stalker?"

"I knew something was up, but until you blew me off last night, I wasn't sure. Then this morning, I got this picture of you two, looking super chummy."

"Who sent it to you?" he pressed on.

"Does it matter?" She returned the phone to her pocket. "I just can't believe this shit. I thought I was important to you."

"You are, Nia." He reached out for her again.

"Don't. I guess it's true what they say." She started to walk away. "Once a cheater..."

Tony jogged to catch up to her and both stood in the middle of the neighborhood street. "Wait. Nia, wait."

"I had to make it look like we had nothing to do with each other. Don't you get that? With all the questions that P.I. lady keeps asking, I couldn't risk her knowing we had a thing. You have to believe me. It was all made up."

"And the kiss? The photo someone sent me with you kissing that—girl. That was made up, too?" Nia pressed on.

"I was playing a part. I had to make her believe it too," he replied. "It's always been you, Nia. I knew that even when I was with Jess."

"You're a liar." She scoffed. "You were with Jess since high school. I know you loved her. I think you were just using me to get back at her." She held his gaze for a moment. "Tell me you didn't have anything to do with why Jess killed herself."

He recoiled. "What? What are you talking about? Of course not."

"You were late."

"Late?" he asked.

"Yeah. You were late that night when you showed up at the bar on the beach. I waited. Kept checking my phone. Finally, you turned up almost two hours late." She stepped back with a slow hesitation. "Where were you, Tony? Did you call her? Jess? Did you call her that day when she was driving home to see her dad?"

"No, I didn't call her," he shot back. "Where is this coming from? I had to pack. I had to get gas..."

Nia peered at him again but said nothing. She turned her back to him and stepped into her car.

"Where are you going?" He started after her. "Nia? Wait. We're not done here."

As she started to pull away from the curb, she peered through her opened window. "I think we are."

16

The casual swagger Detective Brenner displayed as he walked into Professor Lyman's office was an obvious show of strength. To assert his upper hand in an investigation that had so far produced nothing but questions and unproven theories. Nevertheless, Brenner did have an advantage knowing that Lyman screwed up, or at least his attorney had, when they went after the ACL partners the other day.

In a show of defiance, Lyman remained seated at his desk. It was like watching two dogs size up one another before deciding where best to mark their territories.

Lyman's back stiffened and his chin raised. "Good morning, Detective."

"Professor." Brenner continued inside. "I hear you're ready to hand over your phone. I do hope you had enough time to properly whitewash it." He peered around. "I half expected to see your attorney here."

"He's otherwise engaged, not that it matters. I said I would cooperate and I am. Whitewashing comment aside, you'll see I've done nothing wrong." Lyman pulled out his desk drawer and retrieved the phone. "You won't find anything on here that could possibly suggest I had anything to do with Jessica Healey's suicide."

"I'm sure I won't." Brenner reached for the phone and slipped it into an evidence bag.

Lyman scoffed. "You're so convinced I had something to do with what happened." He cocked his head and regarded the detective. "I wonder why you haven't re-opened the investigation. Here you are, collecting so-called evidence, and for what? A closed suicide case."

"I'm still not convinced this is anything else, Doctor. I do, however, find it troubling the efforts you've undertaken to scare off any further probing."

Lyman pulled back. "I don't know what you mean. I'm clearly offering you help."

Brenner nodded, his hands tucked inside his pants' pockets. "Yes, you are. You'd be wise, however, to keep your lawyer on a short leash. Running off the road private investigators who were only doing their jobs? Seems excessive for someone proclaiming their innocence." He turned on his heel. "I'll have this back to you in no time, Doc. I do appreciate your cooperation. Give my best to your wife." He raised his mouth into a crooked smile and walked away.

On his drive back to the station, he made the call. "Ms. Hart, Brenner here. I wanted to let you know that we have Lyman's phone. I'm heading back to the station now to turn it over to Computer Forensics."

"That's great news," Allison replied. "I just arrived hoping to find you."

"You're there now?"

"Yes. I wanted to talk to you about what my partners and I

found on Jessica Healey's laptop in addition to details regarding the burner phone we found at the scene."

"Sounds like you've made some headway. Hang tight. I won't be but 20 minutes or so. I'll see you then, Ms. Hart."

"Goodbye, Detective." Allison returned her phone to her purse and eyed Shane. "I'll need to let him know what the autopsy showed."

Shane sat up at his desk. "I'm sure he's seen it."

"Yes, but he doesn't know about the necklace. Now we have images of Jessica wearing it on the day she and her friends left for Daytona. And the autopsy clearly shows it was no longer on her neck."

"And the ex-boyfriend had it in his possession."

"Sure looks that way," Allison replied. "We don't have material evidence of that, but how else did it end up under the girl's bed neatly tucked away in a little box?"

"Listen, while you're waiting for Brenner," Shane began with hesitation. "And now is probably not the time, but I don't suppose we could talk about what happened last night? Allison, you really threw me for a loop."

Her head dipped. "I know I did. I'm sorry for that. You don't deserve to be jerked around."

"I just want to know where I stand." He waited until she looked up at him again. "You know, sometimes I think I've won you over. Sometimes I feel like you're miles away when you're standing right in front of me."

"Ms. Hart, thanks for sticking around." Brenner approached from the stairs.

Allison swung around. "Detective, no problem at all. We have a lot to discuss." She turned back to Shane. "I'll remember where we left off. I promise." She gathered her things and followed the detective to his office, feeling guilty for brushing off Shane's concerns. However, Brenner's timing couldn't have been better. Allison had no explanation for her behavior toward Shane. Perhaps she did but admitting to it scared her more than anything else.

"So, let's talk about what you and your team discovered." Brenner closed the door to his office and sat at his desk. "It was a smart move getting Mrs. Healey to bring in Jessica's laptop."

"And we got lucky that she hadn't changed the password." Allison sat down. "We were able to see her iMessages that would've synced with her cell phone. Since we haven't been able to gain access to the data on her phone, this should open some avenues for us."

"Did you find anything on there from Lyman?" he asked.

"No. Not yet anyway. My team is still going through the messages, but I wanted to get with you as soon as I had a run on something. I took some screen shots and printed them up." Allison retrieved the file folder from her bag. "In chronological order, you'll find these go back to around Christmas when Jessica and Tony Cruz split up. We highlighted the messages that appeared pertinent to our investigation."

"If you don't mind, this thing goes any further, I'm going to need that laptop. We'll have to scour the whole thing," Brenner replied.

"Understood."

He examined the pages, focusing in on the highlighted messages. "Doesn't look like the kid took the break-up too well."

"No. He seems pretty heart-broken about it. Leads me to believe that his relationship with Nia Brown was his attempt at revenge." She pointed to one of the threads. "You can see here, Tony blamed Sophie for their break-up."

"And it appears he had no idea that Jessica had fallen for one of her professors."

"Not based on these messages," Allison continued. "However, I'm not sure just how close Jessica was to the professor up until around February." She shifted the pages to show him the messages. "Take a look here. There's no mention of Lyman by name, but a somewhat cryptic admittance on Jessica's part in a message to Madison that she had a thing for one of her teachers."

Brenner pulled back. "All this is great, but it doesn't suggest anything other than college drama. I thought you had something worthwhile to show me."

Allison shuffled through the pages. "Here." She tapped with her index finger on the highlighted passage. "This text arrived from an unfamiliar source."

Brenner focused in on the message and shot a glance to Allison. "Leave him alone?" He peered at the message again. "It says, 'leave him alone.' Who is this from?"

"It's an iMessage using an Apple ID, no phone number associated with it," Allison replied. "And it appears to be the only entry."

"I don't see a reply," Brenner added.

"She ignored it or deleted it. Since it's an iMessage, it's recorded as data only. Makes it pretty hard to track back to anyone. It was about three weeks ago, so not long before she died." Allison eyed him. "Detective, I'd seriously consider looking into the possibility of other relationships Lyman might have been having at the time."

Brenner eyed her. "You think he was getting around, huh? Maybe another college girl who learned about Jessica and got jealous."

"Hard to say for sure, but the way he's been acting, I wouldn't put it past him," Allison replied. "It could explain the threatening message. There's one other thing I wanted to ask you about. The burner we found. I know you have your forensics team working on it. Have you discovered where the phone was purchased?"

Brenner appeared to consider her idea. "I don't know if they have that information, but I will find out. However, I'm not sure it's a valuable piece of this puzzle. Now, if you can tell me who bought it, then yeah. But where?" He studied her again. "What's your angle?"

"Right now, we have no idea who left it near Jessica's car. We know it was someone who had been in some sort of contact with her. If we're talking a total stranger who may have crossed paths with her in Daytona, maybe that's where the phone was purchased. The possibility still exists a stalker could have been involved. If it was purchased here in Tampa, that could change our trajectory."

"If those guys are able to find the where, they won't find the when." Brenner rubbed his forehead. "I'll put forensics on that asap. In the meantime, finish reviewing whatever is on the laptop. Who knows? We might get lucky. I'm going to scour through Lyman's phone that he begrudgingly offered up. Not that I expect to find much on it, but he could've gotten sloppy."

"Oh," Allison retrieved the autopsy report. "Have you had a chance to review this yet?"

He took it from her. "Yes. I take it you have too?"

"Briefly. I also have this." She set down on the table a printed picture of Jessica with her friends. "This was the day Jessica left for Daytona with her girlfriends. She's wearing a necklace. According to her mother, she never took it off. And yet..."

Brenner raised his gaze to her. "And yet?"

"Mrs. Healey found that necklace in a box under Jessica's bed the day before yesterday. She believes Tony Cruz left it there. He'd been there that day, saying goodbye in his own way in Jessica's bedroom."

"You should've led with this," Brenner replied. "Can we prove the kid left it?"

"No." Her face wore defeat. "All we know was that Jessica had it in her possession when she died. Then it turned up under her bed in a gift box. We have the word of Mary Ann who said she didn't put it there. Process of elimination."

He nodded. "I'll work on the professor. You and your people need to put the screws to this Tony Cruz. He needs to cough up an alibi and soon."

THE COFFEE SHOP only a block from campus was set to close within the hour. It approached 9pm and Lucy sipped on her chai tea before turning her sights to Nia Brown, who sat across from her. "It sucks to find out like that. I'm sorry."

"Yeah, well, I guess I knew it all along, but didn't want to admit as much. He loved Jess. The rest of us—we didn't matter. Not Hailey and not me. Who knows how many others?"

"Who sent you that picture of Tony with Hailey Buford?" Lucy asked. "Must've been someone pissed at Tony. Like you said, who knew who else he might've been seeing."

"Right. I don't know because it came from an unknown number. How they knew who I was is a surprise to me. Doesn't matter though. They did me a huge favor."

"You mind giving me that number?"

"Sure." Nia handed her the phone. "It's that one there, on the call log."

Lucy keyed in the number on her phone. "Thanks. You said you knew where Tony was that day."

Nia slurped on her frappe, stalling by all accounts. "We were going to tell her that night, Tony and me. We were going to come out into the open and tell Jess that we'd been seeing each other. That was the plan."

"But then everything changed," Lucy replied.

"Yeah. It did." Nia inhaled a slow breath. "He was already on his way. It had been planned and I told him Jess had to go back home. He didn't care. He was coming anyway. So I didn't stop him."

Lucy peered at her. "Can I ask why you would have chosen that particular time to tell Jessica? On Spring Break. That doesn't seem like the best time."

"I don't know. I guess we thought she wouldn't make a scene."

"After what, like 4 months, did you really think she would? It was Jessica who broke things off with Tony." Lucy leaned over with her elbows on the small table. "Nia, are you sure you weren't just trying to get back at Jessica for something? You two argued the night before. What was really going on between you guys?"

Nia retrieved her phone and swiped open the pictures before turning the screen to Lucy.

Lucy pulled the phone closer for a look. Her lips parted slightly as she tried to mute her reaction. "Professor Lyman? Is that you with Lyman? Were you seeing him too?"

"Not *too*, before. He dumped me when Jess caught his eye."

It dawned on Lucy then. "That was the reason for the fight. Lyman was the reason you went after Tony, too?"

Nia nodded almost imperceptibly. "If I would've known Jess planned on killing herself..." She wiped away a stray tear. "What if my actions made her do it?"

Lucy noticed the regret on her face but to answer her question would be impossible. "Nia, do you know where Tony was when Jess pulled that trigger?"

Nia shrugged. "Getting ready to drive to Daytona. He said he was busy packing and getting gas and that was why he was later than he thought he'd be. Whatever. Maybe that's true."

"Did he know about Lyman and you?" Lucy pressed on.

She nodded. "Yes, I told him. It came up when I mentioned that Jess had moved on and that she was into one of her professors. I didn't know for sure, at the time, but I saw the way Jess was around Dr. Lyman. I figured they had a thing going. He looked at her the same way he used to look at me. After me and Jess's fight, I texted Tony and told him about Lyman."

"How did he react?"

"He didn't," Nia replied. "He didn't reply to the text and the next day, the only reason I got him to reply back was because I told him that Jess had to leave to see her dad."

"So he never made mention of it?"

Nia shook her head. "Nope. It was like I never said a word."

———

SHANE WALKED to his apartment door in socked feet, basketball shorts and a t-shirt. He glanced into a decorative mirror that hung in the entranceway and pushed his fingers through his brown hair, checking for anything else that might be out of place. He opened the door. "Hey. Come on in."

"Thanks." Allison let her gaze roam. "I haven't been here in a while. Place looks good."

"It hasn't changed, but thanks anyway." He closed the door behind her. "What brings you by, Allison?" As if he hadn't known.

"I told you I wouldn't forget where we left off."

Shane started into the living room. "Can I get you anything?"

"No. I'm okay for now. Thanks." Allison set down her purse on the side table.

"Then take a seat. I didn't have time to pick up. Sorry about the mess."

"It's fine." She prepared to sit down on the modern, but uncomfortable-looking Ikea sofa.

He sniffed loudly and shrugged before dropping to the couch and pulling one foot over his knee.

Allison finally sat down next to him and appeared ill at ease. "You're mad."

He turned to her, resigned. "I'm not mad, Allison. Frustrated? Yeah. You could've asked Brenner to wait two minutes while we talked."

"Yes, I could have. To be honest, I didn't have an answer for you. Brenner got me off the hook. You have a right to be frustrated. So, about the kiss..."

"Yeah." He felt lighter now that the tension had dispersed, and the conversation set on its path. "I'm not complaining, but what was that about?"

Allison looked down and fidgeted with her hands. "Leo came to me the other night. Unloaded on me about how he thought Jenny was cheating on him."

"His fiancé?"

"Yep. Go figure." She let her eyes roll hard. "Anyway, it brought back a lot of feelings. Feelings about what Leo had done to me. How I felt sort of vindicated that karma had finally hit him." She raised her hands. "I know that sounds awful."

"No, it doesn't."

"Then I started thinking, here you are. A great guy. Handsome. Sweet. Everything any woman would want in a man."

A corner of his mouth raised. "Now you're making me blush."

"You, blush? I doubt that." She laughed but continued. "I started to wonder why I kept pushing you away. I knew how you felt—how you feel. I thought I wasn't ready."

"And now?" Shane asked, turning serious.

"Honestly? I don't know if I'm ready. It took me a long time to become whole again. I let what happened in my marriage define me. I couldn't risk losing myself again."

"Allison, I would never..."

She raised her hand in objection. "No one thinks they would. It's never planned, Shane. It just happens sometimes. I guess what I'm saying is that I'd like to see where this goes. But you have to know that I'm terrified of what it might do to our friendship. If I lost you as a friend..."

"You wouldn't. I promise, Allison. You could never lose me as a friend." The sincerity in his words were real. For the first time, Shane had felt for her something he never really had in another woman. Who would've thought after living the bachelor life for so long that he was capable of feeling this way?

"Time will tell. You know, Shane, you're younger than me. You don't have kids. I realize this might seem strange to mention, but that part of my life is long over. I'm not looking, nor would it be possible at this point, to have more kids. You'd have to be okay with that."

"Allison, I'm almost 41. Kids have never been part of my plan. I'm not cut out that way."

"Well, it needed to be said." She reached for his hand. "I'm sorry about the back and forth. The uncertainty of my actions. But with the agency just getting off the ground, my life getting put back together, I thought jumping into a relationship was the last thing I wanted." She placed her hand on his cheek. "Then you became a bigger part of my life. I started to see you in a new light."

A wry smile played on his lips. "I have that effect on women." He chuckled. "Listen, we can take this as slow as you want. I just know that I want to be with you, Allison. For me, it's been you for a long time."

17

Charlie's white Chevy SUV rolled up onto Allison's driveway and she tapped on her horn. The funeral was slated for 10am and Allison stepped through her front door, wearing a black dress and dark sunglasses. In fairness, it was a bright day, but Charlie did see in Alli a striking resemblance to Jennifer Aniston in this moment. Nice work, if you can get it. Charlie, however, thought of herself as more of a fuller, shorter Jamie Lee Curtis. Allison was a stunner and there was no two ways about it. Leo was an idiot and Charlie secretly, or not so secretly, rooted for Sully to win her heart. She wanted nothing but happiness for Alli.

Allison opened the passenger door and stepped onto the beige cloth passenger seat. "Thanks for the lift. Where's Lucy?".

"She said she'd meet us there." Charlie reversed out of the driveway and started on. "Have you talked to her yet this morning?"

"No. Why?" Allison buckled her seatbelt.

"Nia Brown reached out to her. Asked her to meet at some café near campus."

"Is that so? What did she want?" Allison removed her sunglasses. "I was out until pretty late last night. Is Lucy okay?"

"Oh yeah. No, she's fine. But, um, Nia spilled her guts apparently. Said she'd been seeing the professor before he dumped her and trained his sleezy sights on Jessica."

Allison slammed her hand on the armrest. "I knew it. I knew it wasn't the first time that slime ball preyed on his students."

"Yep. And in fact, Tony Cruz knew it too." Charlie turned to her with a knowing glance. "I'm figuring that he'll be at the funeral today. He needs to come clean because with what he'd told you, that he had no idea Jess was involved with one of her professors, that was a bald-faced lie."

"I don't know, Charlie. I don't want to cause any problems for Mary Ann today. We shouldn't confront him at the service."

"Fair enough. After?"

"Let's talk to Lucy and get a feel for the situation. If Tony knew about Lyman, and we still can't confirm his exact location at the time of Jessica's death, we might want to present that to Brenner. Charlie, I smell a motive."

———

THE QUAINT NON-DENOMINATIONAL church was just ahead. An old, Spanish-style building, common in the area. The Healey family had attended this church off and on for more than 20 years.

Charlie pulled into the parking lot. "I suppose this time around there won't be a need to go covert."

"Not this time, although I am disliking our regular appearances at funerals. Maybe next time we'll come up with aliases." Allison stepped out of the car.

Charlie got out and closed her door. "Dang it. And I had my name all picked out. I was thinking, Raquel Welch. I mean, if we're sticking with the whole celebrity theme."

Allison closed her door and joined Charlie. "First of all, you seriously just dated yourself, secondly, neither one of us could pull off that name."

"Fine." Charlie scanned the area. "We should track down Lucy."

Allison started toward the stuccoed building that displayed a round stained-glass window centered above the wooden double doors. She spotted Mr. and Mrs. Healey and walked up the steps. "Mary Ann. Good morning."

"Allison. Charlie." She politely smiled through the pain. "Thank you so much for coming. I don't believe you've met my husband, Jessica's father, Jim."

"Mr. Healey, it's a pleasure to finally meet you," Allison replied. "How are you feeling? You're looking well."

"Doing better, Ms. Hart. Thank you." He shifted his gaze between them. "And thank you both for what you're doing for our Jessica."

"Of course. I'm Charlie Wells, Allison's partner at ACL. It's very nice to meet you, sir. Please accept our condolences."

"Thank you, Ms. Wells."

A man who appeared to be an usher opened the door and stepped outside. "Mr. and Mrs. Healey, please come in. Pastor Leighton would like to go over a few things before we get started."

Mary Ann turned to Allison. "You'll excuse us?"

"Of course. We'll see you inside." Allison surveyed the grounds. "Let's keep our eyes trained on Jessica's friends. With Nia Brown having come forward with new details, this could be the tipping point."

"It's the ex-boyfriend I want to watch," Charlie added. "Something strikes me as off about this whole thing with him. And until he offers up a concrete alibi, I'm not sure we can trust him." She caught sight of Lucy ahead. "There she is."

As she approached, Allison began. "Good morning. I hear you had an interesting night."

"You could say that." Lucy reached the top of the steps where Allison and Charlie stood. Her black pants and white blouse fit snuggly against her slender frame and her dark hair was pulled back in a tight bun. "From what Nia said last night, the girls are coming here together."

"What are your thoughts on what she had to say?" Charlie asked. "I filled in Alli a little bit."

"Right. Well." Lucy took in a long breath. "It looks like she tried to start up a situation with Jessica and now regrets it. Surprise, surprise. Turned out, it was all because of Professor Lyman."

"Shocking," Allison replied. "Handsome guy with a lot of money teaching young co-eds. Who would've figured?"

"Recipe for disaster for someone with a narcissistic personality like Lyman," Charlie added. "What's our plan here, ladies?"

"We're just observers today," Allison replied. "Mainly here for support of the Healeys. But if we happen to pick up on an interaction among the group, then let's keep our eyes open."

Another usher appeared through the double doors. "Ladies and Gentlemen, if you'll come inside and take a seat. We'll be starting soon."

Allison looked at her partners. "Let's see what happens." She started inside but noticed Tony Cruz approach in a dark suit. "Here we go. Looks like the ex is here."

Charlie noticed his arrival and then her eyes darted farther ahead. "Oh boy."

"What is it?" Lucy asked.

"Over there. Looks like our professor decided to come and pay his respects too."

Allison stepped inside. "Buckle up, ladies. We might be in for a hell of a ride."

———

Tony smoothed down his suit jacket and headed toward the church. His parents had wanted to attend but he had insisted this was something he needed to face on his own. His girlfriend of more than 5 years was gone, and it was his pain to deal with. Of course, Nia would be there and after what transpired between them only yesterday, he wondered how she would react. Tony realized he had no one now. Not Jess. Not Nia. Not even Hailey. It wasn't supposed to go down like that but here he was.

Mrs. Healey had left a message for Tony letting him know about the service. He hadn't seen her since the day he returned Jessica's necklace. He wondered if they'd found it. It was all too personal for him—the note she'd left with the necklace. He couldn't bring himself to tell the Healeys about it. Jessica had kept a photo of the two of them inside it.

As he made his way up the concrete steps, Tony spotted Dr. Lyman approach. He stopped cold. Heat rose under his collar and his pulse quickened. Lyman must've felt his stare because he turned to him. The two locked eyes, but Lyman didn't know Tony. Had no idea who he was. Tony knew exactly who Lyman was and what he had done.

Lyman politely nodded and continued inside.

Tony hurried up the steps and grabbed his shoulder.

Lyman turned to him with concern. "Can I help you?"

"I know you were seeing Jess. I know you went out with Nia

Brown too. Aren't you married, bro?" He struggled to restrain his welling anger.

Lyman pulled away his arm. "I don't know you. You should've learned to keep your hands to yourself back in grade school." He started ahead.

"Hey!" Tony's raised voice drew eyes on him.

The professor turned back and stepped down to meet him again. "Look, I'm here to pay my respects. Whatever beef you got with me, it's going to have to wait."

Tony let him by again and watched as he disappeared inside. He stood still, recalling the moment he'd followed Lyman home that day before he left for Daytona. The day he learned Nia had also gone out with him. He was pissed. Beyond pissed. This 30-something rich dude had used Jess, and Nia, and God knew who else. He had no right to be here now. Not when Tony watched him walk into his home that day, all smiles, with his wife greeting him on the other side. He should've told her then.

———

Sophie, Nia, Madison, and Harriet walked inside the church, two by two with linked arms. The girls dressed in dark clothing, dresses and pants, each one wearing grief. Heads turned in their direction. The church was nearly full for the 20-year-old and a small section in the fourth row was just enough space for the friends to squeeze into.

Allison glanced at them before whispering to Charlie. "It doesn't look like Nia told the others what she knew about Lyman."

"They look closer than ever," Charlie replied in a hushed tone. "And look there, Lyman just walked in."

"Tony's behind him. He looks upset," Lucy said. "I just can't tell if it's because of Jessica or the professor."

"Thank you all for coming today," Pastor Leighton started.

The partners drew their attention to the front as the service began, but Allison let her eyes drift back to Dr. Lyman and Tony Cruz. It was those two men who she was all but certain had a hand in what happened to Jessica. But what she had just wasn't enough. Brenner was right in that it was impossible to overlook hard forensic evidence. That evidence proved Jessica pulled the trigger to end her own life. Lyman wouldn't have left anything meaningful on that phone he turned over to Brenner. She knew that was a pipedream. It was going to have to come down to the burner phone. At least, determine who it belonged to, even if they couldn't access the data on it. It would put the owner at the scene and that would seal the deal. Give them something to run with. Mary Ann and her husband deserved that much.

It was easy to draw on the similarities Allison shared with Mary Ann Healey. Jessica was the same age as Micah. Both were or are at university. Separating herself from her clients' situations was hard for her, but she knew lines had to be drawn in order for her to maintain perspective. Forget the notion that Dr. Jacob Lyman was just some creepy professor who used his position of authority to lure in young co-eds. Forget the notion that Tony Cruz was nothing more than a lover scorned and chose revenge against Jessica by dating her friend. These were things that didn't matter in her investigation and only enforced her biases. Allison needed perspective, not judgement. Otherwise, she might never get to the truth.

As the service continued, there wasn't much the partners could do except observe the mourners. Tony seemed to have kept his composure, though he fired off suspicious glances at Lyman. Lyman, himself, was otherwise oblivious and in fact, hardly seemed present at all. Like he was off in the distance and was only there for someone else's approval. Just to be seen.

When Pastor Leighton concluded his sermon and mourners paid their respects, Allison stood. "Let's try to slip out of here."

"You got it." Charlie nudged Lucy's shoulder and the three slipped out of the pew near the back. As they walked through the doors and into the foyer, she continued. "We did our part for the client. Unfortunately, I don't see that it helped further our cause."

"I agree. However..." Allison raised her index finger and started ahead. "I'll be right back."

Charlie raised her palms as if taken by surprise. "I swear, if she introduces herself as Emma Stone again."

Lucy cracked a smile. "What?"

"Long story. I'll tell you about it someday." Charlie kept her eyes peeled on Allison.

A brief nod back to her partners, and Allison continued toward Tony Cruz. "Tony?"

He turned at the sound of his name. "What are you doing here?"

"Mr. and Mrs. Healey asked us to come. Listen, we're still working to get to the bottom of what happened to Jessica."

"Jeez, lady, what more do you want from me?" He rolled his eyes. "You already had one of your minions pretend to be someone they weren't and almost caused me to break up with my girlfriend."

"And who might that be? Nia or Hailey?" Allison felt a momentary rush of justification, but it quickly vanished as Tony cast down his gaze in apparent guilt. "I'm sorry. This isn't the time. I understand you learned that Jessica was seeing Professor Lyman up until..."

"Yeah, I know all about that. What does it matter?" Tony asked.

"You also know he dated Nia for a while too, don't you?"

"Yeah, so?" He folded his arms in defiance. "Why don't you just ask what you're going to ask."

"Okay," Allison began. "I have a feeling the professor had a lot at stake if word were to come out about his relationships with his students."

"The guy's married, so, probably. What's your point?" Tony pressed on.

"We discovered a phone near where Jessica's car was found that day. Tony, we have reason to believe someone was with Jessica around the time of her death."

"Are you saying someone killed her?" His eyes softened and instilled with fear.

"Not based on the autopsy. What it looks like is that someone was there, possibly threatened her, warned her. I don't know. Tony, we need to know where you were that afternoon. We know you were headed to Daytona to see Nia. The timing is a little suspect."

"You think I was there?" He pointed at his chest and raised his brow.

"Jessica had considered seeing you that day, not knowing you weren't in Tampa that afternoon. Had she reached out to you?"

"No. No, I had no idea she wanted to see me. I swear it. All's I know is that I was getting my stuff together. Getting ready to leave to make the drive..."

"What time was that?" Allison asked.

"I don't know. I'd have to...I really don't know. What I do know is that when I opened my front door to leave, I saw something on my doorstep. It was a box. Like a gift box. No package, no label. Just a box. So I opened it. It was Jessica's necklace. I knew how much she loved that necklace and I thought, 'why is it here?' I thought she maybe came by and left it for me. Like a sign or something saying she wanted to maybe get back together." He swallowed down the lump of rising emotions. "I got confused. I knew I was going to see Nia and yeah, I was pissed about Jess and I guess I wanted to make her jealous. But then I saw that necklace. I took off. Just drove around for a while."

"Why didn't you say anything before about the necklace?" Allison asked. "Do you have any idea how critical that information is?"

He shrugged. "I didn't think it mattered. I don't know. I thought it was maybe a peace offering, or something. Maybe she wanted to get back together. I don't know." Tony grew agitated. "Like I said, I got confused."

"Did you tell anyone else this?"

"No. Nia asked why I took so long, and I just couldn't tell her. I can't tell you how many times I picked up my phone and tried to call Jess. But I never did. She reached out to me and I was too much of an asshole to give in. You don't know how hard it was to hear that she thought about coming to see me that day. Anyway, eventually, I made it to the highway and headed to Daytona, like I told Nia."

"Tony, Jessica couldn't have been the one to give you that necklace. She wasn't back in Tampa at that point," Allison continued.

"I know. That's what was so weird. My plan was to take it with me. Show it to her. Get her to explain it all. But then I found out she took off back home. And then..."

Allison glanced back at Charlie before turning back to him. "Tony, you know she always wore that necklace. You were the one who left it in her room that day, didn't you?"

"Yeah. That was me. I take it her mom found it?"

"They did." She retrieved her phone and swiped open the photos. "This is a picture of Jessica wearing that necklace standing in the student parking lot as she and her friends prepared to leave for Daytona."

Tony examined the picture. "She's wearing the necklace."

"That's right."

He peered at her with concern. "Then who put it on my doorstep?"

"Well, if we can find that out, then I think we'll learn who was there with Jessica that day."

18

It was a wonder how Mary Ann Healey pulled it all together. The funeral and now the reception at their home. The food lay on their formal dining table, buffet style. Flowers that had been sent by family and friends dotted the living room. Jim Healey had to stay off his feet, so he sat on the sofa while people came to him to offer condolences. His eyes were empty, the light had gone out. Meanwhile, Mary Ann dove head-first into her hostess duties, appearing to do her best to keep from crumpling in a heap on the floor.

Allison and her partners huddled together on the screened-in patio out back. The warm sun quickly heated up the room.

"If Jessica didn't leave that necklace on Tony's doorstep, then who the hell did?" Charlie asked in a hushed tone. "Do you think he's lying?"

"You got a polygraph handy?" Allison peered into the back yard. "We're losing our grip on this case, guys. Tony kept a lot from us and now claims the necklace just appeared on his doorstep."

"He's plugging the holes in his story." Lucy stepped in a little closer. "I mean, we still can't confirm his whereabouts during the hours between 1 and 3pm on the day of. He says he was driving around. Okay. Does he have any proof of that?" The subsequent glint in her eye and smirk on her lips meant only one thing. Lucy had an idea. "GPS. Allison, you spoke to Brenner about that right?"

"I did. He thought it could work if Tony was willing," she replied. "He might be more willing now."

Lucy nodded. "That's something we can do without Tampa PD. We have to see his phone. Google Maps tracks locations. Unless he turned off the feature on his phone, but most people don't bother."

Charlie wore a wry smile. "Damn that Google. Love it or hate it, makes our jobs easier."

"Maybe, but let's not jump the gun here," Allison replied. "Even if he left the location services on, I'd need him to volunteer his phone."

"If he wants off the hook, he'll do it," Charlie continued. "He knows we're interested in him. Unless he was there. One way or another, his response will expose his intentions."

"At this point, what are our options?" Allison asked.

Mary Ann approached the partners. Her eyes were reddened from dabbing away tears though she smiled through it all. "You ladies haven't eaten, have you?"

"Not yet," Allison replied.

"Please. There's plenty of food. Everyone brought so much. Jim and I will have leftovers in the freezer for months," she added.

Allison wanted to tell her about the necklace. In fact, she was just about ready to open her mouth when Charlie stepped in.

"Thank you, Mary Ann. I'll make sure we get some food to tide us over. Is there anything we can do for you right now?" Charlie asked.

"Oh, no. You three being there was the best thing you could've done. Is there..." She covertly peered around. "Is there anything new?"

Charlie looked to Allison for approval before answering. "We have a few things we're working on right now, but how about we meet in our office tomorrow and we can fill you in? It's not something you should have to worry about today."

"Yes, of course. You're right. Thank you, Charlie. Please now, please go and eat." Mary Ann turned on her heel and disappeared into the living room."

"Thanks, Charlie," Allison said.

"I just didn't think now was the right time."

———

TONY CRUZ COULDN'T BEAR to sit inside the Healey home and watch Jessica's parents suffer in their grief. Instead, he hunched down in his old Nissan hatchback parked along the palm-tree lined curb near the home of professor and millionaire, Jacob Lyman. With his eyes fixed on Lyman's front door, he waited.

After the service, Lyman had stepped back into his Range Rover and Tony followed him. It turned out, he wasn't going to the reception and instead, went back home. Tony sat there in his car, ready to kick Lyman's ass. Son of a bitch had some nerve showing up at Jess's funeral. Someone needed to put that cheating prick in his place.

The townhome was situated in an upscale neighborhood near campus. At the end of the driveway, iron gates stretched across it while the yards were fenced in with low railings. Lyman's home, with grey Spanish lace stucco, stone columns, and strong modern lines were softened with queen palms and tropical plants.

"Screw it." Tony opened his driver's side door and stepped out in the bright afternoon sky. His heart raced and his chest rose higher with each breath he took. The black suit he'd worn started to suffocate him. Tony ripped off the jacket and threw it onto the driver's seat, slamming the door shut.

"Settle down, kid." An older man, pushing 50, approached from behind.

Tony shot around. His face no longer wearing anger, but surprise. "This doesn't concern you, sir."

"Oh, I think it does." The man wore a heavy 5 o'clock shadow and flicked away the cigarette between his fingers. "The doc up there? He concerns me."

"What, do you work for him or something?" Tony began. "He send you out here to scare me?"

"As a matter of fact, he's concerned because he knows you're grieving. Any man can see that, kid. He doesn't fault you for being here, but that's enough now. It's time for you to move on. Nothing you do here is gonna bring back your friend."

"She was more than my friend. He used her." Tony nodded toward Lyman's house. "He used her; he used my other friend too. He shouldn't be a teacher. I'm going to make sure he gets fired."

The man shrugged and appeared to acknowledge his point. "I can't say anything about that. Point being, you need to go now, son. Get back in your car and drive away. I don't want to have to tell you again."

Tony locked eyes with the large and intimidating man. Tony was on the tall side at 6 feet and a solid 180, but this guy was at least 2 inches taller and 30 pounds heavier. He turned around and opened his door again. "This isn't over. He won't get away with it."

"Uh-huh. See you later, kid." The man turned on his heel and walked away.

Tony looked into his rearview mirror until the man disappeared around the corner. He didn't see a car. "Son of a bitch." He glared at Lyman's house again. "You made her feel like shit, didn't you? Jess killed herself because of you." Tony turned the engine and pulled away.

He made his way out of the neighborhood and back onto the road that led to the center of town. As he checked the time, he knew the reception was probably winding down and going back there wasn't the right decision anyway. Those private investigators would probably hound him again and right now, he was too pissed to see anyone. "Who does that guy think he is, anyway? The Godfather?" Tony scoffed as he rolled to a stop at the intersection. "Son of a bitch."

The light turned green and Tony set down his phone as he pressed lightly on the gas pedal. He pulled out into the intersection when a glimmer caught the corner of his eye. He'd already begun to turn left before a ghastly sound erupted from his throat as he sucked in all the air.

The oncoming car slammed into his door, pushing his compact Nissan onto its passenger side tires. Tony rattled inside. His arms flailed and his neck whipped around while his body was held back by his seatbelt. Finally, the cars came to a screeching halt near the edge of the intersection. Burnt tire marks were left on the street. Smoke billowed and the smell of hot metal filled the air. There were no more sounds. No horns. No one screaming. Just silence.

Tony's head leaned against the steering wheel. His airbag hadn't deployed. It had been disabled when he worked on the dash a year ago and he never bothered to get it fixed.

"Hey? Hey, are you all right?" A man pounded his fist on the driver's window. "Hey, can you hear me?" The man turned around and spotted the other driver. Bruised, bloodied, he spilled out of his car and stumbled until regaining his balance. "Hey? Hang on. I already called 911. Just sit tight." He pounded on

Tony's window again. "Can you hear me? I can't open the door. It's smashed in. Hey, are you awake?"

A bystander jogged to Tony's car and pointed back. "That guy's leaving! Dude got back into his car and is pulling away!"

"Wait! You can't leave! The cops are coming. You need help, man!" He turned back to Tony's car. "Shit. Shit. Dude just left. Car's all busted up and everything!"

"Is he alive?" The bystander peered inside. "Man, I don't think he's still alive."

———

Professor Lyman sat behind the desk in his home office. Student papers were strewn about on top of it. His laptop sat in the center, lid open, and he stared at his home screen. A moment later, his attention was diverted.

"I see that car is gone." Brianne walked inside holding a bottled water, wearing a ponytail and athletic wear as though she'd just finished a workout. "Ever since that student of yours committed suicide, it's like you've been under some kind of scrutiny. Should we be concerned?"

"What?" He turned his sights to her as if caught off guard. "Oh, no. Of course not. It's just," he hesitated. "It's just that the girl's parents refuse to accept the truth. They're looking for a reason why and hired a private investigator. This will all be over soon. I promise you. There's nothing for you to worry about, Brianne."

"You have to admit, it's a little scary." She continued inside.

"What is?"

"All of it. What's the school said about any of it?" she pressed on.

"Nothing. There's nothing for them to say. The police called it suicide. Case closed." Lyman pushed up from his desk and approached his wife. With his index finger, he tucked a few loose strands of her bleached blonde hair behind her ear. "Look, honey, I'm sorry about all this. I guess the reason why the P.I. is coming around is because the girl had a crush on me." He took her hands. "We both know this isn't the first time and it probably won't be the last. I know that sounds narcissistic, but it's only because we have money. I'm not blaming these girls. Part of it is the age. But look, there's nothing to any of this and the police see that too. That's what's most important." He peered into her eyes. "I don't want to worry you about any of this, okay? Once this P.I. finishes her so-called investigation, she'll come to the same conclusion as the police."

Brianne nodded and revealed a demure smile. "I'm sure you're right. I'll let you get back to work. I need to post the video of my workout on Insta."

He kissed her cheek. "I'm just checking my emails. I'll be finished in here soon. Hey, you know what? Why don't we go see a movie tonight?"

"I'd like that. I'll go see what's playing." She turned on her heel and left his office.

The smile on Lyman's face faded as he returned to his desk and sat down. He glanced at his phone as a call appeared. "Yeah?" Lyman held the phone to his ear as he turned stone-faced. "Is he alive?" He turned to gaze through is office window, still unreadable. "Make the calls and find out. Call me as soon as you know more."

———

SHANE ROLLED to a stop in his police-issue black Dodge Charger and stepped out in the afternoon sun. He retrieved his badge.

"Detective Sullivan. Where's the responding officer?" He asked the man who stood outside.

"In there. I think he's talking to the cashier."

"Thanks." Shane entered the convenience store and spotted an officer speaking to one of the employees. "Afternoon."

The cop turned to him. "Detective Sullivan. Nice to see you."

"Officer Garcia. It's been a while. You called this in?"

"Sure did." He gestured to a frightened looking petite woman with dark hair. "This is Sharon Dumas. She was working when the suspect came in."

"Ms. Dumas. How are you holding up?" Shane asked.

"Okay, I guess. Can't believe he came in here in the middle of the day. I'm just thankful no one else was around."

Shane nodded. "Me too. Was he masked?"

"Yes, sir. And armed. Came right in, gun pointing right at me, and demanded I open the register. So I did."

"You did the right thing." Shane reached for his phone as he felt it vibrate in his pants' pocket. "Excuse me for a moment?"

"Sure thing," she replied.

"Sully here." Shane started back out of the convenience store and squinted as he pushed through the doors to step outside. "Are you sure? Damn. Thank you. Yes, she'll want to know about this. Do you know if he's okay?" He inhaled a deep breath. "Okay. Yeah, I'll let her know. I'm on another scene right now, but I'll get in touch with her." Shane ended the call and immediately dialed Allison. "Hey, it's me. Where are you?"

"At the Healey home, just getting ready to leave the reception."

"Listen, Allison, I just got a call from a friend who works in Traffic. Apparently, there was an accident at Jackson Heights and Palmetto Avenue. T-bone."

"Okay," she replied, waiting for some sort of elaboration.

"Tony Cruz was involved in the accident. In fact, he was hurt pretty badly. They took him to Tampa General. He's in the ICU."

"What?" Her tone raised an octave. "Oh my God. This just happened?"

"Within the last 20 minutes or so, yes," Shane replied. "I had feelers out on Cruz's car. My friend called as soon as his name came up when they ran the plates."

"Were you tailing him?" Allison asked.

"Not exactly. You said he didn't have a solid alibi. I had eyes out for his car near your house. I couldn't be sure he didn't have anything to do with the Healey death."

Allison sighed. "I guess I'm grateful you did. I'm with the girls now. We'll go to the hospital and see how he's doing. Thanks for the call, Shane."

"Any time. I'm working an armed robbery now but keep in touch."

"I will. Thanks." She ended the call and turned to the partners. "We have to go."

"Who the hell was that?" Charlie asked as Allison started walking.

"Shane. Tony Cruz was involved in a serious car accident. He's at Tampa General."

"What?" Lucy grabbed Allison's arm to pull her to a stop. "Who hit him?"

Allison peered at them both with a bleak expression. "It was a hit and run. In light of what we know right now, this doesn't look good. Come on. We need to go."

"Are we going to tell Mary Ann?" Charlie hurried along with her short strides.

"Not until we know more. She doesn't need to hear this now." Allison walked outside and started toward Charlie's car. "We were just talking about his cooperation and getting his phone. It's like they knew."

"Who's 'they' and what did they know?" Charlie pressed the remote to unlock her car.

"That's what we need to find out." Allison slipped onto the passenger seat and buckled her belt. She turned to the back where Lucy stepped in. "Do me a favor? You have the contact information for his girlfriend?"

"Which one?"

"Both. Call Nia Brown and that other girl. What was her name?"

"Hailey," Lucy replied. "I'll send them each a text now. Should I tell them he's in the hospital?"

Allison appeared to think on the question before turning to Charlie.

"Unless you want to deal with two young women in hysterics, I don't think that's a good idea," Charlie replied.

Allison nodded. "You're right. Okay." She turned back to Lucy. "Ask them if Tony called or texted them today. See if you can find out where he went after the funeral because he didn't show up here."

"On it." Lucy retrieved her phone.

"What are we going to do when we get to the hospital?" Charlie drove just above the speed limit out on the main road. "We're not family. They won't let us see him."

"Of course," Allison replied. "But I have to think his parents are there already. They would've been the first to be notified. I'll bet they have his belongings."

"Including his phone," Charlie added.

"Yep. I don't want to be a vulture, but we need that phone now more than ever. I don't know the extent of his injuries, but I hope to God he's conscious."

"Nia just replied back to me. Apparently, she confronted Tony about Hailey. It all went to hell after that," Lucy replied. "She has no idea where Tony went after the funeral and is asking why I want to know."

"Don't elaborate. Not yet. Nothing from Hailey?" Allison pressed on.

Lucy checked her phone again. "Oh, wait. Hang on." She read the message. "She must not know about Nia or any of this. She's asking why I want to know too."

"We need someone there who knows Tony's parents and can work on our behalf to make an introduction. If he's not conscious, they'll need to understand what the hell is going on." Allison appeared to consider the predicament. "Okay, tell Hailey Tony was in an accident but you don't know how he is. Tell her we're going and that she should come too. Not Nia, just Hailey. I don't need those two causing any kind of dust up." Allison turned back to the front. "And if anyone believes this was an accident, I have some swampland to sell you."

19

Funny how the people who knew Jessica Healey had begun to behave more erratically now that she was gone. Case in point, Dr. Jacob Lyman. His lawyer sending a thug to scare off the ACL team was one thing. Now, as Detective Brenner learned about the hit and run involving Tony Cruz, he couldn't help but wonder if Lyman's fingers were in this pie too. But why? This was supposed to be an open and shut suicide investigation. Brenner was starting to think Allison Hart might have plucked a nerve. And while he liked what those ladies were doing, he didn't like being wrong.

He marched through the corridor until a voice sounded behind him.

"Detective Brenner?"

Brenner stopped and turned on his heel to see a white coat scurrying toward him.

"Detective, I have forensics back on that necklace you gave me." Papers flapped in his hand as he approached. "Three different prints were on the box and two on the pendant necklace. Partials," he conceded, "but two."

Brenner eyed him before snatching the report from his hands. "Mr. and Mrs. Healey. Yeah. They submitted prints for exclusionary purposes. Fine. I would expect that."

"Yes, but see here?" The tech pointed to another set. "There was nothing in the database on these prints. And it doesn't appear to match anyone in Jessica Healey's circle that we currently have on file."

"And this second set was on the necklace itself?"

"Yep. Now, we could argue that because the set was only partial, the system couldn't pull a match."

"You know what? Come with me." Brenner started back to his office.

The technician hurried alongside Brenner. "What is it?"

"I have a piece of evidence we're working on at the moment. Can you pull prints and do a cross-match against what you found on the necklace?"

"Sure. That won't take any time at all."

Brenner arrived at his desk and picked up the bagged burner phone Lyman had offered up. "Check it against the prints on this phone."

"I'll get on it right now." He took the bag and quickly walked out of the office.

"As soon as humanly possible, yeah?" Brenner called out after him.

"Got it!"

———

ALLISON RETURNED her phone to her purse when Charlie pulled into the hospital parking lot. Sitting in the passenger seat, she grew dazed, light-headed, as though there wasn't enough oxygen. Allison turned to Charlie with a quivering chin. "We're too late."

"What?" Charlie glanced at her.

"That was Shane. The officer on the scene of the accident was just notified that Tony didn't make it."

"Oh no." Lucy's hand clasped over her mouth.

Charlie closed her eyes, still gripping the steering wheel. "Criminy sakes. That poor kid. I'll bet his family is in the lobby right now trying to figure out how their son was here one minute and gone the next. Alli, we can't ask them about the phone. Not anymore. The kid's dead."

Allison met Charlie's gaze.

"No," Charlie began. "I see that look in your eyes, Alli. Come on."

"I'm not saying we'll ask, but maybe Hailey can. Hear me out. The Cruz family will want to know what happened. Why Tony was where he was. We can give them an answer. And in the process, learn whether he was anywhere near Jessica the day she died. Charlie, I get what you're saying, but we have to know the truth. If Tony had nothing to do with it, then all the better."

"I think I agree with Allison," Lucy said.

Charlie shot her a glance. "You too, Brutus?"

"What else can we do to give Mary Ann some answers?" Allison pressed on. "We have to do this. And it has to be now." She opened her passenger door and stepped out.

Lucy joined her as they waited for Charlie, who still sat behind the wheel and stared out into the distance. "For what it's worth, I don't see that we have any other choice."

Allison nodded at Charlie. "Tell her that."

Charlie slowly emerged from her vehicle and locked the door, joining the others. "Alli, I've always supported you, so I sure hope you know what you're doing."

They entered the hospital's lobby where several people lingered. Allison scanned the area. "I have no idea what Tony's parents look like. Anyone see Hailey here?"

"No," Lucy replied.

"Well, we can't wait. This has to be done now." Allison approached the nurse's station. "Excuse me, can you tell me if the parents of Tony Cruz are here? He was the young man brought in..."

"I'm aware." The nurse typed on her screen. "Are you family?"

"No, uh-friends."

The nurse looked beyond Allison. "Then you'll have to speak to that woman over there if you want to know anything about Mr. Cruz."

Allison glanced back. "Is that his mother?"

The nurse nodded.

"Thank you." Allison started toward the plump woman with short dark hair. "Excuse me? Mrs. Cruz?"

Tony's mother locked eyes with Allison, wearing uncertainty on her face. "Yes. I'm Mrs. Cruz."

"I'm Allison Hart. I'm so sorry for your loss." She extended her hand and the woman reluctantly accepted it.

"I'm sorry, do you work for the hospital? I don't need counseling services..."

"I'm not with the hospital, Mrs. Cruz. I am a private investigator."

Her face sobered in an instant. "Then I do know who you are. Tony mentioned that you and your people have been harassing him over what Jessica Healey did to herself. How dare you approach me at a time like this." She turned away.

Allison trailed after her. "Mrs. Cruz, please. I know your son loved Jessica."

She stopped but kept her back to Allison. Her sigh was

distinct. "At first, I wasn't sure what to believe, but Tony made it very clear that he loved her. I am certain he mourned for her up until his last moments."

Mrs. Cruz turned around with slow deliberation. "What do you want, Ms. Hart?"

"I want to get to the truth." Allison took a few steps toward her. "This accident? Mrs. Cruz, there is someone else who we have had our eyes on since the beginning with regard to Jessica's death. And I think that someone else might have something to do with Tony's accident."

"How do you know this?" Her eyes turned dark and serious.

"Because the man who I think might be responsible for what happened to your son also tried to come after my partner and me. I can't be certain, but I would like your help in learning if that could be true."

"If this was intentional, then why aren't the police involved?" she insisted.

"They are. They're operating on the assumption it was a hit and run, but I'd like to change that. I can't do it without your help."

She appeared to size up Allison, wondering if she could be trusted. "What would I have to do?"

"I'd need to see Tony's phone. Specifically, the GPS data contained on it. I don't care who he was talking to or what apps he used. I just want to see where he was earlier as well as on the day Jessica died."

"And what good what that do, Ms. Hart, huh?" she pressed on. "It won't bring my Tony back to me."

"No, it won't, but what I'm hoping it will do is clear any confusion as to where he was when Jessica died that day. It will clear him of any hint of wrongdoing in Jessica's death. That's all I'm looking to do." Allison held her gaze, noting the indecision behind her eyes.

"You said that you didn't think Tony's accident was an accident."

Allison regarded her. "There's only one way for me to know for sure. Mrs. Cruz, I need to see his phone. It's my last option."

———

IN THE SMALL dormitory room at the Tampa university, the friends of Jessica Healey gathered. Still dressed in their dark attire worn for their friend's funeral service, Harriet, Sophie, and Madison sat in silence.

"I can't believe it. First Jess and now Tony?" Madison asked. "What is going on?"

"It was an accident," Sophie replied. "Tony was probably upset, like we all were. Took off after the funeral and was probably driving like a crazy person. You know what he was like. He always flew off the handle at Jess."

"You never liked him, did you?" Harriet asked.

"Tony?" Sophie shrugged. "I didn't think he was right for Jess, if that's what you're asking. The guy was a control freak. I can't be the only one who saw that."

"Maybe," Madison added. "Hey, has anyone heard from Nia? Did she go to the hospital?"

Sophie checked her phone. "She hasn't texted. Not since she gave us the news."

Madison eyed Sophie for a moment. "When that private investigator came by here the first time, why didn't you want to say anything about Professor Lyman?"

"What do you mean? What was there to say about him?" Sophie asked.

"Oh, come on. You know Jess was drooling all over him. Don't you think it's possible she might've been hooking up with him? I hear he has a habit of doing that with students," Madison replied.

"She would've told me. I'm her roommate and her closest friend," Sophie continued. "No way she would've kept her mouth shut about something like that. Besides, what does it matter anyway?"

"It matters because what if he's the reason she's dead?" Madison asked.

Harriet appeared taken aback. "Mads, you can't seriously think Professor Lyman killed her. My God. He's a teacher."

Madison slipped off her black high heels. "Look, we all know Jess somehow got a gun and pulled the trigger. I get that. The police get that. But seriously? What if he, like, blew her off or something? What if she was all depressed about it?"

"Even so, who should be blamed for someone else committing suicide?" Sophie pressed on. "That's like saying, you know, me and Jess had a fight one day and she ended it. Would that have been my fault?"

Harriet raised her hands as if trying to break up a fight. "I think what Madison is saying is that maybe he played a bigger part in her life than anyone knew. And maybe we all missed it."

Sophie shrugged her reply. "What does it matter? She's gone now."

Madison cast down her gaze for a moment. Her breaths grew heavy as though she was nervous.

"What's wrong?" Sophie asked her. "Maddie, are you okay?"

"I was just thinking about that time..." She returned her gaze to Sophie. "That time you and me were talking about the Daytona trip. Planning it out and stuff."

"Yeah, so?" Sophie replied.

Harriet was next to Madison on Jessica's bed and placed her hand on her shoulder. "What is it?"

Madison finally began. "I told you that I would drive. That my car could fit all five of us and that it would be better to drive there together."

"Okay. What are you trying to say?" Sophie continued.

"You insisted that you and Jess take your cars. Even though neither could fit all of us." Madison studied Sophie for a moment. "Why? Why didn't you want me to drive?"

Sophie nervously pulled back her black hair and started to roll it up into a bun. "I mean, like, not to hurt your feelings or anything, but your car is kind of crappy. I wasn't sure it would get us there, you know? Come on, I mean, I thought it was no big deal. Harriet has a two-seater. Me and Jess's cars were newer. It made sense."

"My car would've made it just fine, Sophie. You got all mad when I insisted that we should drive together."

"What are you saying?" Sophie scoffed. "That I wanted Jess to be able to drive back to Tampa on her own? Like I knew her dad would have a heart attack? I mean, seriously?"

Harriet looked at Sophie and cocked her head. "Did you know about Nia and Tony?"

"What?" Her tone raised and her cheeks flushed a light pink.

"Did you know that Tony and Nia were seeing each other behind Jess's back? And that they were planning to come out with it on our trip?" Harriet continued.

Sophie's head shook. "What are you talking about? No, I didn't know they were going out behind her back. How would I know that? You can ask Nia when she gets here. And how do you know, anyway?"

"I saw texts on Nia's phone when we were in Daytona," Harriet continued. "Maybe you knew and because of that, you knew Jess would want to take off. And you would be the one to stand by her side. To go back home with her. Because you two were close like that. At least, that's what you wanted to be."

Madison turned up her gaze and peered at Sophie. "You were always jealous if anyone got too close to her, or something. Like you had dibs on her friendship."

"That's not true. That's not true at all. We were all her friends."

"Sure, but she was closest to you," Madison added. "And it would only prove that Tony wasn't right for her. Because you knew how much he loved her and that he would've done anything to get her back. It was a dumb idea using Nia to get back at her, but you saw an opportunity in that decision."

"Look, I think you both should just go back to your rooms. We're all upset. We all miss Jess and now with what happened to Tony." Sophie stood from the chair. "I'm not going to take offense because I know we're all on edge, but I think I'd like to be alone now."

———

ESTELLE CRUZ, Tony's mother, appeared from the corridor with a plastic drawstring bag in her hand. Allison stood up from one of the lobby chairs, looking back to Charlie and Lucy. "I think she has it."

"I hope you're right about this, Ms. Hart." Estelle opened the bag and retrieved Tony's phone. "This is my son's phone."

"Mrs. Cruz, do you know how to access it?" Allison asked.

Estelle peered at the device and tapped in the code. "Of course, I do. My son didn't keep secrets from me. And he knew I liked to listen to the music on his phone, so he told me the passcode so I could play it while I was cleaning if he was home." She handed Allison the phone. "You need to prove my son had no part in Jessica's death because I already know he didn't."

"That's exactly what I intend to do, Mrs. Cruz." Allison took the phone and handed it to Lucy. "You know how to access the Google locator?"

"I do." Lucy took the phone and within a few seconds, had opened the application.

The look on her face was enough for Allison to know she'd found something she didn't like. "What is it?"

Charlie drew up quickly from her chair as the three examined the screen. "Oh no."

"What have you found?" Estelle asked.

Allison turned to her. "Mrs. Cruz, Tony was at the house of one of the university professors just before the accident."

"Okay." She darted uncertain glances between them. "I don't understand. Is there a problem with that?"

Allison swallowed hard before continuing. "This particular professor, Dr. Jacob Lyman, had been seeing Jessica Healey as well as another of her friends, Nia Brown."

Estelle turned stone-faced.

"This same professor, who is also a very rich and powerful man, hired someone to follow my partner and me the other day."

"The one you mentioned before?" Estelle asked.

"Yes. Now seeing this? Knowing how fragile Tony's emotions were after attending Jessica's funeral." Allison sighed. "He knew the professor had used both of those girls. He knew the professor was married too. There's a chance he confronted Lyman."

"What are you saying, Ms. Hart? That this Dr. Lyman is the reason my son was in an accident?"

Charlie looked at her. "Alli, we don't know anything yet."

"Yes, we do. We just don't want to believe it." Allison turned back to Mrs. Cruz. "I'm saying I think that Dr. Lyman made sure that accident happened. I can't say it for fact. I can't even say it was intended to be fatal." Allison glanced back at Lucy and Charlie. "But what I can say is that I don't believe it was an accident any more than I believe Jessica Healey killed herself."

20

Charlie pulled to a stop at the downtown police station. "You sure you don't want us to go in with you to see Brenner?"

Allison grabbed her bag from the floorboard. "No. I'll show him what we found on Tony's phone. I'd like it if you guys could head over to the university and talk to the administration. Shane's contact had been working on uncovering any complaints issued against Lyman, but I haven't heard anything back. You guys are going to have to run with it now. We're out of time and we need to learn everything we can."

"Got it. The kiddo and I can handle that."

She opened her door. "Good. In the meantime, I'll gauge Brenner's reaction when I show him Tony was at Lyman's house just before the accident. Don't worry about coming back here. I'll hitch a ride with Shane back to the office."

"See you soon." Charlie pulled away from the curb.

Allison walked into the station and stopped at the front desk. "Hi, is Detective Brenner available?"

"Allison, good to see you. He's in his office. Go on up," the officer replied.

"Thanks very much." Allison walked up the stairs that were the centerpiece of the large police station. She made her way back to the offices, noting that Shane wasn't at his desk. "Detective Brenner. I'm sorry to drop by unannounced..."

"Don't be." Brenner waved her in. "Sit. This whole Tony Cruz thing sure as hell gummed up the works, huh?"

"Speaking of..." Allison sat down and retrieved Tony's phone from her laptop bag. "This phone belonged to him. His mother gave it to me."

"That was fast," he replied. "How the hell did you manage that?"

"I just talked to her and asked," Allison replied.

"Well, remind me to bring you along whenever I need something from someone." He folded his arms. "Go on. What do you want to show me?"

Allison keyed in the passcode and retrieved the information. "Tony's location moments before his so-called accident."

"So-called?" Brenner slipped on his readers and took the phone from her before examining the screen. "What makes you think..." He furrowed his brow and pulled the phone closer. "What the hell?"

"Yeah. That's kind of what I thought," Allison replied.

"He was at Lyman's house? Is this for real?"

"As far as I can tell, it's real. The Google locator was on. Says Tony was sitting in front of Lyman's house, then minutes later, ends up in a T-bone crash in an intersection not half a mile away. There's more. Take a look back to the day Jessica Healey died."

He returned his attention to the screen. "Just scroll?"

"Yep. You'll see the day." Allison waited, almost in triumph but she wasn't really sure why. "You'll want to see where he was during the hours of 1 to 3pm the day of."

"Okay." He continued to scroll through until it appeared that he reached his destination. He studied the screen and shot a glance to Allison. "He wasn't there. He was nowhere near there."

"Nope," Allison began. "Detective, Tony Cruz did go to Daytona, but it was after Jessica was gone. He seemed to have no idea. Nia told him Jessica left to return home but asked that he come anyway. So he did. And, of course, none of them knew what happened to Jessica until the next morning."

"Right." Brenner continued to examine the screen. "So the burner wasn't his and now the kid's dead."

"Yes." Allison nodded. "And he just so happened to have died very near a man who still hasn't confirmed his whereabouts when Jessica shot herself."

Brenner set down the phone and opened his desk drawer. "Well, Ms. Hart, I might have some news on that front."

Allison pulled up at attention.

"That necklace you brought me, I had it checked for prints. The box it came in, too."

"And?" she pressed on.

"As you might expect, Tony's prints were on the box. Same goes for her mother's. Partial of her dad's. But there was a partial thumb print also on the pendant part of the necklace."

"Who did it belong to?" Allison's question dripped with anticipation.

"I don't know. The print didn't match any of the ones we have from the people in Jessica's circle. Not her friends, not her family. And now I also can confirm not Dr. Lyman's either. I had our people cross-check that partial against the prints on his phone he turned over."

Allison slumped back in her chair. "I don't understand. What does this mean, exactly?"

"It means we have an unknown."

———

CHARLIE LEANED over the high-top administration desk. "Look, if I'm going to re-enroll my daughter at this school, then I have a right to know who her instructors really are."

"As I said, ma'am, if you'll just tell me your daughter's name, I can pull up her schedule and see who her instructors are."

"I've already told you. I need to know if Dr. Jacob Lyman has a history of complaints. I'm not asking what those complaints are, but if I recall, this is a state school. You are not required to elaborate on the complaints, but I am allowed to know if there are any. That is what I'm asking you now. If you don't want to answer my request, then I'll be left with no choice but to file a complaint against you and the school for withholding pertinent information."

"Ma'am, I just need her name and I will give you what you're asking." the woman behind the counter peered at Charlie.

"I can see that we have reached an impasse." Charlie grabbed her phone. "How about I call the local news station and see if they can get you to do your job?" She opened her screen and acted as though the number was at her fingertips.

"Fine. Fine." The middle-aged woman with blonde frizzy hair put on her glasses and keyed in the commands. "Professor Jacob Lyman." She eyed the screen and the corner of her mouth raised slightly. "I can confirm that Dr. Lyman has zero complaints issued against him by anyone in this school." She pulled off her glasses and peered at Charlie. "Would you like me to print that up for you, ma'am?"

"No, thank you. See? Now was that hard?" Charlie turned on her heel and started back into the tiled floor corridor. She cursed under her breath, certain there would have been something in his file.

"Excuse me?"

Footfalls approached from behind her and Charlie turned around. "Me?"

"Yes. You were asking about Dr. Lyman?" A slim young woman with mousy-hair and a quiet voice appeared.

"I was," Charlie replied. "Who are you?"

"Nobody. But I can tell you that Dr. Lyman has a reputation at this school."

"Is that so?" Charlie moved closer wearing curiosity on her face. "What kind of reputation?"

"He's kind of known as a player. A player is someone..."

"I know what a player is," Charlie replied. "How do you know this?"

The girl looked around for eavesdroppers. "Well, everyone knows it. He's super rich and super cute."

"Uh-huh."

"Anyway, there's this app, website...whatever. You rate the people you, um, go out with."

"Go out with." Charlie nodded. "Okay, go on."

"So there's, like, a whole page on Lyman. Tons of girls rated him. Some good, most are bad. He's definitely a player," she added.

"I'll bet. So what is this app?"

"It's called GoBa."

"Goba?" Charlie asked.

"Right. Like, Good and Bad, you know?" she added.

"Sure. I get it. And how would I go about finding information on Professor Lyman?"

"Simple. Just type in the school, then his name. I'm telling you, there's, like, a ton of stuff about him on there."

"And the school doesn't know anything about this?" Charlie asked.

"If they did, it would be shut down for sure." She peered with wide eyes at Charlie. "You're not going to say anything, are you? I mean, if anyone here figured out it was me..."

"I'm not going to say anything. Thank you for telling me." Charlie started away but stopped and looked back with some confusion. "By the way, why would you tell me this? I'm old. A Mom. Why would you risk it?"

The girl looked down and shrugged. "I don't know. It's kind of mean—the stuff on there. It's not just the teachers. I mean, students, random people. I guess I feel bad that it even exists."

Charlie held her gaze for a moment longer. "Did someone say bad things about you on there?"

She shrugged again and walked away.

———

ALLISON BELIEVED ONLY one option remained. It was time to re-open this investigation and call it what it was. "Detective, based on what we've discovered, the death of yet another young person who happened to have been involved with Jessica Healey. You must be thinking what I'm thinking."

Brenner cast his gaze to the ceiling and took in a long breath. "I still don't see how this is a homicide, Allison."

"Maybe not, but Jessica was influenced by someone there that day. At that moment, someone convinced her to take her own life. Maybe they had threatened to come out with her relationship with Lyman."

"That wouldn't have done anything to her life, only Lyman's," Brenner added.

"Possibly, but it likely would've driven her out of the school for it going public. Look, what I'm saying is..."

"I know what you're saying. Someone got the necklace from Jessica that day. Someone was there on the side of the road with her. And now another kid is dead. Yeah, it doesn't look good regardless of what forensics show." He dropped his gaze and shook his head. "If I go this route, I fully expect Lyman to bring in a team of lawyers. Whatever evidence he had either on this phone or another is long since destroyed, which will make this all that much harder."

"Jessica's family deserves to know the truth about what made her daughter do what she did. Detective Brenner, please. I've given you all that I have. It has to be enough."

A slight nod of his head and he locked eyes with Allison. "It is. It's enough to re-examine the case, however, we still have no legal cause to charge Dr. Lyman with anything. Nothing. I want you to be aware that reopening this case will not do anything more than attempt to find whoever was with her that afternoon. And in the event we are able to do that, it will be up to the D.A. to determine if charges are filed."

"There is precedent, like you said." Allison asserted her case. "Involuntary manslaughter charges against the Massachusetts woman."

"I'm well aware. But make no mistake, Allison, what Jessica Healey did was commit suicide. That won't change."

"I understand. So you'll re-open the case?"

"I will. And if I still have a job after this, we'll have to see." Brenner stood from his desk. "I'll go talk to the higher-ups. I'll be in touch, Allison."

She pushed off the chair. "Thank you, Detective. I do know what's at stake for your career and mine."

"Good God, I hope so."

Allison left his office and walked into the bullpen to find Shane. "You're back. I've been in with Brenner."

"I'm so sorry about Tony Cruz, Allison." Shane stood from his desk.

"I'm sorrier for his family." She pulled out a chair across from him and dropped down. "Brenner is going to re-examine the case."

"Re-examine?" Shane returned to his seat. "A politically-correct way of saying re-open without actually reopening the case."

"Seems that way. But it's better than nothing and I hope it will be enough for Mr. and Mrs. Healey," she replied.

"What's the next step?" he asked.

"I need to get back to the office and get with Charlie and Lucy. They were working on details on Lyman. Do you think you can give me a lift if you're not too busy?"

"Yeah, sure." He reached for his keys. "You ready?"

She nodded and got to her feet. "You know, I should feel relieved by this. I got what I wanted. Sort of."

Shane started toward the stairs. "But you don't."

They reached the first-floor lobby and walked through the doors to the parking lot.

"I don't really know what I feel. I guess I feel that Tony Cruz died because he confronted Dr. Lyman."

"You don't know he confronted Lyman, just that he was at his house." Shane unlocked his door and slipped behind the wheel."

"Seems like a hell of a coincidence." Allison sat atop the leather bucket seat and buckled her belt. "I know none of that really helps Jessica's case."

"Sure it does. It all ties together, Allison. You just need to figure out how." As Shane drove over the bridge and toward the ACL office, he glanced at Allison while she peered through her passenger window. "You sure there's nothing else bothering you?"

She turned to him. "You'd think this was enough, right?" A small chuckle escaped her. "It's a lot of things, I guess. What's going on with Leo. I haven't heard from Micah in almost two weeks. Nolan's gone, playing ball in random small towns. And here I am, trying to find someone to blame for the suicide of a troubled young woman."

"Someone does share that blame, Allison. And I'm not convinced it was suicide."

She narrowed her gaze. "What? Since when?"

"Since Tony Cruz died in a car accident." He turned down the road leading to the ACL office building in the small plaza. "Since you discovered Jessica wasn't alone that day. A phone was found. Her necklace was taken."

"No prints matched what Brenner found on that necklace," Allison added.

"Exactly. Look at the facts, Allison." He turned to her. "Brenner's a hell of a detective, but he's only looking at the forensics. Who's to say someone didn't pull that trigger and make it look like Jessica committed suicide?"

Allison considered his notion. "I have thought about that, but it would have to be someone with extensive forensic knowledge. They'd have to know exactly how to stage it. Like you said, Brenner isn't stupid. He knows what he's doing."

Shane nodded. "Yep. But I'll guarantee you, he's starting to see this in a new light, thanks to what you and the team have uncovered. He just won't admit it. Trust me, Allison, none of us likes to be wrong, especially on an investigation." He pulled to a stop along the curb fronting the building. "This is your stop."

"You don't want to come up?" she asked.

"I can't. I'm slammed with that armed robbery case." He reached for her hand. "Let me know if you need anything. I'm always here for you."

She opened her door. "I know." Allison watched as he drove away, feeling a little better after his affirmation that she was on the right track and to stay the course. Allison never really thought she needed to hear that from any man, but there was a side to her that questioned her actions at times. After all, she was still a relative novice and Shane had years of law enforcement experience.

Allison walked into the office to find the girls at Charlie's desk. "Please tell me you had some luck."

Charlie approached her. "My Irish ancestors are smiling down on us today, Alli. What about you?"

"Brenner's reexamining the case." Allison set down her things at her desk.

"What exactly does that mean?" Lucy asked.

"It means he's considering what we've uncovered as a possible motive to ensure Jessica Healey took her life. But after talking to Shane, he's of the opinion it might have been murder after all."

Charlie returned to her desk. "I'm starting to like him more every day. Come take a look at this."

Allison walked around to peer over Charlie's shoulder. "What's that?"

"Consider it what Facebook used to be when Zuckerberg first created it. Or those other guys before he stole their idea," Lucy laughed.

"What do you mean?" Allison pressed on.

"This website was created by some nerd genius who was probably turned down by a bunch of girls," Charlie began. "It rates hook-ups, as Lucy calls them. Only it apparently has evolved a little since its inception."

"How so?" Allison peered at the screen. "What am I looking at here?"

"This is the so-called ratings page on one Dr. Jacob Lyman," Charlie replied.

Allison's mouth raised into a half-smile. "What?"

"That's right. Alli, you won't believe what we found on here."

21

Milo Nash opened the front door of his restored Queen Anne revival in the heart of Tampa's historic district to find Allison and Charlie on the other side. The glow of the setting sun behind them, he smiled. "Well, well, well. Aren't you two a sight for sore eyes? Looks like you have halos floating above you. Good thing I know better." Milo, still dressed in his suspenders and button-down shirt, stepped aside. "Do come in."

"It has been a while, Milo." Allison wrapped her arms around his sizeable girth. "Thank you for making yourself available."

"Anytime, my dear Allison. Anytime." He turned his sights to Charlie. "And you are looking just as fine as ever, Ms. Charlie Wells."

"Flattery will get you everywhere, Milo." She laughed and offered an embrace. "Good to see you."

"And you." He closed the door. "Shall we take a seat in the lounge?"

Allison delighted in his choice of words. Milo Nash, the 50-

something Special Assistant to the Tampa District Attorney, looked like he'd climbed right out of the pages of a Mark Twain novel. A true southern gentleman with a knack for verbosity unmatched by anyone Allison had ever known. And smart as a whip too. He had helped see her out of the deep waters of her first few cases and this was why she had called on him again. It was time to take another look at just what happened to Jessica that day.

"I hope we didn't cause you to have a change in plans." Allison walked into the living room.

"Not at all. Based on your call and preliminary details, I took the liberty of asking a good friend of mine to join us. I hope that's all right. He's considered an expert in the field of forensic science. Particularly, ballistics." A knock on the door sounded again. "And it seems as though he has just made his arrival."

Allison sat down on one of the two linen wingback chairs that faced a long beige sofa while Charlie sat down on the other. "I feel like I should be smoking a cigar or something."

"You got one?" Charlie asked with a smile.

Milo returned with another man next to him. "Ladies, I'd like to introduce you to Dr. Theo Granger. Theo, this is Allison Hart, P.I. extraordinaire and that little spitfire is Charlie Wells, her partner."

"Nice to meet you two." Granger continued into the room and took a seat on the sofa.

"I've taken the liberty of brewing up some coffee if anyone's interested," Milo began. "Course I always have a beer in the refrigerator when I'm expecting Allison Hart."

"I could use a beer," Allison replied.

"Make that two," Charlie added.

"Uh, how about we make it three?" Granger hiked up his black dress pants and sat down on the sofa. Rolled-up sleeves on his Oxford shirt, and the top button opened, he looked as though he'd just finished a job in the office. "I hear you were hired by a client to investigate the suicide of their child."

Allison let her eyes rake over him. Dark hair, clean-shaven. Roughly 40, and not unappealing. "That's right. It's taken several twists and turns, and we're here now, as are you, I imagine, to review the forensic evidence regarding the conclusion of suicide," Allison replied.

"This forensic report came from the police?" Granger asked.

"Yes, and I hadn't considered disputing because, well, those guys know what they're doing. However, new evidence has emerged that a colleague of mine suggested ought to allow for another look at that evidence."

"Why not go back to the investigating officer then?" he continued.

"We will, once we learn if we have a leg to stand on." Charlie peered up at Milo as he returned with bottles of beer in his hands. "Thanks, Milo."

"Of course. Allison?" He held out the bottle for her. "And Dr. Granger."

"Theo's fine." Granger took the bottle from his hand and twisted open the top. "I was just getting the details on your friends' investigation. Sounds interesting. And challenging, I'm sure."

"Yes, well, that is why I asked you here." Milo sat down. "You see, the fine men and women in blue with the Tampa police are quite effective and efficient. However, I understand another detective, who happens to be a good friend of mine and theirs, suggested that perhaps another look might be warranted."

"And do you have the forensics report in hand?" Granger asked.

"As a matter of fact, Allison, why don't you show the good doctor what you have?" Milo replied.

Allison reached into her carrier bag and pulled out the file folder, setting it on the table. "This is the autopsy report and the accompanying ballistics report."

Granger leaned over and opened the file.

"As you can see, the report suggests suicide by gunshot as the cause of death. Point blank. On the right temple," Allison went on.

Granger flipped through the pages and grunted his acknowledgement. "Interesting. It does look to be a pretty open and shut deal here." He peered at Allison. "What is it you want me to do?"

"I think what my friends are ruminating is this," Milo began. "Some recent developments have occurred that, frankly, put a new light on this situation."

"That's right. Today, a young man was killed in a car accident," Allison began. "And that happens every day, as we know. However, moments earlier, this same young man was at the home of a professor who was involved with that woman there, Jessica Healey. Long story short, Dr. Granger—Theo—my other detective friend thought it would be a good idea to look at this report again. Get a second set of eyes on it and see if it is still as definitive."

Granger picked up the files. "I see. You think the Tampa police might've overlooked something."

"The girl was found alone," Charlie began. "On the side of the road. A gunshot wound on her right temple. No other evidence to suggest anything else. I believe those guys over there do know what they're doing, but I also think they were predisposed to consider suicide because that was exactly what it looked like."

"And if it wasn't?" Granger pressed on. "Do you have a suspect in mind?"

Allison sighed. "Actually, no. We have exhausted our leads and everything we know right now is speculation."

"That's not a strong case you have, then, Ms. Hart," Granger added.

"It is not."

Granger was silent for a moment while he viewed the reports.

Allison glanced at Milo. This was a last-ditch effort to uncover a new lead. After reviewing the information contained on the website Charlie and Lucy discovered, they learned that Lyman had quite the history with co-eds at the university. No information was publicly available on his previous company. It was disheartening to see all the people named on that site. Allison wondered how much of it was true and how much of it was posted by spurned lovers or disgruntled students. Still, she couldn't dismiss that what they found on Lyman was troubling. A serial womanizer, she wondered how much the wife knew about all this.

"Hang on." Granger cocked his head as he studied the photo of Jessica's wound. "Burn mark and gunpowder residue around the wound suggests point-blank range. Okay." He squinted and pulled the photo closer. "But this here. The shape of the wound." He set down the folder and turned his attention to Allison and Charlie. "A self-inflicted gunshot fired at point-blank range leaves a very particular shaped wound. The angle at which this bullet entered is straight on and left a semi-star-shaped wound on the victim's temple. Take a look."

Allison took the photo and leaned toward Charlie as they both gazed at it with an uncomfortable stare. "I—I guess I'm not seeing what you're seeing. It looks like a gunshot wound."

Granger walked around behind their chairs and squatted between them. "Here. You see this?" He traced his index finger around the wound. "The way this bullet entered suggests no angular projection. And this here, this should be a definitive star-shaped wound signifying point-blank entry, striking the skull. And the angle should be ever so slightly raised. Those are signatures of a self-inflicted gunshot. That's not what we're seeing here."

"What are you saying?" Allison peered at him. "Jessica didn't pull the trigger herself?"

"How would that explain the gunpowder residue on her hand?" Charlie added.

Granger stood again and returned to the sofa. "I can absolutely see why the conclusion was made as a suicide. Everything points to just that. But it's this photo, the one in your hand, that doesn't match that conclusion."

Allison felt a renewed hope build in her chest. "This wasn't suicide? Jessica Healey was murdered. That's what you're saying."

"I don't know the ins and outs of your investigation or the one the police conducted. Frankly, when all signs point to a reason..."

"They are predisposed to accept that reason," Milo added.

"Yes, sir," Granger replied.

"What do we do with this?" Charlie asked. "It would explain everything. The necklace. The phone we found. Alli, Lyman is the only one without an alibi."

"He hasn't submitted an alibi because this hasn't been an active murder investigation," Allison replied.

"Well, I'll tell you one thing, ladies," Milo began. "If it wasn't before. It must surely be now."

––––––––––––

THE FOYER of the Lyman home opened up to the family room on the right and a formal dining room on the left. To the rear lay the kitchen, an office down the long corridor, and a guest bedroom. Upstairs were four other bedrooms. There was no reason for the large home as it was currently only occupied by Jacob Lyman and his wife. But there had been plans for a family and they bought accordingly. Regardless, he was in no rush. After all, he was barely in his thirties. There was still too much to do before being saddled with kids.

As Jacob sat on his plush white sofa, proof he had no children at the moment, his wife sat next to him as they watched television. His phone buzzed on the side table and when he viewed the caller ID, he stood. "I have to take this."

"Who's calling this late?" she asked.

"It's Will. I'll only be a minute." He stepped through the French doors that led to the covered patio outside. The cool air felt nice, but it had warmed in the past few weeks as late spring prepared to make way for summer. "Yeah, what's up?"

"They're reexamining the investigation," he replied.

With his phone to his ear, Lyman stepped out onto the deck toward the heated pool. Lights illuminated the rear yard and the pool lit up with a soft blue-green hue. "What are you talking about?"

"Jessica Healey. What the hell do you think I'm talking about?" His voice hardened. "Jake, you screwed up, man. That kid. That Cruz kid. He's dead."

"No shit. Like that was my fault?"

"You can't play me, Jake. Now, Detective Brenner thinks it's all just a little too coincidental, Cruz dying the way he did."

"How do you know this?" Lyman asked.

"A friend of a friend, okay? Trust me, it's coming down. They're going to open it and look at it with fresh eyes. It's time we sit down and hash out a plan because if we don't come up with something, it's game over for you. You hear me? Game. Over."

Lyman walked around the pool, pushing his hand through his thick brown hair. "What the hell am I supposed to do, then? Throw my hands up and call it quits? Come on! You can't tell me I can't find a way out of this. How much, huh? How much is it going to take?"

"Buddy, you ain't got enough to get you out of this one."

ALLISON KNOCKED on the apartment door. It was late and coming here was probably a bad idea, but she had to tell him.

Shane opened the door. "Hi."

"Hi." Her smile widened at the sight of him. "Can I come in?"

"Yeah, of course. Sorry. I was caught off guard by your smile." He cringed and stepped aside. "That didn't sound right. What I meant to say was that you look much happier than when I saw you earlier today."

"It's because of you." Allison walked in and set down her purse. "It's not too late is it?"

"Allison, it's 9:30. I don't have a bedtime." He closed the door and walked into the kitchen. "You want something to drink? Beer? Wine?"

"No, maybe just some water." She sat down on the edge of his sofa, hardly able to contain herself.

He returned carrying a couple of bottled waters. "What's the good word?"

"Shane, it was murder. I know I shouldn't be happy about this." Allison paused for a moment. "I mean, I'm not happy about it. But now we know. We know the truth. Jessica didn't kill herself. Someone else pulled the trigger."

"What? Really?" He sat down next to her on his too-firm sofa. "How did this come about?"

"Well, what you said when you dropped me off at the office today. About reconsidering the idea it could have been suicide. I called Milo. He, in his infinite wisdom, brought in a guy."

"A guy?" he asked.

"An expert in ballistics. Anyway, he reviewed the report. The autopsy and the ballistics. He said something to the effect about the angle of the wound or the shape of it, or something like that. Anyway, I can't remember exactly what he said, but he said it wasn't a suicide."

"Wow, okay. Have you told Brenner about this yet?" Shane asked.

"I called him as soon as I left Milo's house. He said he wanted to meet with Milo's friend and talk to him about it first, but he's on board so long as his team will confirm it. I told Milo and he's going to arrange the meeting for just as soon in the morning as possible." She smiled and shook her head. "This is it, Shane. This is the break we needed. Mary Ann was right. Her daughter didn't kill herself."

"You might've figured that out, but you still don't know who did. Not to rain on your parade, but this is only half the work."

"There's a long road ahead of us, but honestly, we've made a lot of progress. Lyman is looking guiltier by the day."

"Looking and proving are miles apart," he added. "Still, this is good news, Allison. Very good news."

"I'm not sure I would've pushed for this, Shane, if it hadn't been for you. I believed the report. Everyone did."

"Well, those guys make mistakes sometimes too. Especially when all else points to a conclusion."

"I get that." She took a long drink of her water. "How's your case going? The armed robbery?"

"It's going," he shrugged and held Allison's gaze. "I'm just really glad you're going to get that girl justice. Somehow, someway, you'll bring her justice."

"I think so, too." She set down the bottle. "Listen, I know what I said about putting us on the back burner until this is over..."

"Yeah?"

Elation was too strong a word for how Allison felt in this moment, perhaps it was vindication. Everything she had learned about Jessica Healey seemed to point far away from suicide. Everything she had learned about Dr. Lyman led her to believe he used that poor girl along with others, including Jessica's friend,

Nia Brown. But as she sat here now, staring into the eyes of a man who was undeniably handsome, kind, and most of all, a man who cared about her, denying her feelings any longer was only hurting him. And her. It was time for Allison Hart to remember who she was. No longer wife to Leo. No longer the essential figure in Nolan and Micah's lives. She was just Allison. And she deserved happiness like everyone else.

Allison leaned into Shane. His subtle cologne, like fresh-cut wood wrapped in leather, was intoxicating. His deep-set brown eyes widened as he watched her draw near. An innocence masked his face, as though this was his first time. She knew better but it made her feel like she was all he ever wanted.

"Allison...Are you sure?"

She touched his lips with hers before he could continue. What started as a gentle touch grew into a fiery passion the likes she hadn't known in far too many years. Allison thought those feelings were long behind her now as she pushed 50, but Shane drew them from a place she hadn't known still existed.

He pulled away. "Are you sure this is what you want?"

His words were sweet but unnecessary. "I think we both know what we want. It just took me a little longer to realize it." A tender smile danced on her lips. "Should we?" she nodded toward his bedroom.

He returned an impish grin. "I'll have to think on that."

"What?" Confusion masked her face.

Shane chuckled. "What do you think, Allison?"

She stood and offered her hand. "I think you can be funny when you want to be."

———

ALLISON STOOD at the door and turned the handle. "I promise I'll text you when I arrive home."

"Am I being overprotective?" Shane quickly turned sheepish. "You're a grown woman, I'm..."

"It's okay. Yes, you're being a little overprotective, but I'll forgive you this time." Allison kissed him again and hadn't wanted to leave, but with so much at stake tomorrow, she needed to get home and prepare for what lay ahead. "Good night, Shane. Get some sleep." She headed out the door.

"You too, Allison."

She heard the door close behind her and stopped for a moment in the hall that was too bright for this late at night. A smile that stretched ear to ear appeared from nowhere and her heart soared. It felt right. Long overdue, and right. Allison started walking again and reached the elevator. "Charlie's going to be pissed I didn't tell her sooner."

The doors parted and she stepped inside. Her mind replayed the evening and her cheeks flushed. As Allison stepped off the elevator, she reached for her keys and walked into the parking lot. A press of the remote and the lights flickered on her old blue Honda while the doors unlocked.

"Ms. Hart."

Allison swung around at the voice behind her. "What the?"

Jacob Lyman held up his hands. "I didn't mean to scare you."

"Well, you sure as hell did. What are you doing here? How did you find me?" Her eyes glanced up at Shane's balcony.

"I need you to understand that I had nothing to do with what happened to Tony Cruz or Jessica Healey."

"You shouldn't be here." Allison opened her car door.

"Please." Lyman stepped closer.

"Stop. Don't make another move." Allison reached into her purse. "I have a gun."

"Please, you have to believe me. I'm not here to hurt you. I just need you to understand."

"Understand what, Dr. Lyman?" Her fingers laced around the butt of the gun still inside her handbag as she prepared to retrieve it.

Lyman glanced at her purse and returned his gaze. "It was the Cruz kid all along."

22

Shane stared at his phone, noting that she should have texted him by now. The late show was on television, but it was only background noise. What he wanted to do was to call Allison and make sure she was okay. Her car wasn't in the parking lot, so he knew she left. But an unsettled feeling consumed him, and he didn't want to be *that* guy. Allison wouldn't want him to be that guy either. "She probably forgot. She's probably curled up in bed snoozing away." He peered again at his phone. "Don't do it, man. Don't do it. She's fine. She's a grown woman."

His head knew he was right, but his heart felt differently. Shane had squelched his feelings for Allison pretty much since the day he met her. He'd tried everything in his book, but she would never succumb to his charm, until now. And he didn't think he'd used his charm this time. Maybe he finally wore her down. Shane chuckled. "Just do it, man. She'll think it's nice." He picked up his phone. "She'll think I don't believe she can take care of herself."

He knew Allison needed a man like she needed a hole in the head, but it didn't stop him from worrying about her. Shane typed the message, let his finger hover over the "send" button, and finally pressed it. "There. It's done. Whatever she thinks, it's done."

Shane kept his phone in his lap, waiting for her reply. Five minutes went by. Ten minutes went by. "She's asleep, man. I told you, she's asleep."

———

ALLISON STOOD inside the office of Dr. Jacob Lyman, in the building he owned near Downtown. "Okay. I'm here. You said you can prove Tony Cruz was responsible for Jessica's death. Show me." She folded her arms and widened her stance. "By the way, why didn't you hunt down Detective Brenner about this? Why come to me?"

"Because I need to stop this before he reopens the case. I knew that if I could convince you, you could bring that information to Brenner and this entire nightmare would be over before it shows up on social media." Lyman pulled out his desk drawer and retrieved a phone.

"Another phone? How many phones do you have, Professor?" Allison asked.

"Until all this happened? Two," he replied. "I'm not the man you think I am, Ms. Hart. I promise you."

"I know exactly the man you are." She shook her head. "I saw the website where kids post about their hook-ups. Do you have any idea what your girlfriends have said about you? Frankly, I'm surprised you're still married, let alone an instructor at the university."

"What are you talking about?" Lyman asked. "What website?"

"Doesn't matter right now. You'd better show me what you have. I'm not sticking around here for my health."

"What's on this phone will prove I had nothing to do with Jess's suicide."

Allison glanced at her purse as her phone buzzed inside. "I need to see who this is."

"No. Don't."

"What do you mean?" She stopped cold.

Lyman held up his hands. "Just, please. Just wait two seconds."

"If that's one of my kids..." Allison peered at him. She knew it wasn't and figured it was Shane because she hadn't texted him yet. "Fine."

Allison picked up her phone and saw the text message. *"Just wondering if you made it home safely. I'm sure you did, but you know..."* She returned her phone to her purse. "Okay. Show me."

"This is video surveillance that proves I was nowhere near Jessica Healey when she killed herself."

"She didn't kill herself, in case I failed to mention that earlier," Allison replied.

"Well, whatever. Just watch." He pressed play.

Allison slipped on her reading glasses and peered at the screen. "Is that your car?"

"Yes, it is. Keep watching," Lyman replied.

After a few moments, Allison glanced at him. "I think I know now why you haven't shown this to anyone." She pulled off her glasses. "Where was this?"

"Right there." He pointed to the screen. "The Palmview hotel in St. Pete's."

"And the girl with you?"

"Just another in a long line." He turned away, feigning embarrassment. "It's the same place where I took Jess about a month ago. That glass mermaid? I picked it up from the lobby gift shop. It was just a cheap trinket, but she wanted it. So I got it for her."

Allison pursed her lips and studied him.

"You think I don't know I'm a piece of shit?" Lyman asked. "Believe me, I know."

And all at once, Allison watched her case burn to the ground. The only person who hadn't offered an alibi was this man before her now. And he'd just confirmed without a doubt that he was a cheater, but he was not a murderer. "That doesn't prove you played no part in Tony Cruz's car accident. You said it was all him, but he was at your house minutes earlier. We know that for a fact."

"Look, I don't know what to say about that. I had nothing to do with it. The kid came here, threatening me."

"He threatened you?" Allison asked.

"Not directly. I had one of my security staff go out and talk to him. The kid was sitting outside my house and freaking out my wife, okay? And it wasn't the first time he came around." Lyman paced up and down his office.

"Calm down." Allison noticed his growing agitation and exaggerated hand gestures. "The guy who hit him took off. Did you know that? It was a hit and run. The car didn't have any plates on it, which was really convenient, too. So there was no way to track down the driver or determine if he owned the vehicle."

"Like I said, I don't know anything about that. What I've shown you is that I was somewhere else when Jess killed herself."

Allison considered his plea. It explained why his prints weren't on Jessica's necklace or the box. "We found a phone on the scene very near where Jessica's car was found with her dead inside. Brenner's people are working on learning who that phone belonged to."

"You think it was mine?" He reared back with indignation. "I just told you, showed you, I wasn't there, lady. What more do you want from me?"

Allison swallowed down a rising lump of fear in her throat. Lyman's eyes had darkened, and he grew more distressed. "Fine.

Okay. We'll take this to Detective Brenner in the morning. I can't dispute it. It'll be in his hands to deal with."

Lyman rifled around his desk. "And I have other stuff too. Like I said, Tony Cruz had it in for me. The kid threatened me. He came to my house. I know he followed me when I was seeing Jess. You should've been after him, not me."

"Then that's something Brenner will have to look into. Unfortunately, Tony's dead, so he can't defend himself." Allison couldn't risk provoking him further by suggesting she had the evidence that Tony was nowhere near Jessica that day. She needed to get out of this alive.

Lyman eyed her with blunt resolve. "You still don't believe me, do you?"

She stepped back. "I'm not the one you need to convince, Dr. Lyman. Now, I think it's time for me to leave. I have a family at home. They're going to wonder why I haven't returned." Allison reached for her purse.

Lyman threw his hand on top of it. "Wait. I have to know that you believe me."

Allison's heart jumped as she tried to remain calm. "Dr. Lyman, please remove your hand. I understand why you feel angry. I see that you have proven your innocence as it relates to Jessica Healey. You need to present the evidence to Detective Brenner."

Lyman appeared to return to calm and removed his hand. "You're right. I'm sorry, Ms. Hart. This has been a very difficult time for my family. Please, forgive me."

She retrieved her purse and started toward the door. "Good night, Dr. Lyman." The moment Allison stepped outside, she wanted to burst into tears. She'd faced angry people before and especially in her former line of work as a fraud investigator, but there was something in Lyman's eyes that truly frightened her.

As she reached her car and pulled away, Allison picked up her phone. "It's me. Did I wake you?"

"No. Did I wake you? I got a little worried when you didn't text me back. Sorry. I hope you're not mad."

Her voice faltered and she cleared her throat. "No. I'm not mad."

"Allison, are you okay? Where are you?"

————

CHARLIE PULLED onto Allison's driveway and rushed out of the car. The front door was already open, and Allison stood on the other side. "Good Lord, Alli. What were you thinking?"

Allison peered outside to confirm no one had followed Charlie before closing the door. "I was thinking the rich guy wouldn't do anything stupid. It turned out that I was right."

"Still..." Charlie trailed her into the kitchen.

Allison opened the fridge and grabbed bottled waters. "I had no reason to think he wanted anything other than to clear his name, which he did. Sort of." She handed a bottle to Charlie and chugged back half of her own. "Dr. Jacob Lyman is a man used to getting his own way. Used to his people falling in line and when I showed resistance, he didn't handle it well. But I'm fine, Charlie. More importantly, Lyman offered up a rock-solid alibi."

Charlie dropped to the stool at the kitchen island and patted at her spiky hair. "Where does that leave us? We now know Jessica didn't pull the trigger, so who the hell did?"

Allison leaned over with her elbows resting on the counter. Her hair hung over her shoulders and her face wore exhaustion. "I don't know where our part in this goes from here. Mary Ann hired us to get to the truth. I suppose we did, in a way, and now Brenner will reopen the case. He'll run forensics again in a new light and confirm what Granger said. But as far as us?" She shook her head. "I don't think there's any more part in this."

"What does Shane say about all this? You told him about your encounter with Lyman tonight, right?"

Allison pulled up again and took a long drink of her water.

"Alli? Have you talked to Shane?" Charlie asked.

"Yes."

Charlie appeared to wait for her to continue and when she didn't, she pressed on. "Well? What's going on? What are you not telling me?"

The number of details Allison left out of her story piled high to the ceiling. And having just slept with Shane was right at the top, though it paled in comparison to the real issue at hand. "I was going to tell you tomorrow, then Lyman found me."

"Where did he find you?" Charlie cocked her head and narrowed her eyes.

"I had stopped by to see Shane and when I left, Lyman was waiting for me in the parking lot."

She raised her hands. "Let's put a pin in that for just a second and jump back to why you were at Shane's apartment. Look, I don't want to dismiss any of what happened tonight, but Alli, you gotta tell me, did something happen between you two?"

Allison's cheeks blushed and she shrugged her shoulders.

Charlie sat up at attention. "Oh my God, you slept with him. You had sex with Shane Sullivan."

"Like I said, I was going to tell you tomorrow, then all this other stuff happened."

"Shane obviously didn't know Lyman followed you there because he never would've let you leave with him."

"He didn't. It all happened so fast," Allison began. "And there'll be another time to elaborate, which I will, I promise. But right now, we have bigger problems to deal with."

Charlie nodded. "You're right. Don't think you're off the hook, by the way, but we need to figure out where we go from here. It pisses me off that Lyman followed you. Makes me wonder if he's got eyes on us right now."

"I don't think he does. He was acting pretty desperately, but I think he regained his senses. We're scheduled to meet with Mary Ann in the morning. We'll tell her what we know and that's all we can do. Brenner will talk to her soon enough about the fresh look at the reports." Allison peered at Charlie for a moment. "The only pieces of evidence we have now that will confirm who killed Jessica are the burner phone, and a partial thumbprint on the necklace that didn't match anyone she knew."

"That burner might as well be a paperweight for all it's worth to us right now," Charlie added.

"Brenner said it was purchased in Tampa. So we know it's local. It was a store in Tampa Heights. That's all he can tell us."

"No idea of when it was purchased?" Charlie asked.

"If only..." Allison sighed. "We'd have to convince the store owner to let us look at their surveillance and then we'd have to scour through days, weeks, months. Who knows? And since we don't know who killed her..." she scoffed. "We wouldn't know who to look for in any case."

"And Brenner's sure that he can't trace the purchase date by the serial number or the IMEI number?"

"He hasn't so far." Allison turned up her gaze for a moment. "But I wonder...That store would have a record of inventory. They must use an identification of the phone, either the serial number or another number. There must be a record of when the phone was purchased."

"Say you're right," Charlie began. "You'd have to consider that the phone was probably bought with cash."

Allison stopped and turned back. "There has to be a way. It's our only lead until Brenner can rerun virtually their entire evidence log. That'll take too long. Meanwhile, whoever killed her might be on their way to Mexico."

"Face it, Alli, I think we're done here," Charlie said. "As much as I hate to believe that, I just don't see how we get more information on that burner."

Allison pressed her hands against the island top and leaned in. "Then we find someone who can break into that phone. I don't know who or where, but you can't tell me there's no one out there with that skillset. No, someone knows how to do it and we're going to find that person."

———

Nia Brown wiped the tears from her eyes when she heard the knock on her door. "Are you expecting anyone?"

Madison was curled up on her bed, gazing at her phone, and peered up at her. "Huh?"

"Someone's here." Nia stood from her bed.

"It's not for me."

"Okay." Nia cleared her throat before peering through the fish-eye security lens. With a furrowed brow, she opened the door. "Sophie. What's up?"

"Can I come in? Unless you guys were going to bed or something." She peered inside.

"No. We're good. Come in." Nia stepped aside and closed the door.

Madison noted her arrival. "Hey, what's going on?"

Sophie released a heavy sigh and sat down at Nia's desk. "I had to come talk to you, Nia."

"You want me to leave or something?" Madison asked.

"No. No, it's fine," Sophie replied. "You know, Mads, you were right about what you said before. About me wanting Jess to myself. I loved her like a sister, and I guess I was jealous that others would take her away from me."

"Like Tony?" Nia asked as she lowered herself onto her bed.

"I thought he was out of the picture. That she was done with him," Sophie added.

"I know he never loved me the way he did Jess," Nia said. "I knew it from the first day that I was just a way for him to get back at her. Thing is, I never should've gone after him in the first place. I was Jess's friend, and she was mine. I betrayed her. Now they're both gone."

Madison pulled to the edge of her bed and eyed Sophie. "What did you want to say, Sophie? You look like you want to get something off your chest."

She peered at Madison and then at Nia before casting down her gaze. "I did something a while back. Something I knew was wrong at the time, but I did it anyway."

Madison and Nia traded glances before Madison continued. "What did you do? Something to Jess?"

"No. I mean, I didn't...I wasn't there. I loved her, Maddie, I'd never hurt her. Besides, we were together the whole time. Jesus, do you think I made her kill herself?"

Madison shrugged. "You did say you guys were texting right before it happened."

"Yeah, because she wanted to see Tony and I told her it wasn't a good idea. I didn't even know about you two." She peered at Nia. "No, look..." Sophie took in a long breath. "Jess never told me she liked Professor Lyman. I guess I kind of saw it whenever she ran into him, but I never thought anything of it."

"I knew he was dating her," Nia jumped in. "Because he went after me and I was so stupid...I thought, here's this totally rich guy, totally hot, and he wants to date me."

"Even though you knew he was married," Madison replied.

"Be sure and tell me what it's like up there in your ivory tower, Mads," Nia added.

"Sorry. I didn't mean..."

"Whatever. Anyway, when he dumped me, I knew he wanted to go after Jess. He practically told me so. I thought, maybe I should go after Tony, then." Nia shook her head. "I know how shitty that sounds. But when Tony said he was interested too, we hooked up."

"We already know this, Nia," Madison added. "No offense, but what are you getting at?"

"I'm trying to say that I told Tony about Professor Lyman hooking up with Jess and that he was the reason she broke up with him."

Sophie peered at her. "Well, I guess we both f'ed up. I saw that Jess was all into him and I knew then she must've been seeing Professor Lyman. So, I kinda followed him a couple times. Saw where he lived. Even saw his wife in their doorway once."

Madison eyed her. "Sophie, what did you do?"

She shrugged and looked away for a moment. "One day I drove to his house, knowing he was in class, and knocked on his door. His wife answered. She's super pretty. Really nice. I sort of..." Her breaths sounded shallow. "I told her that her husband was cheating on her. And that I knew who the girls were."

"What? Oh my God." Madison stood from the bed. "Holy shit. What did she do?"

"Nothing. She just looked at me. Like right through me, like I wasn't even standing there anymore. It was weird and I got freaked out, so I just took off."

"I wonder if Lyman tried to break it off with Jess after that?" Madison asked. "Do you think she told him she was coming back to Tampa because of her dad and wanted to get him to change his mind?"

Sophie shook her head. "I don't know. If she did, she didn't tell me."

"When did you tell the wife?" Nia asked.

Sophie peered at her. "The day before we left for Daytona."

23

———————

Lucy hung up the phone wearing a smile and plenty of tenacity. "I think we got someone." She stood from her desk and snatched the sticky note from its pad. "Kendall got back to me with a name. Apparently, this person is some kind of genius White Hat."

Charlie pushed back from her desk. "I'm sorry, a what?"

"A White Hat," Lucy replied. "A good hacker, I guess you could say. See, they have Black Hats and White Hats…"

"How very Wild, Wild, West," Charlie quipped.

"No doubt. There's also Grey Hats, but I won't go into that."

"So Kendall offered a name," Allison jumped in. "Great. Who is he or she?"

"She is Emily Raines, or EmRay to those who know her in the hacking world. She left Anonymous a few years ago…"

"Anonymous?" Allison asked. "Aren't they the ones who wear those masks?"

"The very same," Lucy replied. "But like I said, she left them a long time ago. She has her own firm now and helps businesses beef up their software security."

"And this woman can break into the phone left on scene when the cops can't?" Charlie asked.

"According to Kendall, she's the best. He couldn't guarantee she could help, but there was no one else he could think of who could handle a job like that."

"How do we get hold of her?" Allison picked up her phone. "I'll need to get the burner from Detective Brenner if he'll agree to it."

"He gave me her contact information. I'll send her a text now and see what she thinks." Lucy returned to her desk. "But if you can't convince Brenner, then there isn't much point."

"I'll convince him," Allison replied. "After last night, he's going to be in it up to his eyeballs. I'll make the call now."

———

ATTORNEY WILL HARRIS stood up and faced the window of his office. His left hand was shoved into his pants' pocket and his right hand held a bourbon neat. "So let me get this straight. You followed the P.I. to some apartment complex. Waited almost two hours for her to come out. Then you came up from behind and practically threatened her."

"I didn't threaten her." Lyman crossed his legs as he sat on the sofa in the lawyer's office. "I told her I had an alibi and that I could prove it. But that it was at my office."

The lawyer turned back. "You're lucky she didn't shoot you. Frankly, after what happened with the kid, I'm surprised as hell she followed you back and didn't have the cops in tow."

"I didn't do anything wrong, Will. We both know that. After you called and told me the case was going to be reexamined, what choice did I have? I proved that I was nowhere near Jessica Healey when she killed herself."

Harris joined him on the sofa. "Except now it appears, based on some expert forensics guy, that she was murdered."

"No way are they going to prove that. They have zero suspects. No video, nothing," Lyman added. "I just needed to clear my name and that's what I did."

"Maybe so." He tossed back the last of his drink. "But in the process, you're now turning their heads in a direction that you won't like."

"You're my lawyer," Lyman said. "That $1000 an hour rate I pay you, along with a $100,000 retainer means it's time for you to step up and do your damn job." He stood. "Nothing in the death of Jessica Healey points to me. Nothing. Do your job, Will."

"I'll tell you what, Jake. I'll do my job on one condition, keep it in your pants from here on out. If you had, we wouldn't be having this conversation and two young kids wouldn't be dead."

Lyman slammed the door behind him and headed into the parking lot. As he stepped into his car and pressed the ignition, he peered through the windshield. "Jesus!"

Standing in front of his Range Rover was Sophie Matthews. He opened his door. "What the hell are you doing? Get out of the way."

Sophie walked toward the driver's side door. "Do you remember me, Professor Lyman?"

Lyman appeared to search his memory banks. "Uh, yeah. You're Jess's friend."

"*Was* Jess's friend. Her best friend, actually. Sophie Matthews."

"Right. Yeah, I remember you. What are you doing here? How did you find me?"

"Your wife told me."

His expression turned cold. "My wife? You talked to my wife at my home?" Lyman stepped out of his Range Rover and stood before her. "Who the hell do you think you are?"

Sophie looked up at him, her petite frame barely reached his shoulders. "I'm Jess's best friend. I know all about you, Professor. Everyone knows about you." She held up her phone that displayed the website."

"What the hell is that?" he asked.

"It's called GoBa. It's a website that rates hookups. And Professor Lyman, your name shows up on here lots of times. You have quite the reputation with the female students at the university."

He peered at it again and swallowed hard. "When did you see my wife?"

"Earlier today. But that wasn't the first time. I've seen her once before. Not that long ago, actually. She's really pretty. Too bad she married a piece of shit like you."

Lyman stood within inches of her now. "What the hell do you want from me? You'd better stay away from my wife."

"I don't need to see her again." Sophie remained unaffected. "She knows you were seeing my friend. Well," Sophie scoffed. "Both of my friends. You should really consider staying away from girls who know each other. Tends to backfire."

Lyman gripped her throat. His fingers tightening with each word. "What did you say to my wife, huh? What lies did you spread, you little bitch."

Sophie's eyes widened. His grip was tight enough to stoke fear in her, but not so tight as to induce pain. "Let go of me. I'll scream. I swear it." She clawed at his hand.

And in that moment, Lyman appeared to regain his senses and let go. "If you think you're going to blackmail me, you're in for a shock. I don't give two shits about what some juvenile website says about me. I have enough money to shut it down by tomorrow." He stepped back into his car. "And by the way, my wife already knows all about me."

———

DETECTIVE BRENNER ACCOMPANIED Allison and the team as they arrived to see Emily Raines. The young woman of only 28 had a studio above a warehouse and they waited while the gate opened to the elevator.

"Thank you for agreeing to this, Detective." Allison stepped on and waited for the others.

"I just hope it gets us to where we want to be," he replied. "And so long as you know why I couldn't let you do this without me."

"I understand. We want the same thing." She peered at Charlie and Lucy. All we wanted was to know what really happened. And so does Mrs. Healey."

The gate creaked open to reveal a stark hallway with a concrete floor and unfinished walls.

"This is it." Allison stepped out. "Lucy, what did she say her unit number was?"

Lucy checked her notes. "319." She peered into the hall. "Looks like it should be this way."

"I'll tell you one thing, Ms. Hart, you and your team don't give up, do you?"

Allison walked beside him. "Not if we can help it."

Lucy knocked on the door and a moment later, a young woman with short dark hair with a purple streak stood on the other side.

"Hi. I'm Lucy Boyce with ACL Investigations. We spoke on the phone."

"Right, Kendall's friend." She eyed everyone. "Who are these guys?"

"Detective Brenner, Tampa PD."

"Allison Hart. I run ACL."

"Charlie Wells. I run it too, but this one here, she pays the bills." A half smile crept up on her lips.

A faint grin appeared on Emily's face. "Come in." Her eye makeup was dark and her lips, bright. The eclectic fashion was a mix of emo with a hint of punk. "How's Kendall doing? I haven't talked to him in a while. He still working on that drone company?"

"He is. He's doing well with it," Lucy replied.

"Good." Emily started in and brushed by them. "He dating anyone yet?"

"Um, not that I'm aware of."

Emily sized up Lucy. "Interesting. Figured you'd be his type."

"I'm actually seeing someone." Lucy's face flushed a little as she cleared her throat. "So about the burner phone, you think..."

"Let me see it." Emily held out her hand.

"Detective?" Lucy turned to him.

Brenner set down his laptop bag on the futon that lay in the middle of the room. He reached inside and pulled out the evidence bag. "We ran prints on it, but it had been sitting in the dirt and grass for a while. We didn't get anything usable on it."

Emily grunted as she took the bag from him. "You want me to use gloves?"

"That won't be necessary. Like I said, we've run forensics on it already and came up empty-handed. We did manage to track down where the phone was purchased."

"Where?" she asked.

"Tampa Heights. My forensics team has been working on gaining access, but no luck."

Emily walked to a folding table where a laptop rested. "I'm not surprised. Shit ain't easy. Otherwise, everyone would do it." She opened her laptop and keyed in commands and then reached for a USB cord. "I'm going to plug it into my computer and run a program that I'm testing right now. Can't say for sure it'll work, but I think we got a better than 50% chance."

Allison eyed Charlie and both shrugged.

"Ms. Raines, that's a 50% better chance than I had," Brenner replied. "Do your worst. I won't ask questions."

"Y'all might as well take a seat. This is gonna take a while."

———

ESTELLE CRUZ, mother of the now deceased Tony Cruz, stood in the doorway of her son's room. She grinned and shook her head at the mess he'd left. Socks on the floor. A candy bar wrapper on his nightstand. Two cans of soda on his dresser. Dr. Pepper. Estelle couldn't stand Dr. Pepper but, boy, did Tony love it.

In the back of her mind, she could hear the screeching tires and crashing metal. Estelle wondered if he felt any pain. Of course, he must have because he lived long enough to make it to the hospital. Just not long enough so the doctors could stop the bleeding. His abdomen had filled with blood. There had been too much damage. Now, her 20-year-old son was gone and all she had left of him was what was in this room.

Estelle noticed his laptop sticking out of his backpack. It leaned against the back wall of his room and she approached it and set it on the bed. It hadn't been with him yesterday because, of course, he was attending the funeral of his former girlfriend. Estelle liked Jess Healey until she decided to break her son's heart. But it happened. It was part of life. Tony hadn't handled it well and she watched as he went through girlfriends like they were sticks of gum in a pack. Spitting one out right after the other. Tony had a future. He could've played ball for a big college. Now he wouldn't get that chance.

She pulled out his laptop and began to empty the contents of his backpack. These were the things he used the most, except for his phone. The police still had possession of that, thanks to the private investigator. Not that it seemed to do a lot of good, from what she could tell. No one had contacted her about anything yet. It was like Tony had already been forgotten. Tears ran down her cheeks as she sifted through his things. She spotted a folded note inside one of the pockets and pulled it out. A half sheet of paper folded over twice, and she opened it. And written in blue ink, Estelle read the words.

"*I wanted to give you something so that you might remember what we once meant to each other. I hope you have a good life, Tony. That's all I want for you. Love, Jess.*"

Estelle peered at the note again and then searched inside the backpack, but she'd taken out everything inside. "Give you what?" she asked herself. With her hands on her hips, Estelle surveyed his room. "What did you give him?" She opened his dresser drawers, his closet, his desk drawer, rifling through all of it, but turned up nothing. Not that she knew what she was looking for, but Jess had left something for him. Where was it? What was it?

When nothing obvious surfaced, Estelle knew this note from Jessica Healey might mean something to the private investigator. After all, Mary Ann Healey hired her and right now, she knew exactly how Mary Ann felt. Maybe it was nothing, but maybe not."

Estelle walked out of the room and back down the stairs. She reached for her phone that rested on the living room side table and pulled out the card from her purse. "Allison Hart. ACL Investigative Services." She dialed the number, but the line rang with no answer. Estelle checked the time. 2 pm. They should have been open.

Another number was listed on the card. Looked like a cell phone, so she tried that. After two rings, the line was answered. "Uh, is this Allison Hart?"

"Yes, it is."

"Ms. Hart, we met at the hospital yesterday. My son is Tony Cruz."

"Oh, yes, of course, Mrs. Cruz. What can I do for you? I know the police still have your son's phone..."

"That's not why I'm calling, Ms. Hart. I found a note inside Tony's backpack. It was from Jess Healey."

"It was? I see. Can you tell me what it says?" Allison asked.

Estelle relayed the message and waited for a response.

"Do you know what it was that she gave him?" Allison continued.

"I'm afraid not. I had a look around Tony's room, but nothing appeared obvious. I know you're still looking into Jess's suicide. I thought this might help. It's all just such a shame." Estelle choked back her emotions.

"Yes, it is, Mrs. Cruz. I'm in the middle of something right now, however, I will discuss this with the detective in charge of Jessica's investigation. Maybe I can reach out to you later to discuss a time we might pick up that note if that's okay with you."

"Yes, that's fine. I do hope it will help. I'll speak to you soon, Ms. Hart. Goodbye."

———

ALLISON RETURNED her phone to her purse. "You're not going to believe who that was."

Charlie turned to her.

"Estelle Cruz, Tony's mother. She was going through his things and found a note from Jessica."

At this, Lucy and Brenner's attention turned to her. Brenner continued. "A note?"

"Yep," Allison said. "She read it to me. It appears that Jessica left something for Tony, she didn't know what it was, and that Jessica had wished him a good life."

"That's it?" Charlie asked. "And we have no idea what she gave him."

"Not a clue," Allison replied. "What do we make of that, Detective?"

Brenner rubbed his stubbly chin. "I don't know. Is she willing to hand it over to us?"

"She is. Maybe we should go there once we're finished here? I'd like to see it for myself. Not that I expect the words to change, but I don't know. That's a little strange that he wouldn't have made mention of it before," Allison continued. "I'd talked to him twice. Lucy talked to him, what, once or twice?"

"Twice," Lucy replied. "Never said a word about it."

"Maybe he forgot about it? Maybe he'd had it for a while?" Charlie asked. "Could be anything from any time."

Allison nodded. "True. Thing is, Tony kept a lot from us, including the fact that he had the necklace."

"Uh, hey guys, you might want to come check this out." Emily rolled back in her chair, slouched down and wearing a smile.

"You got in?" Brenner asked as he hurried toward her. "If you did that, young lady, you need to work for the FBI."

"Ha! As if!" She scoffed. "Look, this software isn't reliable, but I'm working on that. I was able to break the passcode and see the apps that were running. The apps that had been closed, I can't get into. I hope it's what you're looking for."

"Did you find a messaging app on there?" Lucy asked. "A private, encrypted chat app, not SMS."

Emily keyed in a few commands and the screen on her laptop changed. "You mean this one here?" She eyed Lucy. "You got lucky. It was open. See for yourself." She stepped out of the way.

Lucy moved in and gazed at the screen. "I think this is what we've been looking for." She shot a look to Allison. "We're about to find out who this phone belonged to."

24

A win on the armed robbery investigation would set off Shane on the right foot inside his new department. While he had no one in custody yet, the evidence pointed to a known career criminal. However, he let his focus remain fixed on what had happened last night to Allison. He should have walked her to her car. It was a mistake he wouldn't repeat.

"Hey, Sully."

Shane was pulled back into the moment and turned his sights to the uniformed officer at his desk. "Adelson. What's up?"

Officer Tom Adelson worked in Traffic and had been the responding officer for the deadly accident involving Tony Cruz. "Got some news on the owner of the car in that hit and run yesterday."

"The Cruz accident?"

"Yes, sir." Adelson dropped a file onto Shane's desk. "The plates had been taken off the vehicle, but we picked up the VIN."

Shane opened the manila folder. "How the hell did you manage that?"

"The red-light camera snapped the picture when the car ran into the intersection. Got a look at the driver, not enough to figure out who he is yet. Son of a bitch wore a hoodie and sunglasses. But more importantly, the camera captured the VIN on the driver's side dashboard. You can see it through the windshield clear as day when you zoom in on it. From there, it only takes entering that number to pull up ownership details."

"Who owns the car?" Shane asked.

"Check it out. It's right there in the file."

Shane quickly scanned the details. "Who is this guy?"

"No one, as far as I know. But when I scratched around for more info, I discovered the car had been repossessed and sold at auction."

Shane nodded as he re-read the details. "Who bought it?"

Adelson pointed to the notes in the file. "This guy, right there."

———

ALLISON STUDIED the messages contained on the burner that appeared on Emily's screen. "It has to be her. Who else would've threatened Jessica like that?"

"No mention of names. Whoever it was made a point of that," Brenner added.

"You're right, but it's implied. Come on, Detective," Charlie pleaded. "We know it was the wife. Lyman's wife had to send those two messages. And look at the earlier ones?"

"I know, Charlie. I saw them."

"There were other girls, and she knew about them. She knew about all of them. Only this time, she decided to do something about it," Charlie added.

Brenner turned to Emily. "How do we keep this open so the phone doesn't lock again, and I can access it?"

"Now that I'm in, I can wipe the passcode. You'll be able to access it without one. I can back all this up onto a flash drive too if you want."

"Please do." Brenner turned back to the partners. "I'll concede that these messages suggest Mrs. Lyman made the threats, however, the gun found in Jessica's hand only had her prints on it, and it was unregistered. We have nothing tying the murder weapon to Mrs. Lyman."

"How do we prove it belonged to her?" Allison asked.

Brenner eyed her. "Assuming you're right, I don't know. And it won't be easy to find out."

———

ALLISON HAD STUCK to her guns and got the answers she needed. This case was still far from over, but they learned the truth that Jessica Healey hadn't committed suicide. The problem was, they had no proof that it was Mrs. Lyman who pulled the trigger. But the client needed an update, now Allison had to figure out just what to tell her.

She gazed through the passenger window of Charlie's SUV when Charlie called out to her.

"Earth to Alli," Charlie said.

"What's that? Sorry, I was just thinking about what to say to Mary Ann."

"I need to know if we're heading back to the office," Charlie replied.

"Might as well. Brenner's working on a way to get Mrs. Lyman in for questioning. We can't do that for him." Allison glanced at her phone as a call rang in. "It's Shane." She answered. "Hey."

"Allison, we know who owned the car that hit Cruz and killed him."

"Who?" She tapped Charlie's thigh to gain her attention. "Whose car was it?"

At this, Lucy pulled up from the back seat and both waited for Allison to reveal the news.

"It was registered to a man by the name of Raymond Chavez."

"Who is that?" Allison deflated quicker than a balloon in the hot sun.

"Don't know yet, but here's the real kicker. The car was sold at auction after it got repo'd and the bill of sale shows it was purchased by Dr. Jacob Lyman about a month ago. He never registered it, so the old owner's details were pulled up. After my buddy in Traffic discovered Chavez lapsed on the bank payments and the bank turned it over to auction, he contacted the auction house to find out who purchased it. The new owner paid cash, but by law, was required to show ID. I'm betting Lyman never thought it was that easy to track down a car purchase."

"So it was Lyman's car." A measure of hope resurfaced in her tone. "Who was driving?"

"They don't know yet. Of course, Lyman can try to talk his way out of it. Claim it was stolen or whatever, but it'll be a tough sell, all things considered."

"That, along with the fact that we know the burner belonged to Lyman's wife."

"His wife?" Shane asked.

"That's right. Lucy pulled a rabbit out of a hat and tracked down someone who unlocked the phone for us. We found two threatening messages via an app. She was smart enough not to reveal her name, but the contents of those messages suggest it was Lyman's wife. Brenner was with us and now he's going to bring in Mrs. Lyman for questioning."

"Then I'll stick around here until he gets back and give him a head's up about the accident. He'll need that information," Shane replied. "I'll catch up with you later?"

"Yeah. Sounds good." Allison ended the call.

"Lyman owned the car, huh?" Charlie asked. "I don't think any amount of money Lyman has will be able to get them out of this one."

"There's still a lot to prove on our end. Well, Brenner's end," Allison added.

"There might be something we can do to help things along."

Allison lifted a brow. "Okay, Ms. Wells, what do you have up your sleeve?"

———

THE NOTE WRITTEN by Jessica and found in the backpack belonging to Tony Cruz was handed over to Detective Brenner. But not before Estelle Cruz emailed a picture of that note to Allison. Thanks to Charlie's idea, it was time to confirm the details.

"First thing we need to do is determine whether Jessica wrote this note herself," Charlie said. "Sadly, Tony isn't here to let us know when he received it. And at this point, I don't want to make assumptions. The idea Lyman's wife had concocted a plan to track down Jessica makes more and more sense. So, let's not assume she had no part in planting this note to reinforce the whole suicide story."

"Mary Ann said it looked like Jessica's handwriting, but we have enough here to corroborate that." Lucy retrieved a box provided by Mary Ann Healey that contained several examples of Jessica's handwriting. Class notes, birthday cards written to her family members. They'd gone down this road once before, but for a different reason.

"But she has no idea what Jessica left for him?" Charlie asked.

Lucy stopped for a moment and froze in place.

"What is it?" Allison asked her.

She slowly turned her gaze to them. "The necklace. It has to be. Tony admitted to finding it on his doorstep. The note said she wanted to leave something for him to remember their time together. That necklace had a picture of the two of them inside the pendant."

"Then the necklace turns up in Jessica's room shortly after Tony's visit," Allison added. "Lucy, you're right. The note had to be in reference to the necklace. Which makes it all the more important to confirm what we're looking at is Jessica's handwriting, because if it isn't..."

Lucy's gaze turned serious. "Then it has to be her killer's."

———

SHANE STOOD behind the guest chair in Brenner's office, his hands pressed against it. "So, what do you think?"

Brenner eyed him. "I think without tire tracks on the side of the highway where the Healey car was, it's a long shot to prove it was the same vehicle."

Shane nodded. "I get that. What if we make a trip to the auction house and take a look at their records? Particularly, the bill of sale for that car."

"What good will that do? Adelson already confirmed the car was purchased by Jacob Lyman."

"Yeah, but something doesn't fit. Lyman has a solid alibi. He was with some girl at a hotel. We know he didn't kill Jessica Healey. Yet he bought a car, more than a week prior, doesn't get it titled or registered in his name, then all of a sudden, it's used to ram Tony Cruz's vehicle in the middle of an intersection? That would mean Lyman knew Cruz was going to sit in front of his house and threaten him." Shane shook his head. "It doesn't make sense."

Brenner stood from his desk and swiped his keys. "I think I see where this is going. This was your idea, you want to check it out with me?"

"You bet." Shane followed him through the station and swiped his keys along the way. "It's the Car Market Auction House in South Tampa."

Brenner pushed through the doors and into the bright afternoon daylight. He slipped on his aviator-style sunglasses and unlocked his car. "Get in."

Shane stepped into the passenger side of the black Ford Fusion. "Nice car."

"Got it at auction." Brenner cracked a smile before slipping behind the wheel. "You have a copy of the bill of sale?"

"I'll have Adelson text it to me now." Shane typed the message.

"So, you and Hart have something going on?" Brenner asked, pointedly.

"I'm sorry, what?" The question hit Shane like a brick wall.

"Oh, come on, man. I see the way you are around her. I hear you two have been through a lot recently. You helped her out of a jam or two."

"She's done the same for me."

"I heard that," Brenner added. "So, you two together or what?"

Apparently, he wasn't going to let this go and Shane feared letting the cat out of the bag. Allison wouldn't want anyone in the department to know because she'd worked hard to establish a professional relationship with the detectives. The ones who had already worked with her respected her, but in one fell swoop, Shane could wipe all that away if he were to answer in the affirmative. On the other hand, he wanted to tell the world he was in love with Allison Hart. She was smart, beautiful, and had more determination in her pinky than most people had in their entire bodies. So, yeah, he was proud as hell.

"Uh, no, man. We're friends. Been friends for a long time. We got a little closer since she opened her firm, but nah, it isn't personal."

"Huh," Brenner nodded. "So, you wouldn't have a problem with me asking her out?"

"What? Uh, no. Why would I?" Shane unleashed a nervous laugh. "Hey, that's the place up ahead."

"What gave it away? All the shitty cars in the parking lot?" Brenner chuckled and turned into the lot. "They keep the good ones in the back guarded by their attack dogs." He stopped the car and stepped out, pushing a hand through his brown hair and smoothing down his dress shirt.

Shane joined him as they walked atop the crushed gravel lot toward the construction trailer with a metal staircase leading to the door. Behind the trailer appeared to be a large warehouse.

Brenner walked inside where a waft of stale cigarettes and flatulence gave him pause. He turned back to Shane with raised brows.

Shane tried to hold back his amusement.

"Afternoon. What can I do for you boys?" A man who appeared to be in his sixties and was heavy-set, pulled up at attention. "Auctions are Tuesdays and Thursdays, 7pm."

"We're not here for a car." Brenner retrieved his badge. "Need to check out your paperwork on a car you sold a few weeks ago."

The man raised his hands preemptively. "Look, once a car rolls off this lot, it ain't my responsibility no more."

"But you are responsible for keeping records of purchases,"

Brenner continued. "We're looking to see who bought one of your cars."

"Fair enough. You got a make and model? VIN would be useful if you got that," the man replied.

"I have a VIN for you." Brenner retrieved a slip of paper and set it down on the man's worn desk.

He slipped on his reading glasses and typed the number on his keyboard slower than a dog playing piano. It didn't help that his computer looked to be ten years old. "Okay, let's see what we have here." He raised his chin and looked down on the screen where his bifocals would magnify the information. "2008 white Nissan Altima. Buyer paid cash."

The man spoke about as expeditiously as he typed, and Brenner's fuse burned to the quick. "I understand that an ID is required for purchase. Do you have the buyer's ID scanned in?"

"Well, not exactly. We have a driver's license number." He typed again and pulled up a new screen. "Looks like it belonged to one Dr. Jacob Lyman."

"But you didn't copy the license?" Shane asked.

"No, sir. So long as we have a valid driver's license. Is there a problem here?" He looked down his nose at them.

"Yes, there is," Brenner began. "Let me ask you this, do you have security footage around here?"

"Well, sure. We got lots of money sitting here in this lot. Tell me what you need. I'll get it for you."

"The day that car was purchased. We need to see the footage from the auction," Brenner replied.

"You got it. It'll take me a few moments. Can I offer either of you a cup of coffee or a soda pop while you wait?"

"I wouldn't mind a soda," Shane replied.

Brenner gave him the side-eye. "Nothing for me thanks. We

are, however, in a bit of a hurry. How long you think this will take?"

"Oh, not long," the man replied. "Just need to go into the back room over here and pull up the files. We keep them up in some cloud or something. I don't know exactly. Had my nephew set it up for me last year. To be honest, I never really needed to take a look at it, so I'm not sure of the process." He shrugged it off.

Brenner pursed his lips. "Great. Well, please just do the best you can." After the man walked away, he turned to Shane. "Christ Almighty, we're going to be here a while."

25

With each comparison made, it became clear that the note given to Tony was not written by Jessica Healey. It was close, like someone had studied her handwriting before attempting the forgery, but it was not hers.

Allison studied the papers before her. "Who wrote it, then? And when had it been left for Tony?"

"I think we know, Alli. I think this was a set up all along. Jessica was targeted. I don't know what part Tony Cruz played in that or why he's now dead." Charlie eyed her partners. "Do I need to state the obvious? We're all thinking it. We know Lyman has an alibi. Tony Cruz clearly wasn't there, so who's left?" She peered at them. "The friends were together. We now know it wasn't a random road rage incident."

"If it had been, the killer wouldn't have taken care to make it look like a suicide," Lucy replied.

"Exactly." Charlie laced her fingers on the table. "Come on, ladies. It's time to face facts. The only one left is Lyman's wife."

"Her prints were nowhere to be found. Not in Jessica's car. Not on the gun. Not on the burner," Allison replied.

"But the messages are from her," Lucy said.

"We know that, but we still can't prove it." Charlie inhaled a breath. "It's going to come down to this note. Lyman's wife somehow tracked down Jessica. Got her to pull off to the side of the road and then she killed her. We just need to prove it was the wife who left the necklace and this note for Tony Cruz in attempt to reinforce the suicide theory. It's the only way to firmly place her at the scene. The burner is great, but too easy to answer for. She tossed it out the window, it wasn't hers, whatever excuse she can think of."

"The partial print," Allison said.

"What print?" Charlie asked.

"The partial on the necklace that Brenner couldn't match to anyone in Jessica's circle. He has to get the wife to submit prints. The phone? The note? She's done." Allison gauged the partners. "That's the answer."

The front door opened and drew the partners' attention. Lucy stood from the conference table. "Hello?"

"Ms. Hart." Harriet Torres walked inside and trailing her was Madison and Nia. "Is it okay if we come in?"

"Of course." Allison stood from the table. "What can we do for you girls?"

Charlie started toward them. "Is everything okay?"

"Um, yeah," Madison replied. "We just got together and decided we should come talk to you guys about something."

"Okay. Why don't you three come and take a seat here?" Allison gestured to the table. "You want anything to drink?"

"No, thank you." Harriet sat down.

"I think we're okay, Ms. Hart." Madison sat down next to her, followed by Nia.

"All right. "So, what can we do for you?" Allison returned to the table.

"Well..." Harriet glanced to the others for approval before continuing. "Um, our friend, Sophie."

"Yeah." Charlie pulled out a chair and took her seat.

"We were all hanging out last night. She came over kind of late. Harriet was working," Madison said. "But we told her what happened."

"What happened?" Allison pressed on.

"Sophie confessed to us," Nia cut in. "Not like she did something...well, she did do something."

"Just tell her," Harriet pressed on.

"Okay. Sophie told us that she went to Dr. Lyman's house a couple of times and the second time she went, she told his wife that he hooked up with Nia, Jess, and others," Madison continued.

"I see," Allison began. "And did she say what his wife did after that?"

"Just that she kind of looked dead or something. Like she had no reaction," Madison replied. "So Sophie took off. She said she was freaked out and just drove away."

"Lyman's wife knew." Charlie peered at Allison. "Falls right in line with what we just discussed. I wonder if she confronted her husband after that."

"Lyman doesn't strike me as a man who fesses up to his transgressions," Allison replied. "Although anything's possible."

"If she didn't confront him, maybe the wife learned about the website. Saw everything right there in black and white, then started threatening Jessica," Lucy replied.

"That website isn't something you'd just happen to stumble on. That's not to say the wife didn't do some digging after that and found it." Charlie turned to Allison. "We need to let Brenner know about this, especially if he's preparing to talk to her."

"I agree." Allison looked to the girls again. "Is there anything else you can tell us?"

Madison shook her head. "Is Sophie going to be arrested?"

"Arrested? No. She didn't do anything wrong," Allison replied.

"Sophie told us she was jealous of Tony and then Dr. Lyman," Madison said. "She said they tried to take Jess away from her."

"So she tried to implode Lyman's personal life," Charlie added. "But in the process, it might have been the catalyst."

"Catalyst for what?" Harriet asked.

Allison glanced at her partners before turning back to Harriet. "For Jessica's murder."

———

THE OLDER MAN meandered back to his desk. "I am sorry about that, fellas. I think I have what you're looking for now. You want to come on back and have a look-see?"

Brenner pushed off the chair. "Yes, sir. Thank you."

Shane followed him, tossing back the last of his Pepsi.

They entered a small storage room where boxes of files were stacked on rolling metal carts. A folding table was pushed against the wall under a window and held two monitors and a keyboard. Beneath it was a CPU.

"I had to call my nephew," the man began. "Which was why it took me so long, but he was able to point me in the right direction. I pulled up the day in question. Please have a seat and see if it'll help you boys out with what you're looking for."

Brenner sat down in the putty-colored metal folding chair and slipped on his glasses.

"You need me to take a look?" Shane asked.

Brenner glared at him. "I got it."

Shane held up his hands. "Sorry, just trying to help."

"Besides, you aren't that far off from needing these either, brother." Brenner pointed to his reading glasses.

Shane raised his shoulders and cracked a smile. "We'll see."

Brenner shook his head and turned back to the screen. "This is the day?"

"Yes, sir. Just like you asked," the man replied.

He played the video, noting the time. "Hey, is there a time written on the bill of sale?"

"No, sir, but the auctions don't start till 7pm. That might narrow things down a bit for you."

"Of course, yeah. Thanks." Brenner sped up the frames until the time reached 7 o'clock. "Here we are." He peered at the screen. "How long before the auction ends? Is that when you do all the paperwork?"

"Yep. I'd say a good hour. Maybe 90 minutes."

"Then let me just speed through all this."

"Wait," Shane jumped in. "Don't you want to see if he's in there? Lyman?"

"I'd rather see him signing the paperwork." Brenner pushed the fast-forward button again. "I'll go a little slower in case something pops out."

Shane stood behind Brenner and viewed the screen while the old man stepped out into the main office again. He let out a long sigh.

"You got someplace else you'd rather be, Sully?" Brenner asked. "I thought you wanted to see this through?"

"I do. I just hope we aren't wasting our time."

"You and me, both." Brenner slowed down the video. "All right. We're getting close now. Looks like people are leaving. Got a few hangers-on. Probably buyers."

"You see Lyman in there?"

"Not yet, gimme a second." Brenner leaned in a little closer and pressed the plus sign on the screen to zoom in the video. "There's a line there. I hope to hell we can get a closer look."

Shane squatted down. "I can see them."

Brenner glared at him once again. "What's your point?"

"Nothing. Absolutely nothing."

They turned their attention to the screen again. Shane narrowed his eyes. "Hey, you have a picture of the wife?"

"What? Not on me, why?"

"I don't see Jacob Lyman in that line right there. What I do see are two women." He turned to Brenner. "What if one of them is Lyman's wife?"

"Shit. Pull out your phone. Google her. With as high-profile as he is, there's bound to be a picture of his wife with him at some event."

Shane retrieved his phone and typed in Lyman's name. The screen populated with several articles, including one that stated he was joining the University of Tampa teaching staff. "Here! Right here." He turned the phone to Brenner. "That's his wife according to the caption below."

They both returned to the monitor when Shane continued. "Brenner, that's her. Right there."

"Wouldn't you know? She used his driver's license number to make it look like her husband bought the car. Was she setting him up to take the fall?"

"Why else use his name? But if that's the case, then who drove the car right into Tony Cruz?" Shane asked.

"Hell. Could be anyone." Brenner studied the now-frozen image of Mrs. Brianne Lyman. "One thing's for sure. This makes it pretty damn clear she knew the shenanigans her husband was up to and appeared to have a plan to handle it."

———

BRIANNE LYMAN, the 28-year-old former software executive, walked to the foyer when her front door opened. "Where have you been? We need to figure this out before the detective arrives."

Jacob Lyman walked inside and set down his carrier bag. "I had a class. I can't just skip out on it without having a sub in place. I already told you that there's nothing to worry about, okay? He's just coming over to talk about the car accident."

"Because it was the guy who sat in front of our house?" she asked.

"Yes."

Brianne headed into the kitchen. "Well, I don't know what that has to do with us anyway. I didn't know him. I have no idea who he was." She grabbed a water from the fridge. "Ever since your student decided to off herself, it's like everyone's looking at us. Why is that, Jacob?" She set her sights on him and moved toward the kitchen island. "Why is it that every time something happens at that school, they look to you?"

"Me?" He scoffed. "What the hell is that supposed to mean? I didn't cause Tony Cruz to get into an accident and I didn't make my student take her own life."

Jacob grabbed a beer from the fridge and twisted off the cap. "This is just them giving me more grief because everyone wants to go after the rich tech guy. Well, screw that, Brianne. I'm not their punching bag anymore. Assholes." He tossed back a long swig.

She walked toward him and placed her hand on his shoulder. "You know, maybe it's time you step back from the school. It's not like they pay you a lot and we certainly don't need the money anyway. It's more trouble than it's worth, Jacob. Look at us? Look at what they're doing to us?" She kissed his shoulder. "Go back to what you do best. You're far too brilliant to teach those spoiled little brats. You could get into another startup. I could help you, just like before. We could do it together. Just the two of us."

Jacob turned to her. "They're going to reopen Jessica Healey's investigation. It's no longer considered a suicide. Brianne, they're saying someone murdered her."

"What?" She pulled back. "Is that the real reason why the detective is coming here?"

"Partly. It is about Tony Cruz too, but he's in charge of the Healey case as well."

"What does this mean? Are you a suspect or something? Jacob, what the hell?"

"I didn't kill her, Brianne."

"Do they think it was you? Jesus, Jacob, were you sleeping with her?"

———

THE DETECTIVES RETURNED to the station and Brenner marched on toward his office. "Let's see if we can match up the tires of that Altima to what you and Hart found on the scene of Jessica's murder. The immediate area came up a bust for me when we first looked into it. Found some that tracked back to police-issue patrol cars, but that's it."

"If you're able to put the same car that hit Tony Cruz at the scene of the Healey murder, then it's over for Brianne Lyman." Shane hurried to keep up with him when his phone buzzed. "Hang on." He placed it against his ear. "Yeah, Allison, what's up?"

"We're at the office and a couple of things popped up. The note that Mrs. Cruz found in Tony's belongings was not written by Jessica."

"What?" he stopped in the hall.

"We compared it to several writing samples we had of Jessica's and I know we're not experts, but they don't jibe," Allison replied. "Then something completely unexpected happened."

"Another shoe? Okay, tell me." Shane peered up again and noticed Brenner had disappeared and had probably gone into his office.

"The girls came by. Jessica's friends. All but one—Sophie Matthews. Apparently, Sophie came to them last night and mentioned she had gone to the Lyman home twice and confronted the wife. She told her about Lyman's conquests."

He inhaled a breath. "Brenner and I tracked down the buyer of the car that struck Tony Cruz and killed him. Allison, Mrs. Lyman bought that car with cash and used her husband's driver's license number to do it. I'm just now walking into Brenner's office to see if the tires on that car match the tracks we found at the scene of Jessica's murder."

"The pictures you took? They aren't the best considering the rain afterward."

"I know, but it's all I have, and we need to put that car at the scene where Jessica died."

"So that would put this car at the scene of both murders, Cruz and Jessica," she pressed on.

"The evidence is mounting, Allison. The phone, the car, the note."

"And the necklace," Allison cut in. "I was going to call Brenner and ask him to get Mrs. Lyman to submit prints. He pulled a partial off the necklace. Shane, it looks like we have Mrs. Lyman on the hook."

Shane noticed Brenner peek his head out of his office. "I gotta go. Brenner's waiting. I'll keep you posted."

"Okay, bye."

Shane hurried into the office. "That was Allison. Looks like Mrs. Lyman knew about her husband's infidelities."

Brenner cocked his head. "Motive."

"Yep. But why not target the husband instead of the girls?"

"Based on what we found, it sure looks like she was trying to frame him. Well, while you were on the phone with Hart, I pulled the photos initially taken at the Healey scene. I gotta tell you, I can't tell my ass from my elbow on those pictures. Track marks everywhere and nothing discernable. If we were looking to get a link to the auction car, we ain't doing it this way."

"Don't throw in the towel yet." Shane opened his phone. "I have my photos from the scene."

"Send 'em my way. I'll need to input them into the database," Brenner said.

Shane typed on his phone. "Done."

A moment later, they appeared in Brenner's inbox. "All right. Maybe you guys saw something we didn't."

"In all fairness, you guys weren't looking for a suspect."

"Thanks, but you don't need to sugar-coat it for me, Sully. We were all certain what it was based on the evidence presented. As you know, it doesn't always work that way." He pulled up the images and loaded them into the database. "Okay. Let's see what she spits back out at us."

Brenner pulled back and folded his arms across his broad chest. When the results appeared, he slipped on his glasses again. "Well, what do you know? 75% match." He looked at Shane.

"Close enough?"

"Hell yeah, it's close enough for me. With everything else we have? It's about as close as we're going to get." Brenner stood. "Thanks for the help, brother. I gotta run. I'm late for a very important date."

26

Allison wanted to be there to hear, first-hand, what happened to Jessica Healey. But this was Brenner's deal now and the time had come to question Mrs. Brianne Lyman.

The video evidence Jacob Lyman presented to Allison was sent to Brenner, so he was going in knowing there was only one person who could've killed Jessica. Still, barring a confession, most of what they had was circumstantial unless Brianne Lyman's prints matched the partial on the necklace. Even the tire tracks were a stretch for any D.A.

"She must be there by now." Charlie perched on the edge of her desk, drinking a can of soda.

Allison paced the office. "There is still something that I don't get. When Tony's car was hit, the driver fled. We all know that. It wasn't Jacob Lyman or his wife driving. So one of them had to have someone ready and waiting, essentially. Like they were expecting Tony to show up."

"There's no indication it was planned," Charlie replied. "The kid took off from the funeral and drove to Lyman's house because he was upset. He blamed Lyman for Jessica's death."

"Did someone set him off?" Lucy asked. "At the funeral. Do you think someone talked to him and convinced him of Lyman's guilt?"

"Nia?" Charlie asked. "She was dating him. And had gone out with Lyman, which we knew Tony wasn't happy about."

"That would mean Tony had to tell her where he was going," Lucy replied. "And maybe she warned Lyman?"

"Sure, but that would give him mere minutes to arrange for a driver." Charlie tossed her soda can into the trash and joined Allison in the center of the office. "And why would Lyman then jump to the conclusion that Tony posed as some sort of threat."

"Because he told me." Allison stopped pacing. "When I went back with him to his office, he said Tony had threatened him before."

"I can't wrap my head around it," Charlie began. "Maybe Brianne Lyman was at the funeral, tracked down Tony to talk to him, and convinced him this was all her husband's fault and that he should do something about that."

Allison nodded. "It would be a good way to get herself off the hook and Tony onto it. I don't recall seeing her there but that doesn't mean she wasn't. That would be a question for Brenner to ask."

"Except Tony wasn't at the Lyman home for very long. We don't know what transpired, but he left. So if Brianne had hoped Tony would take care of Lyman, he didn't. Then he died," Charlie replied.

Allison returned to her desk and studied the image of the note left for Tony. "The only ones who know what happened to Tony and Jessica are the Lymans. It's this note." She eyed Lucy. "Can you help me with looking into something?"

"You got it. Tell me what I need to do."

———

BRENNER WALKED into the interview room where Jacob and Brianne Lyman waited. "Your lawyer is here."

Will Harris walked in and eyed Jacob Lyman immediately. "Neither of you need to say anything."

Brenner closed the door behind them and continued inside. "In the spirit of cooperation, they've agreed to come in and answer a few questions for me. Let's start with the 2008 Nissan Altima that was involved in vehicular homicide as well as its tire tracks found on the scene where Jessica Healey was murdered."

"Murdered?" Harris sat down at the table. "It's murder now, is it?"

"Since a ballistics expert reexamined the autopsy report of Ms. Healey, yes, sir, it is." Brenner leaned against the wall. "Mr. and Mrs. Lyman, now is the time to offer clarification. We have evidence that Mrs. Lyman purchased the Altima at auction more than 3 weeks ago but failed to get it registered in the State of Florida."

"Look, that car was stolen," Lyman began. "Probably by the same person who let it get repossessed."

"I figured you might say something to that effect," Brenner added before eying Mrs. Lyman. "Brianne, a phone was found near the scene where Jessica Healey's car was discovered. Messages were recovered from that phone. Do you know anything about that?"

She turned stone-faced. "Why would I? I have no idea what you're talking about. I don't know what any of this has to do with me. I didn't buy a car at an auction. Why would I?"

Brenner pulled out his phone and swiped open the video

showing her at the auction house. "You sure about that, Mrs. Lyman?"

Jacob glanced at the video and to her. "Like I said, the car was stolen, and we just hadn't had a chance to call it in."

"Yet it was at your house the day Tony Cruz showed up and then died in an accident involving that same car only minutes later." Brenner sized them up. "Mrs. Lyman, you can come clean now, or I can get a warrant for your bank records, search your home, your car. And most importantly, I can make you submit fingerprints and DNA. I can make life very uncomfortable for you, ma'am. Unless you are 100 percent certain you didn't leave any evidence behind, then I suggest you make this easier on yourself."

Harris eyed Jacob Lyman and Lyman shook his head.

Brenner picked up on the exchange. "You have something to say, Jacob? The warrant will cover everything of yours too. Think about it."

Lyman turned defiant. "Whatever you have to do, Detective. My wife and I have nothing to hide."

"Is that so?" Brenner scoffed. "Then I guess we'll do things the hard way." He walked out of the room and into the hall where Allison and Charlie waited. "What are you guys doing here? I'm kind of in the middle of something."

"We've been trying to understand how Tony Cruz got caught up with the Lymans and died as a result," Allison said.

Brenner eyed them with reservation. "Someone hit him with a car owned by the Lymans and killed him."

"Yes, but we'd been going back and forth trying to figure out how the Lymans knew Tony would be at their house right after the funeral," Allison continued. "Then we came up with something."

"Detective Brenner, we were convinced that Brianne Lyman used Tony to prove that Jessica had killed herself," Charlie began. "We were sure she wrote the note for Tony and left it along with the necklace Jessica was seen wearing the day she and her friends left for Daytona."

He folded his arms across his chest and held Charlie's gaze. "And what do you think now?"

"It wasn't Brianne Lyman's handwriting. We went back to the mermaid trinket Jacob Lyman gave to Jessica and the note attached to it," Charlie replied. "Detective, you can see for yourself, but it matches Jacob's handwriting."

"So the two were working together, is that what I'm hearing from you?" Brenner asked.

Allison and Charlie traded awkward glances before Allison continued. "Yes and no. We think Brianne Lyman confronted her husband about his infidelities because we learned Sophie Matthews told her. And we're sure he denied them. But we don't think she gave up so easily."

"You ladies are going to have to speed this up. I got three people in that room with more money than I'll make in my life-time. Tell me where this is going," Brenner demanded.

"Alli, you go on," Charlie said.

"We're pretty confident Brianne Lyman followed Jessica back to Tampa. The logistics of that, I think, we need to confirm with the woman herself. However, when she returned that day, I believe Jacob found the necklace, knew it was Jessica's, and then discovered the next day that Jessica had died. I think Jacob has been trying to hide what his wife had done, but we got to the truth anyway."

"I'll tell you what, how about we go back in there and see what those two have to say about this?" Brenner asked. "It needs to come from them and I sure as hell hope you two are right."

The Lymans conversed with their attorney when Brenner opened the door. "Sorry to keep you waiting. There's something these ladies would like to ask you about, Mrs. Lyman." He gestured for Charlie to begin.

"What the hell is this?" Harris asked. "You're the private investigators."

"They are." Brenner held up his hands. "Let them speak."

"Mrs. Lyman, are you aware of a website called GoBa?" Charlie asked.

"GoBa? No."

"It's a website built by someone who attends the university. It essentially rates hookups from those at the school."

"Okay. What does that have to do with me?" she asked.

Allison appeared to note Lyman's shifty expression. "I think your husband is very familiar with it, aren't you, Jacob? In fact, when you showed me the footage of you and another pretty young woman at a hotel the day Jessica was murdered, I mentioned it to you then."

Jacob Lyman remained stone-faced.

Charlie continued. "Mrs. Lyman, I think you do know about that site because you have an account on it." She pulled up the information on her phone. "One of our partners happens to be whip-smart when it comes to all things computers and social media. She was able to find your account, even though you used a fake name. It appears you learned a lot and discovered Jessica on that site too. You friended her, then followed her on other social media sites. And of course, we all know kids these days document every single thing in their lives, including their travel plans. Jessica posted that she was going to Daytona Beach for Spring Break. You followed her there, didn't you?"

"You were planning on confronting her then, weren't you, Mrs. Lyman?" Allison added.

"You then discovered she was leaving and followed her as she headed back toward the city," Charlie added. "Did you know she was going home to see her father who had just had a heart attack?" She eyed her. "Didn't think so."

"THAT WAS when you sent her the messages via a burner phone with an encrypted app while she was driving back to Tampa. You threatened her, Mrs. Lyman," Allison said. "I'll bet when Detective Brenner pulls the warrant, he'll find that it was you who purchased the burner. I'm guessing you didn't think to use cash because you hadn't planned on killing anyone. Just wanted it to track down those who you thought were responsible for your husband's wandering eye."

"You came up on her in the Altima, scared her until she finally pulled over," Charlie added. "That was your chance."

"I think we've heard enough here," Harris began. "You have zero proof of any of this. Is this how you run your investigations, Detective Brenner? By allowing hacks like these two run the show?"

"Sounds like they hit a nerve," Brenner said. "That left Mr. Lyman to find a way to cover it up. I'd say using Tony Cruz as cover was a smart move. You found the necklace, or your wife confessed to what she'd done and gave it to you. Either way, you wrote that note and left it and the necklace on Tony Cruz's doorstep. Things went a little south from there, didn't they? You decided the kid needed to die too."

"We'll see you in court." The attorney stood and turned to his clients. "It's time to go."

"The picture you sent to Nia Brown of Tony and another girl was a nice touch, Dr. Lyman," Allison jumped in. "You did your best to try to point everything at Tony Cruz. Nia handed over her phone and showed us."

"Don't say anything." The lawyer escorted them out of the interview room.

Brenner turned to the partners. "I guess that's it then. All we need to do is figure out who drove the Altima that killed Tony Cruz. But I suspect those two will be all too willing to cooperate on that front. They'll try to take down with them everyone they can. Those two have a lot of money and folks are willing to do all sorts of things for money."

Brenner inhaled a deep breath through his nose. "I'll be the first to admit we screwed up here. I'm not sure I've seen anything quite as sad as this situation. Mary Ann Healey did a fine job bringing you all into this." He extended his hand. "Allison, Charlie. I'd be happy to work with you guys anytime."

Allison took his hand. "Thank you, Detective. A friend once told me all it takes is to see something in a new light. We weren't convinced of anything other than your initial conclusion. So, we understand where you're coming from. Thank you, though, for putting your faith in us."

He returned a grin. "Be sure to tell Lucy I'd love to hire her out some time for her social media expertise."

———

CHARLIE TURNED off the ignition and peered at Allison. "You ready?" She turned back at Lucy. "And you?"

"Ready," Lucy replied.

"Same here." Allison stepped out of the SUV and waited for her partners to join her. "Let's give them the news."

They approached the Healey home where Mary Ann stood behind the screen door.

"Good afternoon," Allison began.

"Please come in." Mary Ann stepped aside. "Jim is in the

living room. Please, go on ahead. Can I get you all anything to drink?"

"Thank you, no. I think we'll just be here for a few minutes." Allison walked into the living room to find Jim sitting up on the sofa. "You're looking better every day, Mr. Healey."

"I'm recovering from the surgery. I suspect the rest of the healing will take some time."

"Of course." Allison took a seat across from him and waited for Lucy and Charlie to join her. As Mrs. Healey entered, Allison continued. "As you know, we just left the station where Mr. and Mrs. Lyman were being questioned."

"Yes. And?" Mary Ann asked.

"Where can I start but by saying that your instincts were on target, Mrs. Healey," Allison began. "From the moment you walked into our office, you knew Jessica hadn't taken her own life. And we were able to pull together enough to prove that you were right."

"Oh, my." Mary Ann grabbed her husband's hand while her eyes welled.

"Mary Ann, your daughter's life was taken by a woman who was angry at her husband. I'm sorry to say Jessica got caught in the middle," Allison continued. "But she will pay the price for what she's done."

"I don't understand. How could someone do this to my Jess?" Jim asked.

Allison considered for a moment how she felt when she learned of Leo's affair. How angry she had been. How she had wanted to beat the living hell out of the woman he'd slept with. But what it boiled down to was Leo himself. It was Leo who made the decision. So she could understand how Brianne Lyman felt, but the tragedy that resulted was inexcusable.

"All I can tell you, Mr. Healey, is that some people can't

control their pain. They lash out, even against those who weren't responsible for it. Jessica was young and made a poor decision. A man who was in a position of authority over her aided in that decision. He should've known better. And who among us didn't make poor decisions in our youth? She didn't deserve to die for it."

Charlie appeared to notice Allison's voice falter. "The fact remains, Mr. and Mrs. Healey, is that Jessica will get the justice she deserves. I hope that will provide you with some solace. Some closure."

"I suppose I had resolved myself to the fact that my baby wasn't coming home again," Mary Ann began. "I just knew that she would have never done what they said she had. I want to thank the three of you for making everyone see the truth. I know that someday I will be able to forgive, but today is not that day."

Allison stood. "We should go. Detective Brenner will be in contact with you soon. Everything is in his hands now. But please, don't hesitate to call on us for anything."

"Of course." Mary Ann offered an embrace to Allison. "Thank you, Allison." She hugged Charlie and Lucy. "Goodbye for now."

27

A fternoon gave way to evening as the partners returned to the office. Questions remained on the Healey investigation, but Brenner had it under control. Allison had contacted Estelle Cruz to let her know that Brenner would be in touch with her now that Tony's death was considered a homicide. Two young kids were gone because of another person's decisions.

Lucy sat at her desk and noticed a text arrive on her phone. She smiled as she read it. "Nolan's coming home tomorrow. Just for a few days, he says."

"He is?" Allison checked her phone and had no messages. "Oh, he hasn't texted me."

Charlie glanced up from her desk with a wry smile. "And so it begins...the phasing out of the mother in favor of the girlfriend."

"Guess I should have expected that, huh?" Allison replied.

"I'm sure he'll call and tell you," Lucy said.

"Thanks, it's okay, Lucy. I know he's coming home to see you. Hopefully, he'll want to spend a few hours with his old mom too."

She laughed. "I'll definitely have to make a trip to the grocery store tonight, then. Kid eats everything in sight."

"You guys want to do dinner tonight?" Charlie asked. "Seems to be a growing tradition for us when a case is over."

"Sure. I could use a drink—or five," Allison replied.

"Me too. That sounds good, Charlie."

"Great. Listen, Alli, if you want to bring Sully..."

Allison cast her a sideways glance. "I can ask him. Last I checked, he was busy with an armed robbery investigation."

"Last you checked?" Charlie cocked her head and smiled. "Not ready to get into it yet, huh?"

"Get into what?" Lucy asked.

"Nothing. It's just wishful thinking on Charlie's part." Allison returned to her laptop, pretending to work, but then sighed. "Do you think it's a mistake?"

"Me?" Charlie asked. "Hell no. I've been waiting for this for months. Are you kidding me?"

"Okay, what am I missing here?" Lucy gazed at them. "And don't say I'm just a kid and wouldn't understand, or any of that crap. We're partners, right?"

Allison nodded. "You're right, Lucy. We are partners. Charlie tends to stick her nose where it doesn't belong sometimes."

"Alli, this nose, right here, has gotten you out of plenty of trouble," Charlie replied.

"Fair enough. Lucy, Shane and I have decided to start seeing each other." Allison held up her hands. "It's a trial run. Nothing serious. No strings."

Charlie scoffed. "No strings. Yeah, we'll see how long that lasts."

"Oh my gosh, Allison. That's great. I mean, it's been kind of obvious the way you two look at each other," Lucy added.

"I didn't realize it was obvious. Anyway, it's too early to know just how it's going to work out. I only hope it doesn't ruin our friendship," Allison replied.

"Alli, just because Leo screwed you over, doesn't mean Shane will too. Give him a chance or it won't work."

"You're right, Charlie. Speaking of, I should find out how things are going between Leo and Jenny."

"There's your problem, right there." Charlie walked around her desk and approached Allison. "Leo isn't your concern anymore. And I'm pretty sure you told him that yourself. Look, I get he's the father of your kids, and I know you'd never want to see him hurt, but jeez, act like an ex-wife once in a while, would you?"

Allison threw back her head in laughter.

The office door opened, and Sophie Matthews walked inside. "Hi."

"Sophie." Allison sobered in an instant. "Hi. What can we do for you?"

"I heard that Mrs. Lyman might be charged with Jessica's murder." She continued inside. "Ms. Hart, I was the one who told her about what her husband was doing. She killed Jessica because of me."

"No." Allison approached her and took her gently by the shoulders. "You hold no responsibility for what happened. Brianne Lyman is a disturbed woman who was in pain. You didn't do that, her husband did. I'm just sorry Jessica paid the price for it."

"What about Tony?" Sophie continued. "The accident. They say it wasn't really an accident."

"Look, Sophie, this was a situation that spiraled out of control. Tony and Jessica got caught up in it. Is there someone you can talk to who can help you through your feelings?" Charlie moved in.

"I just miss her." Sophie pulled into Charlie and held on. "I didn't mean for any of this to happen."

Charlie's eyes watered as she glanced to Allison. She gently pushed Sophie away and captured her gaze. "You didn't do anything wrong. The Lymans did. Sophie, you're going to have to stay strong because your friends are going to need you as much as you need them."

"They blame me, Ms. Wells. They blame me for all of it." Sophie wiped away her tears and turned back to the door. "I'm sorry I bothered you. I am glad that you gave Jessica justice." She walked out the door.

"Should I go after her?" Lucy asked.

"No. I'll call Harriet. Ask her to make sure she'll be okay and that she should get some help," Allison replied. "All the lives those people ruined."

"Look, it's almost five. Let's close up shop and get the hell out of here, okay? Go get some dinner and try to put this behind us," Charlie said.

"I agree." Allison returned a smile. "Let's get out of here."

———

It was still early in the evening when Allison returned home. She was grateful to have Charlie and Lucy and understood the comradery among the five young friends at the university. Female friendships were invaluable as it was really only women who understood other women. As much as men tried, and Allison loved that they did, it wasn't the same. She suspected male bonds occurred in much the same way.

With each case they took on, they grew closer, even with Lucy, the youngest. Yes, Allison and Charlie both treated her a little bit like their daughter, but also an equal. It took a strong constitution to take on these cases and each of them had one. As far as the remaining college friends, Allison didn't know what would become of them. Would they survive the tragedy? Would it make them stronger together or would it divide them? One thing was certain, it would change them. Fundamental change was inevitable.

Life-altering events tended to do that to people. It re-writes their code. It would change those girls as Allison had been changed by her own life-altering events. Fortunate to have never lost a friend in that way, Allison still felt a sense of loss from her marriage. But now she had stronger bonds with her son, her friends. Maybe someday with Micah too.

For now, Allison had to close the book, as the saying went. For their part, it was over, and it was time to move onto the next case. She wondered how Detective Brenner, or anyone in law enforcement, including Shane, was able to close the book. Maybe they never closed it completely.

A knock on the door sounded and Allison smiled, knowing who waited on the other side. Another change she wasn't quite sure yet how to accept, or if it was in her best interest. She opened the door. "Hey."

"Hi." Shane walked inside and kissed her lips.

She pulled back. The unexpected gesture caught her off-guard. It wasn't how they usually greeted each other, but then again, they'd slept together so maybe this was how things would be from now on. "I'm glad you could stop by. You should've joined the girls and me for dinner earlier." She closed the door and started into the kitchen.

"I'm still pretty busy on this robbery investigation. Waiting on forensics to come back and hopefully open it up for me." Shane followed her. "I'm glad you three took the opportunity to step away and have some downtime."

Allison opened the refrigerator and pulled out two bottles of beer. "Well, our part is done. We gave everything we had to Brenner. It's up to him to get a conviction." She twisted off the caps and handed one to Shane.

"Thanks. I'll bet you hope your next case will be searching for a missing dog or something, huh?" He chuckled before tossing back a swig.

"Something like that would be nice." Allison smiled and paused a moment. "I told them."

He set down the beer. "About us?"

She nodded. "I hope that's okay."

"Um, yeah. Of course. I'll bet Charlie had some wisecrack about it."

"Not really. I mean, yes, but she's happy for us. So is Lucy. Lucy said it was about time."

"Is that so?" he replied. "No, it's good. I'm glad we don't have to keep it a secret. Brenner asked me if we were going out." He held up his hands. "I didn't tell him. I think I know better. I know how hard you're working to establish a professional reputation with the guys at the station. But don't be surprised if he asks you out. Just sayin…"

She smiled. "Thank you. Just know that it's not about you…"

"I know that." He held her gaze for a moment. "So where do we go from here, Allison?"

She pressed her lips together in a tight grin and raised her shoulders. Her long blonde hair still piled high on her head. "How about upstairs?"

Shane threw back the rest of his beer. "Lead the way."

The End

ABOUT THE AUTHOR

Robin Mahle has published more than 30 crime fiction novels, many, of which, topped the Amazon charts in the US, Canada, and the UK. And most recently, she has delved into the world of psychological thrillers.

Also a screenwriter, she has adapted some of her works into teleplays, which have gone on to place in film festivals nationwide.

From detectives to federal agents, and from killers to corruption, her page-turning tales grab hold and refuse to let go. Throw in tense action and thrilling twists, and it becomes clear why her readers come back for more.

Robin lives in Coastal Virginia with her husband and two children.

If you enjoyed Ms. Mahle's work, please share your experience by leaving a review on <u>Amazon.</u>

ALSO BY ROBIN MAHLE

The Kate Reid FBI Thriller Series (17 books)

The Chef (stand-alone psych thriller)

The Man in My Attic (stand-alone psych thriller)

The Compound (standalone psych thriller)

The Remy Fontaine Fugitive Hunter Thrillers (4 books)

The Det. Rebecca Ellis Thrillers (5 books)

The Allison Hart PI Thrillers (5 Books)

The Lacy Merrick Thrillers (4 books)

**Visit robinmahle.com and sign up to receive Robin's Newsletter so you can stay up to date on her new releases, events, contests and even exclusive new material!